The Sound of Gematria

Judith Field

LEAF BY LEAF

Published by Leaf by Leaf
an imprint of Cinnamon Press,
Office 49019, PO Box 15113, Birmingham B2 2NJ
www.cinnamonpress.com
The right of Judith Field to be identified as author of this work has been asserted by her in accordance with the Copyright, Designs and Patent Act, 1988. © 2023 Judith Field.
Print Edition ISBN 978-1-78864-974-2
British Library Cataloguing in Publication Data. A CIP record for this book can be obtained from the British Library.

Designed and typeset in Adobe Caslon Pro by Cinnamon Press.
Cover design by Adam Craig © Adam Craig
Cinnamon Press is represented by Inpress.

About the Author

Judith Field was born in Liverpool, lives in London and has been writing since 2009. She is the daughter of writers. Her grandson inspired her first published story when he broke her laptop keyboard. Unlike in the story, a magical creature didn't come out of the laptop and fix her life.

Her short stories, mainly speculative, have been published in the USA, Canada, UK, Australia and New Zealand. Her short story collection, *The Book of Judith*, was published by Rampant Loon Press in 2014. She was shortlisted for the Cinnamon Press Literature Award in 2022.

Judith has had several stories published about Euphemia, the protagonist in *The Sound of Gematria*, and her struggle to make her mark in a Victorian man's world. The idea for a longer work came to Judith during a synagogue service when she was reading the Bible. She came across the section about ritual impurity and wondered what would happen if this was an actual force – what might its effects be?

Judith is also a pharmacist, freelance journalist, editor, medical writer, and indexer. She was awarded an MA in Creative Writing from the Open University in 2018.

For Ruth, Laura and Jack

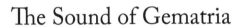

The Sound of Gematria

Twenty heads, you're dead

London, October 1899

As I trudged from the graveside after Aunt Ada's second funeral, rain soaked through my clothes, chilling my skin. Water dripped from the faceless statues of praying children and sorrowing angels.

The birds, perched in the moss-hung trees, fell silent. It grew dark and the yellow fog oozed up through the earth, snaking towards us, as though exhaled by the thousands of bodies buried beneath. I could no longer see my feet. The vicar picked his way towards me through the fallen leaves, along the gravel path winding between graves.

'My condolences, Miss Thorniwork.' He coughed.

The fog, smelling of rot, caught in my throat. The air tasted sour. The other mourners, muttering to each other, remained clustered by the wrought iron gate. My shoes clicked along the path as I stepped, shivering, towards the waiting carriage. I must be the first home. Mother would not be able to answer the door, and I would have to receive the visitors.

The clocks in the house had been stopped at the time of Aunt Ada's and Pearl's deaths. Mirrors were draped or turned to the wall and the curtains were drawn, as though my poor aunt and cousin had just died. I stepped inside the parlour and a blast of stuffy air hit me. I moved to the window, where fog crawled up the outside of the pane. It must remain closed.

'Why Aunt Ada?' Cousin May put her plate of Chelsea buns on a side table, knocking a pile of condolence cards onto the floor. I knelt to gather them, and when I stood and faced her a tear pooled in her right eye, overflowing until it ran down her cheek. She did nothing to check it. 'And why Pearl? Why did the horse have to bolt?'

She pulled a black-edged handkerchief from her sleeve and dabbed the corner of one eye.

'Why not?' I said. 'There is a one in a million chance any of us might meet an accidental death.'

'Is this supposed to ease my grief? How could God let it happen? Or what came afterwards? Poor Aunt Ada. Poor Pearl. To think that they... I cannot speak of it.' She reached for a bun.

'Not God.' I pursed my lips. 'Events, unpredictable and uncertain. The odds are the same as of throwing a coin twenty times, and its landing on heads, upon each occasion.'

'Do not speak of gambling. Where are your tears? If you do not shed them for Aunt Ada, then for poor Pearl. You and she were as thick as thieves.' She clutched the brooch, pinned to the neck of her blouse. A swirl of bright auburn hair, mounted in rock crystal. I reached to touch it, for contact with something that had been part of Pearl. She jerked backwards. 'You shall not have it.'

'May, I'm not trying to rob you, I just...'

'Just what? This is all I have of her, now. Father gave it

to me, to try to ease my grief. Of course, it could not. My sorrow is inextinguishable. Your dry eyes reveal your indifference. You care not a jot where her... her body is.'

'May, that is unkind.' I clutched my hands to stop them shaking. 'Nobody wants to find Pearl more than I. But we must leave such matters to the police.'

May turned to Uncle Jacob who had come to stand next to her, a teacup in one hand and his hat in the other. She grabbed his arm. Tea slopped into his saucer. 'Father, the police, she says. Bungling blue-bottles who could not catch a blindfolded burglar!' She burst into tears and buried her face in her hands.

Uncle Jacob put down his cup and patted May's arm. 'She thinks of nothing but numbers and her studies.' My fingertips brushed the outside of my skirt pocket, where I kept, like a touchstone, the miniature copy of Burkhardt's *Theory of Functions of a Complex Variable*. The last thing I had bought in Oxford. 'Come, we will leave now.' He turned back to look at me, as, tutting and shaking his head, he led her away. 'Show some respect, Euphemia.'

As you did, in deciding on a sixth-class funeral costing only three pounds and five shillings? Their bodies would not have been taken, had you agreed to cremation. A gasp from Jacob, and a further sob from May told me that, worse than simply thinking the words, I had spoken them.

'You are cold, young lady. It was a mistake, holding the wake in your house. With your poor mother so unwell that she could not leave her bed.' He strutted into the hall, dragging May after him. I followed them and heard Mother's bedroom door close on the floor above.

Aunt Emily, Uncle Jacob's wife, came down the stairs. 'Poor Agnes is no better, Jacob,' she said. She turned to me and took my hand. 'Your mother ought to be in a sanatorium. Of course, we do not begrudge her a minute of our time and will continue to visit her each day. We will be back tomorrow. Will you be here?'

Jacob pulled her hand. 'Come!' he snapped, before I could reply. 'We depart.' He opened the door and stepped into waist-deep fog. 'This foul vapour! It comes earlier each day.' He coughed, making a sound like a clogged drain, and glowered at me as though I were to blame.

The yellow fog had appeared from nowhere, about six months earlier. Every night, it seeped from the ground, causing sickness. When we awoke it would be gone, but it persisted for longer each morning.

The last guest stepped out, holding a handkerchief over his mouth and nose. The laurel wreath hanging on the outside of the front door clattered as I shut it. I moved aside the black crepe covering the mirror in the hall. To stop Aunt Ada's soul getting caught up in it, as she tried to leave, Aunt Emily had said. But more likely, so we would not have to see our own expressions. My face was pale, with shadows under the eyes. We had buried Aunt Ada, again. But Pearl's only memorial was an emptied grave.

I went upstairs and put my head round the door of Mother's bedroom. She lay in bed, next to the window. The fog rose up the outside of the glass, edging toward the open casement. I ran across the room and shut it, before the choking tendrils could creep in. Mother turned her head towards me, her alabaster face scarcely darker than the pillowcase.

'I'm sorry to have woken you.'

'I wasn't asleep. But... have they gone?'

12

'Yes, thank goodness. A gaggle of ghouls, trying to outdo each other's grief.'

She took a deep breath. Her chest rattled. 'I forbid you to speak of our family in such terms.' She tried to sit up.

'Let me.' I plumped her pillows and managed to move her to a semi-recumbent position. Her counterpane slid down. Under her nightgown, her skin stretched over her ribs and her hip-bones protruded. It required no more effort to move her than to lift a cat. I replaced her cover and straightened up. 'I'll make us some supper.'

'I have no appetite. This fog... I feel I could get up and come downstairs, if only I could breathe.'

A resonant cough left her shaking. 'I'm sure our relatives mean well, although they are overwhelming in large numbers. Your Aunt Emily and Uncle Jacob are kindness itself, looking in on me while you are away at your studies. Which opportunity I do not, of course, begrudge you for so much as a second.' She coughed again, deep, shattering, and leaned back against the pillow.

After a few moments, she drew breath. 'I shall be better, once this fog lifts. Will you return to Oxford soon? Emily asked me.'

'Perhaps. I don't know.' I stroked a wisp of damp hair from her forehead. 'You'd rather I stayed?'

Mother put her hand on mine. 'Euphemia. You look as gloomy as Emily.' She smiled. 'The truth is, while no mother would choose the life of a bluestocking for her daughter, your father would have been proud of your mathematical ability. Although I can see no practical application of your skills, they're not bestowed on many.' She drew a wheezing breath. 'I only pray that you may meet a young man who will value them.' She closed her eyes.

I pulled at the starched collar of my black dress where it chafed my neck. My head ached. I had no appetite either. It might help Mother if she could sleep.

I went downstairs into the kitchen and drained a glass of water, to which I had added a few drops of laudanum. The bitter taste fitted my mood as I turned down the lights. I went to bed.

I lay, staring at the ceiling. The clock in the church across the square chimed the quarter hour, half, three quarters, the hour. Thoughts chased each other inside my head. Pearl. Aunt Ada. Why had I not told May and Jacob that my grief was of the heart, rather than a brash outward display? Why did I not defend myself?

Normally, when sleep eluded me, I would be soothed by the elegant logic of a mathematical text. I turned my head to the shelf next to the bed. There were several books there, but tonight the thought of reading such a thing repelled me. Why had I ever thought mathematics engaging? I had no skill in the subject. I had managed to trick everyone into thinking I did, but soon my duplicity would be discovered. How could I leave Mother here in London, and return to University? How could I be beholden to Jacob and Emily? I would leave Huxley College. I had no skill in any subject. So much of what I had to do in daily life was unpleasant. Why add the unnecessary to it, by deluding myself that I had an academic mind? I must give up this fancy and find sensible employment—sufficient to pay for Mother's care. But where could I find it? I wanted no more than to stay in bed forever. If only I could sleep. I counted backwards, in threes, from one thousand. My eyelids, rough from fatigue, grew heavy.

In my dream, I stood in an unlit street I did not recognise. Chimney pots belched coal smoke, leaving a layer of soot on the ground and the terrace of seven wretched buildings to my left. Dampness squelched under my feet as I walked, looking at the numbers on the doors. First, a shuttered house numbered zero. The next, number one: a shop with empty, unlit windows. Then, a miserable tenement, all in darkness, also number one. I passed buildings two, three, and five: houses in darkness. Curtains drawn, as though in mourning. Each building numbered with the sum of the two preceding it. A Fibonacci sequence. The next would be number eight.

I stopped outside the seventh building, an alehouse. I looked at the door. 341. Breaking the sequence. I shivered. The door swung open. Gaslight shone out. A blast of voices and hot, sweat-laden air. A voice called my name. I pushed inside and forced my way past sweaty bodies to the bar. Wooden stools butted against a brass rail. A leering man grabbed my hand. 'Tug me off, Miss Numbers? I'll give you a simultaneous equation.' I tried to step back, but the crush of bodies held me in place.

A woman stood behind the bar, her back towards me as she replaced a bottle on a shelf. She turned. It was Pearl. The clattering of glasses and the sound of conversations slowed, and lowered in pitch. I looked around. The people had stopped in mid-movement. A man held a tilted glass to his mouth. Liquid stopped in mid-flow. Complete silence. Motes of dust hung motionless in the air.

I dropped to my knees and wept. My nose ran. Tears dripped off my chin. I screamed and cried for my cousin. My friend. She bent and touched my hand. I shivered as a chill ran up my arm. She reached down, lifted my chin and looked into my eyes. 'By stopping them, you'll find me.'

'Pearl…who are *they*? Stopping them? What've I to do?'

'I know you. You'll have memorised the number on the door.'

'Three hundred and forty-one. It breaks the sequence.' I rose to my feet.

She nodded. 'You must break the sequence. Don't you know the name of this hostelry?'

I found myself back in the street, outside the alehouse. I looked up at the sign, creaking in the cold wind that blew my dress around my ankles. A cow, bright auburn. And the name beneath it, The Red Heifer.

I awoke to the sunlight filtering through my thin curtains. My headache had gone, and I felt my spirits lift, the previous day's tribulations behind me. I threw back the bedcovers, arose and went to the window, half expecting to see the dark street and alehouse from my dream. The fog had vanished and I saw clear across the square to the church. The clock on the tower chimed seven.

I went into Mother's room. She sat on the edge of her bed, but stood as I entered. 'I breathe so much more easily when the fog is absent.' Her cheeks had more colour. 'I believe I could eat a piece of toast.'

The Magic of Nine

'Wait, Mother—I'll bring the toast up to you,' I said.

'Don't be silly, Euphemia, I will come downstairs. Just as soon as I'm dressed.'

I stood in the kitchen, wondering what it was the maid used to do each morning, lighting fires, scuffling around like a little mouse. I hoped Mother would not try to persuade me to go back to Oxford. I shivered. This was too cold for her, but lighting the range was such a complicated business involving bits of wood and half-burnt ashes. Perhaps she could be persuaded to summon all the patience she possessed and show me what to do, yet again. A bucket of coal and kindling sat next to the range. One of our visitors must have filled it for us yesterday, hard as it was to imagine which of the family might believe in doing good by stealth.

The range needed black-leading, and its steel parts polishing with emery powder. More for me to learn now we had no scullery maid. The dull metal felt warm against my fingertips; it must still be alight. I opened the hatch and threw pieces of kindling on top of last night's glowing coals, hoping the fog had not choked the chimney. The wood burst into flame, so that was unlikely. Seven pieces of coal should be the right number to start with. More would be needed later, but to add it now would snuff out the flames. Fewer would not maintain the fire. As the smell of wood smoke pervaded the kitchen, I filled the kettle and put it on the hob.

The glass from which I had drunk last night stood on the scrubbed wooden table next to the laudanum bottle, which I put back in the cupboard. It would take more than a headache before I swallowed any more of that. Such a disturbing dream. Pearl. In an alehouse called the Red Heifer. I took the glass into the scullery and returned with the butter.

Now, how best to prepare Mother's breakfast? There was tea to brew and toast to make. Perhaps she would eat a whole slice this time. I remembered Mrs Beeton's advice on feeding invalids: 'You cannot be too careful as to quality in a sick diet'. The thought of having to make bread gave me a jittery stomach. Perhaps it was just hunger, but I would have to buy bread, and goodness knew what else. Meanwhile the remains of yesterday's loaf ought to be acceptable for toast. How did a housewife find time to think?

Mother's hesitant footfall pattered on the floor upstairs. I rummaged in a drawer of the dresser and pulled out a tablecloth. It was creased, but I did not have time to heat the iron. Next, the best plates from the dresser shelf, then cups from the hooks above it. A posy of some sort would have added a decorative touch, but we had no flowers for me to throw together. Pearl would have known how to arrange them.

Metal-tipped toes and heels clattered along the pavement outside the window, breaking into my flight of memory. Children ran up and down, playing a chasing game that involved shouting 'Tick, fog's got you, you're it' at maximum volume.

The running stopped. I looked through the window into the sunlit street. A boy and a girl, about ten years of age, had tied one end of a long skipping rope to the lamppost outside the house. The boy held the untied end, turning the rope, while the girl skipped. They chanted in time with the rhyme and the thwack of the rope against the pavement.

'One two three four five six seven
All good children go to heaven.
Multiplication is vexation,
Division is as bad;
The Rule of Three doth puzzle me,
And practice drives me mad.
One two three
In comes she.'

Pearl and I had made up rhymes for our games, all about our favourite things. Rhymes about roses and numbers. I turned away and took the loaf and knife from the bread bin. Would Mother manage two slices?

The chant changed.

'Once nine is nine.
Two nines are nine-teen
Three nines are twenty-three.'

I returned to the window. The children stopped skipping.

'No, Gertie, that's wrong,' the boy said. 'Three nines are twenty-seven.'

I nodded.

'Come on,' the girl said. 'That's not right neither. Just turn the rope, Billy. Start from four nines.'

He did as told, reciting 'Four nines are forty-five.'

I shot the window open as far as it would go and put out my head. 'And that's not right, either!' The two looked up at me, eyes wide.

Billy managed a whisper. 'Sorry, Miss.'

'No, *I* should apologise. I did not mean to alarm you. But, don't you know that there are many patterns in the nine times table? It is almost miraculous.'

They shook their heads and stepped backwards, away from the window.

'Be careful!' I said. 'Don't fall into the road. Now, how would you like to learn something that will make you top of the class?'

'Go on, then,' Billy said. 'It'd be a miracle if Gertie got anything but the dunce's cap.'

She punched his arm.

I smiled. 'Now, stop your squabbling and listen to me. This is sensational. It'll amaze you, and your teacher.' I felt like a fairground barker. 'In the nine times table the first digit, I mean the first number from the right, in all the answers it goes down from nine to zero in steps of one, then repeats.'

'Eh?' Gertie said.

'Hang on.' Billy pulled a lump of chalky stone from his pocket. He squatted, and wrote '1 x 9' on the pavement. 'Say that again, Miss.'

'Write this down.' I drew a breath. '2 x 9=18, 3 x 9=27, 4 x 9=36, 5 x 9=45, 6 x 9=54, 7 x 9=63, 8 x 9=72, 9 x 9=81, 10 x 9=90, 11 x 9= 99, 12 x 9=108.'

'Hold on!' He scribbled, the tip of his tongue protruding from the side of his mouth. 'Phew. Now what?' He finished and looked up. 'Well?'

'Now, the second number goes *up* from zero to nine in

20

steps of one. Do you see? Then that repeats.'

Gertie shrugged her shoulders. 'I don't know a word you're saying.'

Billy hushed her and looked at me. 'And?'

'Look,' I said. 'The third digit is zero for the first eleven multiples, then it'll be one for the next eleven multiples, then two, and so on.' My heart raced. 'But here's the cleverest thing. If you add up all the numbers in the answers, it always makes nine.'

Gertie shook her head. 'Says there, two times nine makes eighteen,' she said. 'That's not nine.'

Billy elbowed her. 'Don't be a twit. Look. One and eight, that's nine.'

I laughed and clapped my hands, feeling more awake than I had for months. 'You are a clever boy. Magic, do you see?'

Behind me, mother stepped into the kitchen still wearing her dressing gown. She inched her way through the cloud of steam coming from the range. As I pulled in my head, Billy said, 'She's loony. Fog on the brain. Got to humour 'em.' I slid the window shut, muting his voice a little. 'Let's play glass ollies instead,' he said. 'Now, you've got nine left, and I've got my nine and your nine what I won yesterday, so that's twenty seven.'

'Clever clogs,' Gertie said. 'I'm going to win them all back.' Their footsteps clattered along the cobbles, fading as they walked away.

Mother tottered towards the table, clutching the back of a kitchen chair. I took her arm and helped her to sit.

'Thank you. My legs are still weak, but I'll feel stronger when I've eaten. Then I will get dressed.' She looked round the kitchen. 'No tea? You have been down here an age.

And where's the toast?' I glanced at the slices of bread, and the butter, still on the scrubbed wooden table. She wafted her hand in front of her face. 'Open the window again. Really, it's a wonder the kettle did not boil dry.'

I seized a cloth and dragged the kettle off the heat. 'There's a splash of water still inside it. I will start again. I'm sorry to have taken so long. I meant to have had the breakfast ready by now.' I reopened the window and headed for the scullery.

Mother called after me. 'No, leave it. Let us talk.'

I sat opposite her. She reached across the table and took my hand.

'I should not have spoken so sharply. The effort of walking downstairs… I should have kept my temper. Now, I know—'

'If you'd called, I would have helped you down.'

'No. I must do things myself. Now, don't interrupt me again. I know you meant to get our breakfast ready. But you were distracted. I heard what you said to those urchins.'

'Idle chatter. I'm sorry.'

'Please. I saw you as you spoke of numbers. You almost… glowed. I cannot remember when I last saw you so animated. Not since before we lost your poor Aunt Ada, and Cousin Pearl.'

'I would give anything to find Pearl.'

She gave my hand a feeble squeeze. 'Wherever her body may be, Pearl's soul is in heaven. There is nothing we can do. I try not to dwell on it, but I know that you often do. You need to occupy your mind. I'm poor company for you.'

'No, that's not true. I will send to Oxford for my

belongings—today.'

'Yes, it is true. You are my flesh and blood, but we are not alike.' She shook her head. 'Numbers are your life.'

'Yes, but I can learn to love opera, as you do. You gave me a most interesting account of—what was it called—*Lohengrim*? Shall we go to hear it together? Isn't that the one about a swan?' Was that the one that lasted three hours, or four? And all about a bird?

'It's *Lohen-grin*.' She smiled as she looked into the distance. 'A mysterious knight... a doomed romance... I am sure you would learn to love it. Or maybe we should start with something lighter. *Puccini*...' Eyes cast down, she squeezed my hand again. 'I would love to, but no. My opera-going has been curtailed by the fog, as you know.'

'Nevertheless, there is so much for you to teach me. And when you're recovered, we will go, and I'll know all about it.'

'I fear my recovery will take some time.' She coughed. 'Don't change the subject. Didn't you tell me that your research might lead to the chance to teach? What could be more fitting? It was your Father's dearest wish that you study mathematics. You must return to Oxford. I would never forgive myself if I prevented that.'

'But, Mother, *I* would never forgive myself... your health...'

'But me no buts, Euphemia. You do not need my permission to leave. Uncle Jacob and Aunt Emily will call later. Perhaps they will bring May, to sing me one of her lovely songs.'

May, at the parlour piano, thumping out 'To a Wild Rose' with a menace half-heard, half-felt.

Mother took a knife out of the table drawer and

buttered a piece of bread. 'I will try to persuade her to play a Chopin mazurka, in order to spare her voice.' She took a bite of bread.

'And our ears.'

She frowned, and tapped my wrist with her finger. 'That is unkind. I will also engage a replacement scullery maid.'

'But if I stayed, you wouldn't need one.'

Mother pursed her lips. 'Looking around this kitchen gives the lie to that. I'll ask Uncle Jacob and Aunt Emily to help in doing so. I'll ask May to consider how best to word the advertisement. It will give them all a means to occupy their time. And, I'd say also their minds, were it not for May.'

I laughed. 'And neither is that kind. Although true.'

'You are right. Tempting as it is to speak my mind, I must practise what I preach.' She dropped my hand, stood and made her way to my side of the table, holding onto the edge. She kissed my cheek. 'Go and pack your bag. Then, you will be able to leave as soon as they arrive.'

'I can't… I won't.'

'You might be prepared to go against your Father's wishes, but it's clearly what God intended for you or he wouldn't have given you such a talent. Don't also go against His will.'

I stood. 'You do not know me at all if you think that will change my mind. Religion? Nothing but a jumble of false assertions. God? A product of the imagination, as I have said before.'

She opened her mouth.

'The subject is closed,' I said. 'I must take care of you. Now, I'll draw up a list of my belongings, and ask for them to be returned from Huxley.'

'Won't you at least have some breakfast?' Mother said.

I shook my head and left the kitchen. There were eighteen stairs in the flight to the first floor and my bedroom.

Book of Numbers

I stood with my back against the closed bedroom door. Uncle Jacob, Aunt Emily and May would arrive soon, all rudeness and chatter. I sank onto the bed and, from the middle of the tower of books on the cabinet next to it, pulled out *A treatise on the calculus of finite differences*. The rest of the heap fell to the floor. I left it there and opened the book. Just a peep. Just enough to calm myself. Then I would stop.

No. I took a deep breath. Time to put away my Oxford life. I might as well throw away all the books. My trunk stood on the other side of the bedroom next to the wall, covered in a blanket with a vase standing on top, containing a few dead twigs. I removed the vase and blanket, opened the trunk and took out a Bible bound in white kid leather, small enough to fit in a lady's handbag. Pearl had carried it with her, always.

'You should read it, Pheemie,' she said, the last time we met. 'Even if you don't believe it, there's such poetry there. It's just the thing for a long journey, like London to Oxford.'

'I'd sooner read something educational.'

She laughed. 'There's more to life than cramming your head with facts.' She took a pack of cards out of her bag. 'Very well—I will teach you to play Patience. Will that be mathematical enough for you?'

After she died, the family gave me the Bible, but until now I had felt unable to look at it. I sat on my bed and opened it at a page marked with a red ribbon. Was it the last thing she had read before she died? I pictured her, sitting in the carriage, Bible open at that page. The Bible thrown to the floor as the carriage crashed in the fog, hit the lamppost, and turned over. The Book of Numbers, Chapter 19: 'This is the ordinance of the law which the Lord hath commanded, saying, Speak unto the children of Israel, that they bring thee a red heifer without spot, wherein is no blemish, and upon which never came yoke.'

It appeared to be some sort of purification ritual. The red heifer. Perhaps Pearl had spoken of it, although I could not recall when, and that was why it had appeared in my dream. I would never be able to ask her what it meant. I closed the Bible and put it on the table next to my bed, next to the pile of mathematical texts. I must pack those. I looked inside the trunk. Something would have to come out, to make room for the books.

The latest volume of *Progress in Mathematical Physics* caught my eye and I took it from the trunk. I would allow myself a short look, then return to packing mathematics away forever. According to the contents page, the journal included 'Some equations of electromagnetism' by Rufus Milton, Jeffrey Spaulding and Leopold Lazarus. Spaulding and Lazarus would have done the actual work, and probably written the article as well. First rate mathematics.

Lazarus, I did not know, but Spaulding inhabited the rooms on the landing below mine, or rather below the ones I used to occupy. I used to see him almost every day when I was a research student. Of course, I did not find him attractive, but now I wished I might see his face again and hear him ask my opinion on his latest findings. Perhaps we would have worked together. I might have been among the authors of the next paper, although Professor Milton would have been reluctant to include a woman's name on the title page. He would have no need to trouble himself with that now.

I turned to a letter from a Dr Simpson. 'The liminal nature of the time of the coming millennium has thinned the veil between the living and the dead. I and my colleagues are developing a method of communicating with the departed, using sound waves. We hope to publish our method and findings in this august journal.' Perhaps the editor would reserve him a place in the edition of the first of April, 1900.

Downstairs, the front door opened and I recognised May's irritating prattle in the hall. Mother called out greetings from the kitchen. My stomach tightened. I told myself to be sensible: it was better that they had a key than Mother had to get up to answer the door. I put *Progress* on the bed, went to the landing and leaned over the banister. What was so important that they had to come at this hour in the morning?

Aunt Emily looked up at me before turning away. 'Fetch a bucket of coal, Jacob,' she said, 'While May and I help Agnes into the parlour.'

'Let me lend a hand,' I called. 'And I will light the fire.'

'No, thank you,' Uncle Jacob said. 'By the time you have placed the coal and wood in the grate all higgledy-piggledy so that it won't light, and we've had to pull everything out onto the hearth and re-lay it, we will all have caught pneumonia.'

Soon, all that sort of work would be done by our new housemaid. 'Very well. Please call me when you are settled. *I* will make the tea. That much I can do, for my own mother.' This time, I would make sure I did not let the kettle boil dry. I retreated into my room and shut the door.

As I picked *Progress* up again, I heard footsteps climbing the stairs. May walked into the room without knocking and closed the door. I felt her hot breath on my cheek as she peered over my shoulder, she smelled of parma violets.

'Don't you read anything but books of boring sums?'

I closed the journal. 'Don't you ever eat anything but sweets?'

She turned away and poked the contents of the trunk. 'Better than having bad breath.'

'You could always try brushing your teeth. I can tell you where to buy a good brush.'

'Oh, bother that. I use a silk cloth and my teeth are like pearls.' She giggled. 'I mean, like in an oyster. Although of course Cousin Pearl's were very pretty.'

I had no wish to discuss Pearl's dentition, particularly not with May. I opened the journal again.

She leaned in so that her head was between my face and the page, turned and looked up at me. 'Leave that and unpack your clothes before they get all creased. I don't suppose *you* know how to iron.'

'No. Do you?'

She stood and wrinkled her brow, as though working out a puzzle. 'I'd probably be very good at it, but I've never had to try. Come on, I'll help you put everything away.'

I stood and opened the door. 'There is no need, thank you. There's not much to do. You may as well go back downstairs. I'd rather be alone.'

May sat on the bed. 'I can't imagine why. Anyway, I can't go back down, Father told me to come up and stay here. He and Mother want to talk to Aunt Agnes in private. I wonder what about?'

I shrugged. 'I don't know. Mother did say she wanted a word with him, though. I think she wants to ask his advice on engaging a housemaid. Perhaps he thought all the talk of wages and duties would bore you.'

'But, if that was it, why didn't he say? He wouldn't tell me what they wanted to talk about. Oh—' She gasped and clapped her hands. 'Euphemia! Perhaps he's found a young chap for me.'

I imagined Uncle Jacob poking through something resembling a giant Lost Property Office, filled with socially respectable young men, with good family names and expectations.

'Perhaps.' And good luck to the gentleman concerned.

May grasped my hands. 'Oh, can it really be true?'

I pulled free and wiped my palms on my skirt. 'You've got plenty of time. You're only 21. Anyway, I don't want to disappoint you, but why should he want to talk to my mother about that?'

Her mouth turned down at the corners. 'I don't know. Oh! Maybe he's got someone for you, too.'

'I can find my own. I mean, I could. If I wanted to. But I don't.'

'Oh, you'll change your mind when you meet the right person.' She pulled armloads of clothes out of the trunk. 'You'd find yourself buying smarter outfits before you knew it. Like mine.' She gave a twirl and her pale pink satin dress swished around her legs. 'And you'd better hurry up. You're 22, after all.'

'I'm happy with these things. They're comfortable and warm.'

May dropped a bundle of woollen skirts, in dark browns and greens, on the bed and put her hands on her hips. 'What am I going to do with you, Frumpy Pheemie?'

'Do? I don't want *you* to do anything.'

She pouted. 'You were only too ready to do what Pearl said. Following her round like a little pet poodle. Never asking me to play.'

I stood. 'May, that's unjust. We did ask you, but you always wanted to play a different game. If you're going to hark back to when we were children, then there are many things that *I* could remind *you* of.' Such as, how long it had taken her to learn to count.

May drew a breath. Uncle Jacob called our names up the stairs, in a tone someone might use for a servant or dog.

I took a pair of electric blue evening dress shoes out of the trunk. Why had I taken them to Oxford? Had I really thought it possible that some invitation might be forthcoming, for which I would need them? There had been none, and nor would I need them here. I held them out to May. 'Let's not quarrel. Would you like these? If they're not too dowdy?'

She turned her head this way and that, examining them from all angles. 'No, thank you. They're too big for me.' She blinked. 'And they're rather... *bright*, aren't they? Where on earth did you find them?'

Uncle Jacob called again. 'May! Euphemia!

Downstairs, now. We have something to tell you.'

May rolled her eyes. 'We'd better not keep him waiting. Come on—I expect he's going to tell us all about our young men.' She grabbed my arm and pulled me to my feet. 'Do you prefer dark ones, or fair?'

'It would depend on what was inside the head, not on it. A meeting of true minds. Like in that poem.'

She raised her eyebrows. 'What are you talking about?'

'Mother read it to me. It starts "Let me not to the marriage of true minds admit impediments". It makes you think.'

May tutted. 'Never heard of it. What's that got to do with love? Do you want to know what *I* think?'

'No, but I doubt that'll stop you.'

She gave me a slap on the arm. 'I think you should let me have the handsome one, as you don't seem to care.'

We walked downstairs and into the parlour. I sat in the middle of the sofa, Mother on my left. May, on my other side, nudged me. 'Isn't this exciting? I bet I'm right.' She put her hand over her mouth to muffle a giggle.

Uncle Jacob stood with his back to the fire, blocking most of the heat. I took Mother's hand in mine, trying to rub some warmth into it.

'Euphemia,' Mother said, 'Uncle Jacob and Aunt Emily have been kindness itself, looking after me. But it can't be sustained.'

'No, I'm afraid not,' Aunt Emily said. 'I have so much work to do these days with the poor. And Uncle Jacob's business expands daily, taking him away from home more and more.'

'Thank you for all your kindness,' I said. 'I shall now take up the reins.'

'Not that you're a horse, of course, Aunt Agnes,' May said.

'Euphemia, you can't,' Mother said. 'Now, listen. We can afford a housemaid, or a nurse, but not both, and nor can Uncle Jacob. He has a housemaid. We have neither.'

A gust of wind blew down the chimney, ejecting a puff of smoke from the fireplace. Uncle Jacob coughed.

Mother continued. 'It is therefore sensible for us to pool our resources. I am going to live in Uncle Jacob's house. My signing over the funds I inherited from your father to him will permit the employment of all necessary staff. Of course, you'll come too. You'll have your own room, next to May's. That will be pleasant.'

I was unable to suppress a gasp. 'With Uncle Jacob and Aunt Emily? And May?' I said, once I had caught my breath. 'But why can't we go on as we have been since my return? I'm not going back to Oxford. I can take care of the house. And I can look after you.'

'No, you can't,' Mother said. 'And nor should you have to.'

May clapped her hands. 'Oh, we'll have such fun, you and me. The first thing we can do is go shopping together. For a new frock, for you.'

'But Mother, *all* your inheritance? Is this wise?' Would I, too, be treated like a child by Uncle Jacob?'

'It's the only way,' Mother said.

Uncle Jacob looked at me, jaw clenched. 'You have no need to worry. I will, of course, continue to pay you the same allowance your mother has done.' I opened my mouth. He raised a finger. 'We needn't dwell on minor misfortunes—let's not forget that my most recent enterprise turned a clear profit.'

'Yes, and your partner absconded to Spain with most of it. It's not just my allowance I worry about, it's all of it.'

'Don't speak to your uncle like that,' Mother said, in a croaking voice. 'Who better to live with than my own brother, and his dear ones?' She coughed, drawing in breath with a whooping sound.

'Now look what you've done, Euphemia, upsetting your poor mother.' Aunt Emily rushed across the room and dabbed at Mother's forehead with a handkerchief. Mother waved her away.

'Consider your mother, Euphemia,' Uncle Jacob said. 'And have no concerns. I will invest your money wisely. Let me explain. This is a brilliant, innovative scheme, called "Shares in Prosperity". Since it all turns on early investment, there's no time to lose.' He launched a lengthy, complex description of money being paid back and forth. May yawned. Mother looked at the floor. Aunt Emily leaned forward and gazed at Uncle Jacob, lips parted. The gist was that returns were paid to early investors using the money put in by people who came later.

'So,' I said, 'One person takes money from someone coming later, keeps some, and gives the rest to those who invested earlier?'

He nodded. 'Exactly.'

'But that's robbing Peter to pay Paul!'

Mother sighed. 'You of all people, Euphemia, must see how the capital will grow. It's basic arithmetic. Now, no more discussion. Money is men's business.'

'Is this really what you want to do?'

'It will be a new beginning. Tomorrow I'll give notice to the landlord.'

'Well, Uncle Jacob,' I said, 'the population of London

is around six and a half million. I only hope you exit the scheme early, before there are no more new people willing to throw their money away.'

He frowned. 'Euphemia, pack bags for yourself and your mother. You're both coming back with us, today, before the fog comes. We will have our lawyer attend tomorrow morning, to draw up the financial documentation. We will see about moving your other belongings later.'

I walked across the room and opened the door.

Mother stood. 'And May will be the sister that, alas, I was never able to give you.'

I stopped and walked back to her. I put my hand on her shoulder. 'I will pack bags for us both. But I won't be coming with you. I'll be going back to Oxford, while I can still afford to do so.'

Mother exhaled. 'Finally.' She looked at me and smiled.

Three Floors Up

I dropped my bag on the floor of my room in Huxley College, raising a cloud of dust. The place was as I had left it. Walls lined with polished oak. Scuffed parquet floor. Chair at a forty-five degree angle to the fireplace. I walked to the window and pushed aside the curtain, bleached from its former royal blue to a perfect shade of turquoise, and looked outside, three floors down onto Broad Street.

It had rained in the night. The water dripping from the honey-coloured buildings glittered as though the weak rays of October sunlight had turned the bricks into barley sugar. I told myself not to be fanciful, that the stones were clean because there was no fog in Oxford. But still, there was something enchanting about the caramel walls of Wagstaffe Hall on the other side of the road. The fog, Uncle Jacob, May and the rest of them, were far away. The pavements shone like spilled mercury.

I recognised Maurice Parbold, fellow mathematician, coming towards me. He rubbed his hands as he waddled along the pavement, his chin seeming to melt into his neck, which melded seamlessly, via his chest, with his stomach. He had, most likely, just come from toadying to Professor Milton. Perhaps he had been given the task of writing another article. But he was not May, Uncle Jacob or Aunt Emily. I stopped scowling and held my arms open wide, as if to hug the whole of Oxford.

Parbold stopped, raised bulbous eyes to my window and waved, his round, flat face split by a broad smile. The sun flitted from behind a cloud and glanced off a window opposite, lighting his head and giving him a brief, halo-like aura. Perhaps we could discuss our research proposals later. I felt that, today, I could hold a conversation with him without wanting to run.

But first, there was much to catch up on. I wandered round the small study, moving clutter into aimless piles. After half an hour I had a heap of mathematical journals, a pile of textbooks and a number of unpaid bills. Those, I would send to Uncle Jacob, while he still had the money to pay them. Although he had given me a small allowance, he had insisted on administering my expenses. And, I had no doubt, would comment on the suitability and probity or otherwise of the way I spent my money, as though each penny were an expression of my values and aspirations. But no matter—he was not here.

I found an envelope and pushed the bills inside. I would have to buy a stamp. Underneath the envelope was a notice I had found shoved under the door of my room on return. It was from Blackwell's Bookshop, telling me to collect my reserved copy of Durège's *Elements of the Theory of Functions of a Complex Variable with Especial Reference to the Methods of Riemann.* I had not collected it and they might have sold it by now. I stuffed the envelope into my bag, put on my coat and hat, locked the door behind me and strode into the street.

There were three people waiting at the counter in Blackwell's. I peered round them, at the reserved books on the shelves behind the shop assistants, but could not see a copy of the Durège book among those waiting for collection. They must have returned it to stock. I found the bookcase marked 'Mathematics' and, jostled and shoved by other students, looked along the shelves. There it was. As my fingers touched the spine, a man beside me reached out from behind me and grabbed it too, his wrist protruding from a too-short jacket sleeve.

'Mine, I think.'

I whipped round. He stood about six feet tall. He looked to be aged in his late twenties, with curly hair and eyes the colour of Uncle Jacob's tawny sherry. 'You are mistaken,' I said. 'I asked for this book to be ordered for me.'

'Then, my dear lady, they'll have saved it for you. Behind the counter.' He cocked his head in that direction and took the book from the shelf.

'I'm not your dear lady. Open the book. My reservation slip will be inside. They must have shelved it by mistake.'

He took the book by its front and back cover, opened it, and shook it. Nothing fell out. 'It most certainly is for sale,' he said. 'And I intend to buy it. Good day.' He strode to the counter and handed the book to one of the assistants. I ran after him and pushed past the queue that had gathered like iron filings around a magnet. 'Excuse me!'

'Madam,' said the other assistant, 'You must take your turn.' A woman in the queue remarked that it was unladylike to push in. A second assistant with an armload of books asked if he could help me.

'I hope so!' I said. 'That man, for I hardly think he deserves the title of gentleman,' I turned and saw him

38

leaving the shop. I was about to continue when I noticed that the next book on the pile to be shelved was Durège. From inside the front cover protruded a card, bearing my name.

'Man, madam?'

My face grew warm. 'Never mind. I'd like to collect that book you have there, Durège.' I pointed. 'My name is Euphemia Thorniwork.'

The assistant placed the book on the counter. 'You are in luck, madam. We were about to place it for sale, since you had not collected it.'

I took the book back to my room. On my way upstairs, I saw Parbold waiting on the landing next to the staircase. 'Welcome back! I am happy to see you.' He was probably merely glad of someone to whom he could feel superior.

'I am happy to be here.' I beckoned him on. 'Don't let me detain you.'

He giggled, tapping the tips of his fingers against his mouth. I thought of May. 'Oh, no, it's bad luck to pass on the stairs. One of us needs to go back and wait.'

I continued to climb the stairs. 'I don't believe in luck. And neither should you.' He remained on the landing. I shoved past him and headed for my room.

He turned and called to me, 'You shouldn't tempt fate. You might need some good fortune. Don't forget our research proposals must be with Professor Milton by the end of the month. After all, you have been absent for the whole of September.'

'There are three weeks to go. I can assure you I have been planning mine the whole time I was in London.' This was true, if you considered mathematics to include calculating how much coal would start the kitchen range, but not extinguish it. That, and teaching the two urchins their nine times table. 'I may do some work around quaternions.'

'It's good that you have plans,' Parbold said. 'Because the last time I saw Professor Milton, he said he wanted to speak to you as soon as possible.'

My mouth dried. What could he want? 'When did he say that?'

Parbold looked upwards and tapped his chin as though trying to work out a puzzle. 'Oh…about a week ago.' He walked downstairs.

I had to see Professor Milton right away. He was probably unaware that I had returned. Three weeks to submit proposals, then a further two weeks for him to consider them. Five weeks for my future to be decided.

I knocked on Professor Milton's office door. No reply. I reached for the handle, reluctantly as though it were red hot, and turned it. The door was locked. I walked along the corridor till I came to an office with an open door. Professor Straughan's. I knocked and stood in the open doorway.

He looked up from his desk. 'Ah, Miss Er… were you looking for Prof Milton?' I said that I was. 'I should have known. Professor Milton and his lady student.' He shook his head and grinned. 'I am afraid that he is not here. He was last seen a week ago, hurrying to the station, suitcase in hand, heading to Lossiemouth with his grandchildren.'

I gasped. 'Oh, no. For how long will he be gone?'

'You worry about the climate? I agree that the Scottish seaside in October is not an enticing prospect.' Professor

Straughan turned from me and rummaged in a drawer. 'He told me that he would be absent for two weeks. I am sure he will be able to withstand the less-than-torrid clime.'

'I don't doubt his resilience. That's not what I'm worried about. Do you have an address where he might be reached?' I would have to send a telegram.

Professor Straughan shook his head. 'No, but your mention of an address has reminded me.' He reached into a desk drawer and pulled out a bundle of envelopes, bearing Professor Milton's characteristic scribble. 'He left some letters for his students.' Frowning, he put them down. 'They might have been easier to read had he asked the grandchildren to write the envelopes,' he said, staring into the distance. 'Now, I know that one is seven years of age, Flora, if memory serves. And the younger, Henrietta, is aged four.' He paused. 'I will see if he left one for you. What is your name?'

'Euphemia Thorniwork.'

'Euphemia. What a lovely name. It means fair speech, you know.'

'So I've been told,' I snapped, placing my hands on the desk and leaning towards him. 'Is there one for me among them?'

'I can't see one.' He rifled through the bundle. He put them down. 'No, I'm sorry.'

'Are you sure? Please look again.'

'I am certain,' he said, 'but to ease your agitation, I will examine them once more.' He picked the pile up again. 'No, I tell a lie.' He raised a finger and put them down. 'The grandchildren's names are Fabian and Harold.'

'To the devil with that,' I said. 'I don't wish to appear

rude, but—'

'Too late, I fear.' Prof Straughan narrowed his eyes.

'I'm sorry, but it's possible that even as erudite a scholar as you needs to read envelopes written by Professor Milton more than once. New eyes might help.' I reached out a hand. 'May I look?'

He snatched up the pile and clutched it to his chest. 'Oh no! That would never do. Confidentiality.' He put the pile down, shielded it with a cupped hand and flicked through the envelopes, squinting. 'Robinson… I suppose this says Smith… Milton certainly believes in corresponding with his students. I only wish he wrote as clearly as he thought.' He held one up to the light coming through the window behind him. 'This might be an algebraic equation, for all I can tell. But nothing for a Miss Thorne. Perhaps he does not wish to communicate with you. Unless of course your name is Miss Scribble.'

I shook my head, grasped the edge of the desk and leaned forwards.

'There must be a letter for me. Please look again. My name is Thorniwork.'

He backed away from me. 'Why didn't you tell me before?' He spread the letters out on the desk as though dealing clock patience and poked through them yet again.

I suppressed an urge to reach across the desk and grab the letters myself.

'Ah, here we are.' Professor Straughan held an envelope out at arm's length and tilted his head to read it. 'Or at least, I suppose it is. Yes, it looks as though it is meant to read "Miss Thorniwork, on return.' He handed the letter over. With all the strength I possessed, I managed not to snatch it. 'From now on,' he said, 'I shall think of you as

"Miss On Return".' He laughed. 'Just my little joke. Do not be offended. I merely attempt to put you at your ease.'

'No offence taken. I apologise for my earlier curtness.'

'Yes, you did some very thorny work. Just my little joke. I have allowed you some latitude. It is, after all, the research proposal season again, is it not? Such pressure on the students. But they do say the cream will rise to the top.'

I left the office, shutting the door behind me. I ripped the envelope open.

To Miss Thorniwork, should you deign to return:
You and Leopold Lazarus are, by October 31st, to submit a proposal for research that you will carry out together. You will supervise him. You will receive my comments on the proposal on November 17th.
R. Milton.

Three weeks, and three days. Leopold Lazarus had been one of Professor Milton's co-authors of the article I had read in London. *Some equations of electromagnetism*, that had been the title. Perhaps we could base our research around that. I smiled. I put the letter in my pocket. Such a ringing endorsement from the Professor. He must think me suitable for the work, despite all his behaviour to the contrary, his remarks about women's brains. Perhaps it had all been some sort of test. Perhaps I had passed.

I walked along the corridor. Perhaps I had misread it. Perhaps, he had told me he wanted Lazarus to do the research, but not me? I pulled the letter out and read it again, running my finger along the page one word at a time. *You will supervise him.*

A door opened to my right. I collided with the man who walked out, making him scatter papers and books across the floor. I dropped to my knees. 'I am so sorry! Do let me help. I do hope I can get them into the right order.'

The man knelt next to me. 'Don't worry. It will probably make as much sense if you don't.' I looked up. It was Spaulding, Professor Milton's other co-author. 'Oh, hello Jeffrey.' I smiled.

'Froggy Parbold told me you were back, Euphemia. You look pleased to see me—has my luck changed? Shall we yet elope to Gretna Green?'

'Certainly not—but I never thought I'd see you again. Or any of you. Even Parbold looks like an angel today.'

'I fear you need spectacles.' He stood. I passed him the papers I had gathered. 'Well, if you're not going to be my sweetheart, I'll bid you adieu for now.'

'Actually, there is something. I'm looking for one of your partners in adversity.' He raised an eyebrow. 'I read the article you wrote with Prof Milton. Leopold Lazarus—do you know where I might find him?'

'That's a coincidence. I just saw him in the Bod. He was asking about you. Something about a letter from Professor Milton. I told him you had gone away.'

'Thank you, but I have very much returned.'

I turned and headed for the Bodleian.

Two Heads

I stopped by the table in the corner of the reading room, beside the window with the broken blind. A man sat at the next table, by the bookcase. Perhaps that was Lazarus. A student stood at the top of a ladder, searching for a book. Could that be him? I scanned Professor Milton's letter again, as though it would somehow have changed between this (its seventh reading) and the ones before. There was no mistake. I cleared my throat. 'Am I addressing Mr Lazarus?'

The ladder-climber descended and strode to the opposite side of the room. The man at the table spoke, without looking up. 'Yes, Leopold Lazarus.' He marked his place in *The heuristic probabilistic argument 'for the strong form of the Goldbach conjecture of prime numbers'* with his index finger and scribbled a note onto the back of an envelope on the table next to the book. A copy of the Durège book lay next to it.

I coughed.

'We must maintain silence here, Madam,' he said. 'May I offer you a cough drop?'

'No, thank you. I'm quite well. But I need to speak to you.'

'What about?' He threw his pen down onto the envelope, splashing ink across it. 'This interruption is most unreasonable.' He looked up at me with a frown. It was the man from Blackwell's. 'Oh. It's you. The book thief.' He snatched the Durège and clasped it to his chest, as though it were some precious jewel he had found among the shelves in the shop. 'But you can't have it. You can't even borrow it—I have not yet finished studying it.'

My throat tightened. 'I am no thief. I didn't realise my copy had been reserved. And that's not why I'm here.' I drew myself up to my full height. 'I am Miss Thorniwork. Professor Milton will have written to you about me, I know.'

He stood, looming over me as he took my hand. It was unusual to find a man so much taller than I. We shook, his hand warm and dry. He held mine in a firm grip.

He smiled. White, even teeth, set in a wide mouth. 'I'm pleased to meet you, and I'm most sorry for what I said. I did not intend to slander you.'

'Let's forget about it'

He frowned. 'Dear lady, you must assure me that you find my apology sufficient.'

I pulled my hand free. 'Yes, yes, I do. Now, in his letter, Professor Milton said—'

'Do you realise,' he said, looking into the distance, 'that legally, if you've said that a man did not have the manners fit for a pig, you make an inadequate apology by saying he did?'

I shook my head. 'I haven't studied the law. And I didn't comment on your manners, so let's speak of it no more. We have no time to lose. We must submit research proposals by the end of this month.'

He rubbed his hands. 'Yes, to work! I've found a most interesting passage in this book about primes. It might be our starting point, although I admit that it will be the first time that I've tutored a lady student. Now, what can you tell me about Peter Dirichlet's work on number theory?'

I gasped. 'You misunderstand. I won't be—'

He raised a hand. 'Stop. Your reputation precedes you. I know you to have a quick mind and a firm grasp of the principles of mathematics and mathematical physics. You may dispense with such modesty.'

I felt my face grow warm. 'No. You stop and listen to me. *I've* been assigned to tutor *you*. Didn't Professor Milton write to you?' I rummaged in my pocket and pulled out my letter. 'He wrote this, to me.'

He took it from me and read it. 'Indeed, he did write to me. But this is rather embarrassing.' He picked up the ink-splattered envelope on which he had scribbled the note and pulled out another letter, which he put down next to mine.

The two letters were similarly written in Professor Milton's near-unreadable scrawl. Similar, but not identical. 'You see,' Lazarus said. 'He asked *me* to tutor *you*.'

'I do not need tutoring in reading. Or in anything else,' I snapped. I grabbed his pen and underlined the crucial sentence in my letter. 'He asked *me*,' at this point I gouged a hole in the page, 'to tutor *you*.'

He ran his hands through his hair. 'Well, this is a pretty state of affairs. We must go to him now and ask him how he wishes us to proceed.'

I shook my head. 'Not unless you have the time and the money for a train ride to Scotland and back. At this precise moment, he's up to his knees in seawater at Lossiemouth.'

'A little cold in October, I'd have thought, for bathing. Although, perhaps, he's eating a strawberry ice?' He looked over my shoulder into the distance. 'My favourite.'

I felt my throat tighten. 'Never mind that!'

A muffled "shh" came from one of the readers at the table behind me, followed by a muttered comment about women.

I sank into a chair. 'The point is,' I whispered, 'that he won't be returning for at least two weeks, or perhaps even until after the date by which the research proposals must be submitted. There's nobody else to ask about what he wants us to do. It is all very well for you, with publications under your belt already. But I can't wait. I must set up my own research, and get published, or lose my postgraduate place.'

He sat next to me. 'Miss Thorniwork, please don't distress yourself. There must be some solution.' I felt his warm breath, inches from my ear. I turned.

'Please? Let us consider this,' he said again, drawing in a breath and holding it. His eyes opened wider and I was put in mind of a puppy pleading for a treat.

'I'm sorry for my brusqueness,' I said, fighting back an urge to pat his head. 'This isn't your fault.'

He exhaled. I smelled a combination of tobacco and peppermint. 'Perhaps Professor Milton has set us a conundrum,' he said. 'And its solution's that he means us to work together.'

'He is not known for such japes and tricks, but it seems we may have little option but to do so. At least, I don't. No research, no place. It is a matter of publish or perish.'

He placed his hand on mine. My heartbeat calmed as I felt its warmth. 'Now, let us consider on what we might work,' he said. 'I know that we're both interested in Durège's theories that so cleverly explain the theory of functions of a complex variable.' He nodded towards the book. I felt my face redden, and I looked down.

'Come, now, Miss Thorniwork. Time is of the essence, we've none to spare on modesty. Your enthusiasm for the subject does you credit. And I know from discussions among the faculty, that you match this with your skill and quick mind. Spaulding, in particular, is impressed by your ability.'

I turned towards him. 'Thank you. It'll be refreshing to work with someone who values what I have to offer. Rather than someone who views me as something to be tolerated.' As I smiled, I felt my heart flutter and I cursed myself for acting like the heroine of one of Mother's gothic novels.

'Yes,' he said. 'I have encountered that reaction from Professor Milton, myself.'

'But you have nothing to prove to anyone. And neither have I. We will demonstrate that in our research.'

He gasped and his voice grew louder. 'Oh, so you agree that we can work together?' More hushing from the table behind.

I nodded.

He leaned towards me and whispered again. 'Capital. Durège is fine, as far as he has gone. And, indeed, there's an almost musical quality to his theories. But, I feel that the time has come not only to probe more deeply, but to take a step in the direction of Mr Faraday. Into the world of magnetism. And from there into the world of dreams.'

I stood. 'I read Dr Freud's *Studies on Hysteria* as soon as it was published last year, but I am no psychologist. And magnets? I fear that we cannot help each other.' It would do me no favours to be associated with what appeared to be the ideas of a mountebank.

He raised a finger. 'No. Listen. Have you ever wished you could master the art of controlling your dreams?'

I would not wish him to think me unstable. I sat again and nodded.

'I see that you have. And you may yet find that you can. My research suggests that, in the presence of a strong magnetic field, the sleeper can do precisely that. I refer you to my paper in *Trigonometric Series* last year. I mean our article, Prof Milton, Parbold and I. *Some interesting findings in magnetism.*'

'That was yours? First rate mathematics.'

'Thank you. It's good to be appreciated. But that presented my preliminary findings only. Work is needed to determine the flux density needed, before we can even consider its alignment with the head... we have much to do.'

We. 'Mr Lazarus, I believe we can collaborate,' I said. 'It can succeed.' And if I had to nail my colours to the mast of an unlikely sounding proposal, then it might as well be with a man who was not completely repellent.

He wagged his finger at me. 'Not only *can* succeed, Miss Thorniwork, but *must.*'

'We will succeed.' I remembered what Freud had said about the power of suggestion. 'Perhaps there is an aspect of prime numbers that we can incorporate into the work.'

'To work!' He pushed up the sleeves of his jacket, revealing shirt cuffs with frayed edges.

'You should ask Mrs Lazarus to get out her darning needle.' The words bubbled out before I could stop them.

His brow furrowed. 'That's true. But I fear that, living in London as my aunt does, she is too far away for me to ask. I must deploy the needle myself, and I'm unskilled in that art. I wouldn't presume to assume that I could ask you to undertake it, simply by virtue of your sex.'

I could not contain my laughter as I shook my head. 'It would be useless if you did. I too am unskilled.' I thought of May, who covered any bit of fabric unable to escape her attentions with embroidered exotic blooms in colours that made my eyes water. 'I have resisted all attempts to change that.'

'I've another proposal for you. In keeping with the times, I put it to you that we abandon the use of unwieldy surnames. My name is Leopold, but my friends call me Leo. And I believe your name is Euphemia.'

'It is,' I said. I waited for him to explain the meaning of the name. We looked at each other for what felt like several minutes.

He frowned. 'Oh dear,' he said. 'Have I said something wrong?'

'No, it's just that, well…' I felt my face grow warm again. 'People are forever telling me that it means "fair speech".'

He raised his eyebrows. 'Do they? Oh dear, I'm sorry to have disappointed you. My aunt is always saying that my social graces are few.'

'They're fine. I'm not disappointed. It is not always polite to tell a person the meaning of their name. After all, according to some people, the name Portia means pig.'

He smiled. 'There we go again, speaking of pigs. Such irony, since I cannot eat them.'

'No? Well, there are many who find their flesh difficult

to digest.' My stomach rumbled. The power of suggestion, again. 'Perhaps we can leave our books here, and go to take refreshment somewhere? I have found an agreeable tearoom in Turl Street. Or do cakes and biscuits also disagree with you?'

He stood up. 'Cakes are always acceptable. Fair speech, you say? How appropriate, for one who is so well regarded. Now, Euphemia—'

I rose too, and put my hand on his arm. 'Leo, call me Pheemie.'

Transcendental Numbers

As I poured hot water from the enamel jug into my basin the following morning, I realised it would be eight hours until it was time to meet Leo. I told myself not to be stupid. I would make good use of the time to draw up research proposals of my own. I would work in the Bodleian. Leo might be there.

He was not. I remembered he had told me he would be lecturing. The morning dragged on and on, but eventually it was time to go out to the Botanic Garden, where Leo and I had finally decided to meet despite the November weather. I scurried along Catte Street into the High, through rain. Would he still come? Where was he?

I stopped and peered across the road, past cyclists and carriages. A man stood by the park entrance reading a book, his face concealed by a voluminous black umbrella with a vicious looking spike at the top. He tipped the umbrella back and looked out. It was Leo. He waved.

I crossed the road. 'Good afternoon. I'd begun to wonder whether you'd come, in all this rain.' He put the book, *An account of the Poincaré Conjecture*, in his overcoat pocket and smiled. 'I would not have left you standing, waiting for me.' We walked into the Garden.

'There are a lot of exotic botanical oddities in the Garden,' he said. 'It is one of my favourite places.'

'Then I will let you be my guide.' I stepped under the umbrella, dislodging my hat in the process. I replaced it and went to take his arm, but thought better of it. Our hands bumped. I apologised. We hurried into the Garden.

'This rain!' he said. 'I think it would be a good idea if we looked at the hothouses, although I fear there may be little growing there.'

The first hothouse we entered had a raised square pool in the middle of the floor, filled with water lilies and fish.

'Let's sit down,' Leo said.

'Why, are you tired?'

'No, but there's no hurry. You don't need to get back, do you?'

We found a bench. 'Some of these fish are incredibly old,' he said. 'They can live for hundreds of years. They might have seen Mr Charles Dodgson, while he was formulating his work on condensation of determinants. Or, perhaps, Mr Edmond Halley.'

'You think of things others wouldn't. Perhaps sitting in such illustrious company, even at many years' separation, will help us decide what research to pursue. We don't have long to draw up proposals. I have some ideas about number theory and the distribution of primes.'

'I too have suggestions. I feel that perhaps the matter of magnetism and dreams may be a little obstruse for Professor Milton. Let's compare and contrast. Talking of Halley, I think we should aim for the stars. I mean, to produce a solution to one of the great unsolved mathematical conjectures. Let me explain.'

He drew closer. A drop of rain dripped off the brim of his hat onto my sleeve. At that moment, two old ladies in black raincoats buttoned up to their chins entered the hothouse and cast pointed glances at the bench. Leo stood and raised his hat. 'Please, do sit.'

I did likewise and rubbed a clear patch in the condensation on a pane of glass and looked outside. The rain had stopped. 'Let's walk,' I said.

Leo strode along a path, holding forth about the Riemann Hypothesis. 'It is of great interest in number theory because it implies results about the distribution of prime numbers.' I ran to keep up with him. 'Many people consider it the most important unsolved problem in pure mathematics.'

'Yes, I think we should concentrate on prime numbers,' I said.

'Very well. Let's pause for a moment, next to these magnificent aconites.'

'My cousin told me that even the colour of a flower had a meaning, that there was a language of flowers. For example, hyacinth is meant to mean "your loveliness charms me". But I prefer the language of numbers.'

'Quite right. Flowers could lie,' Leo said, 'if you put them together in the wrong way. Or maybe the right way. We should make a sarcastic message and send them to Prof Milton.'

The rain started again. We darted underneath a spreading cedar tree. 'They plant evergreens like this in churchyards,' I said. 'It's meant to represent everlasting life, not that I believe in that. Religion is a hodgepodge of false claims, with no basis in reality. The idea of God is a product of the human imagination.'

Leo raised his eyebrows. 'My faith, Judaism, holds that life isn't the end, but there's not much dogma about the afterlife. It seems to be a matter of personal opinion.'

'Well, my opinion is that it is all superstitious nonsense,' I said. Wind gusted along the path, sending yellow-brown leaves scudding before it. I shivered.

'It's too cold to think,' Leo said. 'If you don't find this an improper suggestion, perhaps we can discuss things further in my study.'

'That would be most acceptable. Let us leave, before we get drenched.'

His room was crammed with heavy oak tables and chairs, ill-matched as though he had taken residence in a furniture depository. Books were heaped on every surface; others were scattered across the floor where a pile had overbalanced. Leo heaped a shovelful of coal onto the embers in the grate and the flames grew, illuminating a newspaper lying next to the fireplace. The headline: 'London Enshrouded in Thick Fog'.

On a table by the window stood a square wooden box with a closed lid. I touched the ornately scrolled crank handle mounted on the front.

'Ah, you admire my tone generator. Allow me.' He flipped open the lid. 'My own invention.'

I peered inside at an intriguing series of interconnected wheels and reels of different sizes, ending in two glass bell-shaped devices from which I supposed the sound emerged.

'It generates a pure tone of a fixed frequency.' He operated the crank and the machine produced a sound like a loud violin, rising in pitch as he turned the handle faster. 'I hope soon to find a way to power the device with a dry cell.'

'How interesting for you, but why did you make it?'

'Because I could. If you are interested, I could show you how. Some tones, some notes, are pleasing. It can generate more than one. Some intervals—I mean the gap between notes, are most satisfying to listen to.' He flicked a switch at the side of the box. Two notes. 'This is called a perfect fifth. There's a strict mathematical ratio between the two notes. Music and mathematics are linked.'

I shrugged. 'Perhaps you ought to teach music in your spare time, which we will have in excess if we do not produce a research proposal acceptable to Milton.'

'You are right. To work!' His stomach rumbled. 'I do apologise—unlike the perfect fifth, that is not satisfying to hear.' He wrinkled his brow. 'Although, I could tell you what note my insides sounded.'

'Please do not. But perhaps we should find somewhere to eat?'

'There is no need. Allow me—will you join me in a boiled egg?'

I realised it was many hours since lunchtime. I would help in the only way that I could, by taking the kettle into the scullery.

Leo poured a dark stream of tea into a cup in front of me, decorated on the inside with pictures of playing cards and dominoes, with 'Many Curious Things I See, When Telling Fortunes In Your Tea' written around the rim in curling script. I dipped my spoon into the golden egg yolk. 'This is delicious, Leo. The consistency is perfect. I wish I had a copy of Mrs Beeton to hand; she explains how it is achieved. So that you can replicate it.'

'There's no need.' Leo launched into a complex scientific explanation of egg cookery and protein coagulation, including the effects of atmospheric pressure.

I looked out of the window at the darkening day. In London, the fog would have emerged by now but here it was still clear.

The room grew dark except for the glow of the fire. Leo lit the gaslights, illuminating the photographs on the mantelpiece. I walked across and looked more closely at one, a man and a woman gazing straight at the camera, the woman with a sardonic expression as though remembering a joke. The man looked like Leo.

'Who are they?'

'My late parents.'

'I am sorry—I did not mean to distress you.'

'You did not. They died when I was a child of five. My aunt and uncle took me in. My uncle is no longer with us, but this is my aunt Matilda.' He picked up a photo of a woman in her sixties. 'I live with her when I am in London—in Islington.'

'My father is dead. Mother and I live in Highgate with my aunt, uncle and cousin. Mother approves of my study, but the rest of them take the view that all I think of is mathematics, and they consider this boorish and uncultured.'

He nodded. 'Yes, I am also the victim of this accusation. But I like many other things. Music, walking. You?'

'I think that there is music in numbers. I too like to walk.'

'Then you would have liked a delightful stroll I took on Hampstead Heath last summer, near Whitestone Pond.'

'That's close to where Mother and I used to live, before we relocated to my uncle's house. I… I wish I had been there.'

'You must come with me next time,' he said. I had hoped he would.

I looked at the cup. 'I see that you also collect crockery.'

'Ah, this. It was a present from me to my aunt. She gave it back.'

'I can see that it might not appeal to everyone. What made you give her such a thing?'

'Well, she's always wishing she could see into future, so that she could tell what time I'm going to return in the evening. It was a sort of joke, after an occasion when my watch stopped, and I was late. She returned it so that— she said—I'd have something to remind me to wind my watch.'

'My cousin May, with whom I now live, would find it marvellous—but I'm not suggesting you give it to her. She maintains that you can derive a wealth of meaning from different shapes formed by tea leaves at the bottom of a cup. Really, she makes it all up. She can't tell a skull from a set of stairs. Her predictions always turn out to be about meeting young men.'

'Perhaps she will meet someone who owns a tea plantation.'

'I would be happy if she went to Ceylon to try.'

Leo frowned.

'I'm sorry, I do not wish to be uncharitable. But May and I are so badly suited. It starts as soon as we awake when she sits around the breakfast table discussing dreams.'

'There's little more boring.' He poured out more tea.

'Especially when she tries to interpret them. Like Joseph.' I remembered a Bible story that Pearl told me.

'Yes—Genesis Thirty-Seven. And his brothers hated

him for his interpretations.'

'That is typical in families,' I said. 'Nothing changes. But you seem quite the biblical scholar. My other cousin Pearl was, too.'

'My aunt and uncle insisted I attend religious classes three times a week when I was a child. The Bible is poetic in both the original Hebrew and in translation, but I—unlike some—am not convinced that it can be considered as a history book.'

'Pearl loved it for its language. I miss her.'

'If it would help to talk about it,' he said, 'then consider me to be all ears.'

I looked away. 'I do not wish to bore you.'

'It would not, I'm sure. I wish to know more about you.'

'It might help us work together more efficiently.' I explained about Pearl and Aunt Ada. About the theft of their bodies, the finding of Aunt Ada's, Pearl's still missing. 'And I dream of her,' tumbled out before I could stop it.

'That is natural. She is in your thoughts.'

'True. And it would normally be lovely to see her in my dreams, even if I did have to wake alone. But these are so peculiar.'

He raised his eyebrows. 'In what way? I feel certain that *they* are not boring.'

I did not reply.

'I apologise for prying.'

I thought of the dream I had had about Pearl and the alehouse and remembered the laudanum. 'Dreams are probably just the effects of what we eat or drink.'

'Or what occupies our mind. I confess to dreaming, once, that I was giving a lecture dressed only in my underwear.' His face reddened.

'I believe people look for patterns where there aren't any, to try to make sense of the randomness of life.'

He did not reply, and we fell into silence.

I felt no need to talk. When you can be quiet with someone, that is special. He looked at his watch. Perhaps he felt that, if we had nothing to discuss, our time together had run its course. I cast around for something to say.

'You mentioned attending classes. Do you read Hebrew?'

'Yes. And here is something interesting. You mentioned patterns.' He picked up a book from the floor, opened it and showed me a diagram containing letters, presumably Hebrew, and numbers. 'It's called gematria. Numerology. Each letter has a number assigned to it. So that the letters in Hebrew words can be added together. For example, the word for "life" adds up to eighteen. It's seen as a spiritual number, and some Jewish people give to charity in multiples of eighteen.' He took a pencil and paper. 'Look—this is your name written in Hebrew. And mine.' He looked at the diagram in the first book and scribbled under each letter that he had written. 'Remarkable—they both equal one hundred and fifty-six.'

We looked at each other for a moment. 'Pure random chance,' I said. 'Although it would be tempting to think that it means that our research proposals will be successful.'

'Let me do the same calculation for Rufus,' Leo said. It was Professor Milton's forename, with the total of three hundred and fifty-two.

'No matter; I was not going to suggest we propose it as

61

a topic for research.'

The smell of cooking rose from the kitchens. I went to the window and looked out into the wet, shining quadrangle, crowded with hurrying figures.

'Shall we find somewhere to eat?' I asked. 'It's a pity I'm not allowed to eat in hall.'

'Not a pity. Stupidity. There is no reason why women shouldn't do so. Hall is not a bath-house changing room. But in any case, I regret I have arranged to dine with Parbold, in his rooms. He wants to discuss transcendental numbers.'

'I hope that you can eat quickly. Even as fascinating a subject as that would not induce me to be in his company for longer than five minutes.'

'Fortunately for my digestion, I find him a pleasant enough chap. He has promised that he will serve no meat forbidden by the Jewish dietary laws.'

We left the room and walked downstairs, arranging to meet again the next afternoon, in Leo's study.

I returned to my room. Someone had collected a letter for me and pushed it under my door. The letter was from mother. I snatched it open. Before I left London, she had made some reference to limitations of money. I had asked what she meant but she had not replied. This letter did not answer the question, but merely included some inconsequential account of family life. She had included one from May. I skipped over a page concerning the fog and her supernatural beliefs about it, to the end where she asked if I had yet to meet a young man. I wondered what she would make of Leo. We had failed to discuss our research proposal, but for some reason I had enjoyed myself.

Tea for Three

A few days later, we enjoyed a cup of tea and a slice of seed cake in the tea shop in Turl Street. On the next day, Leo and I met in his study yet again.

Sugar crunched under my feet as I entered. The scent of fruit and spice pervaded it—ginger, lemon and another I could not immediately identify. Leo stood by a table near the fireplace, holding something wrapped in a teacloth. I looked around for something on which to hang my coat and, finding nothing more suitable, draped it over an over-stuffed armchair. He held out a metal cylinder six inches in radius and height.

'You're just in time,' he said, dropping the cylinder onto the table. He threw the cloth to one side and blew on his hands. 'That was close. I really must invest in something to provide better heat insulation. One of those woollen potholders, perhaps?' He raised his eyebrows.

'When you know me better, you won't assume that I can knit,' I said. 'I could ask my cousin to embroider one, perhaps. I would tell her that it was for me.'

'Please do. I will hang it on a nail and think of the two of you whenever I see it. Now, to make the tea.'

He took a soot-blackened kettle from a cluttered shelf.

'Let me,' I said. 'The least I can do is go to the scullery for the water.' From the look of the kettle, I presumed we would have to boil it on the fire, as we had done with the egg.

'I wouldn't dream of it. You're my guest. But if you do want to help, see if you can get my work of art out of the tin.'

He left the room, and I looked at his creation. It was the source of the delicious smell—a cake, golden brown and risen to fill the cylindrical tin. I looked around for a plate and unearthed a large one from underneath a heap of textbooks, its floral pattern faded, a chip in the rim. On the floor to one side of the hearth was a squat wick-bearing metal bottle with a circular frame mounted above, and next to it a screwed-up tea cloth. I used it to pick up the tin, which I inverted over the plate. I shook it once, the cake slid out, and landed upside down. Perhaps if I put my hand right underneath, it might invert. It felt like it was on fire. I jerked my hand away.

Leo came back with the kettle. He put it on the floor and wiped soot from his hands. 'Thank you. But stop! It'll break if you shove it about like that.' He picked up the topmost book on the heap, *Riemann surfaces as bounded domains* and put it on top of the cake. He inverted the plate, put that on the table and slid the cake back onto it from the book.

'Just like a conjuring trick!' I said, picking up the book. 'And no greasy marks on the cover.'

'Grease? You traduce my baking skills.' He gasped and recoiled, the back of his hand against his forehead.

'Now you're being silly. You know I meant no harm. I am sure I couldn't make a cake that would rise more than an inch. And yours looks as though it might float away in the slightest draught.'

He patted my arm. 'I'll make the tea.'

He took a box of matches from the mantelpiece, lit the wick in the metal bottle and placed the kettle on top of the frame above it.

'Is that another of your inventions?'

'I wish it were. I would make my fortune. But no—it's called a Primus stove, my latest purchase. The latest thing. From Sweden. So much more controllable than ramming things into the fire.'

Another smell competed with the cake. 'It is operated by paraffin, presumably?'

'Yes. But I devised this cake-making attachment. You fill this part with water, place the tin with the cake inside, and the entirety on the stove.'

He took two cups from a shelf, one decorated with what appeared to be red and purple cauliflowers, the other without a pattern but coloured a bilious green that I could still see when I closed my eyes.

'I am afraid I have no saucers,' he said, putting the cups on the table.

'I will be most careful not to spill my tea.'

A brown teapot stood on the table. Leo picked up a pottery jar next to it, labelled 'dried beans.' He took off the lid and spooned tea from the can into the pot. 'I hope that Ceylon tea will suffice.'

'Any, as long as it has no beans.'

'Beans? I thought you liked coffee.' His brow furrowed, as though he was trying to solve a conundrum. 'Oh, I see. My aunt gave me the jar as it was surplus to her kitchen requirements.' He tipped some tea into his hand, then into the pot.

The kettle boiled. He took it off the stove and blew out

the flame, which increased the odour of paraffin. That aroma would always remind me of today.

Leo poured water into the teapot. I sat at the table, tottering on a chair with uneven legs. Leo sat next to me, picked up a wooden ruler, wiped it on his sleeve, and used it to cut the cake. He seized a piece of paper from a mound on the other side of the table and put it in front of me. It was covered with equations, in Leo's characteristic scribble. He dropped a piece of cake onto it, then repeated the exercise.

'The ink is indelible. It won't come off onto the cake. Don't worry.'

'I won't,' I said, through a mouthful of feather-light confection. I gulped. 'I apologise for my poor table manners.' I took another bite.

'I shall take it as a compliment.'

'But Leo, I owe you another apology. I asked you to join me in the teashop. And you did. But this outdoes anything we can get in Turl Street—I am sorry that I made you eat inferior cake.'

'I chose to do so. And, the company more than made up for any culinary shortcomings.' He put his hand on my arm again and left it there.

There was a knock, and Spaulding entered without waiting for permission. He strode to Leo, without looking at me. 'Lazarus, do you have my copy of… I say—do I spy teacups?'

'You do, and you have timed your book request to perfection. A coincidence, I am sure. Find yourself a cup and join us.'

He turned his head. 'Oh, hello, Euphemia.' He went to the cupboard and returned to the table with a black cup, spattered with irregular orange blobs around the edging. He sat. 'And delicious-looking cake, too!'

'It doesn't just look delicious, it is.' I licked my fingertip and used it to pick up my few remaining crumbs.

'A recipe of my own composition.' Leo cut another slice, put it on a sheet of paper and handed it to Spaulding.

'Really, Lazarus,' Spaulding said. 'Your crockery does not match—and you have no plates or teaspoons at all. The only sugar I can see is all over the floor. And what of the milk? Will you bring a cow to the table?'

'Are you familiar with the expression about beggars and choosers?' Leo stood and walked to the rain-spattered window, opened it, and picked up a jug striped with yellow and black like a hornet, topped with a beaded fabric lid, from the outside ledge. He put it on the table, lifted the teapot lid and peered inside. 'It is ready, I think. Pheemie—please do us the honour of pouring it.'

'Oh, no—that honour must go to the chef.' The pot looked as though it might drip.

'Quite,' Spaulding said. 'Besides, there's some superstition that if one person makes tea and another pours it for a third person, something happens to the third one, and that's me. I don't know what, though. Perhaps someone shoots them.'

'Or their research proposal gets declined.'

'Very well, allow me.' Leo grasped the pot. 'Sugar?'

'No!' Spaulding and I spoke at the same time.

We sipped our tea. 'It is refreshing. Despite the diluted milk. Of course, one could not keep a milk jug outdoors like that in London. Regardless of what you think the fog's origins, I would not wish to take it in milk.'

Spaulding took a bite of cake. 'Euphemia, this lemon cake is delicious. You made it, I trust?'

'I? No, I can boil an egg, thanks to Leo's expert tuition, but that's all. The cake is his.'

'Of course, I should have known the cake was not yours, because the best chefs are men,' Spaulding said. 'Women can cook, of course, Mrs Beeton and all that. I am sure you do yourself no credit—a boiled egg, indeed! I imagine you are adept at plain food.' I decided not to enlighten him. 'Bread pudding, potatoes, that sort.' He ticked them off on his fingers. 'But think of the great Escoffier. Peach Melba!'

'You have tasted it?' I said.

'Well, no, but I have eaten Melba toast. Also, one of his creations. Named after a great operatic soprano. Such a voice!'

Which, I would wager, he had never heard. 'Then we must call this "Lemon Cake Lazarus",' I said.

'Quite so,' said Spaulding. 'Now, what are your research intentions? Remember, we have little time to present our proposals.'

'Prime numbers.'

'In the generation of a magnetic field of a particular flux density,' Leo added.

Spaulding raised his eyebrows. 'Really? I can't see Milton agreeing to such a hotchpotch of mathematics and physics, even if you bake him a cake.'

I felt my face grow warm. 'That remains to be seen. Anyway, when you go far enough back, you really can't tell who's a physicist and who's a mathematician.'

'This is true,' Leo said. 'In order to reach the pinnacle, Newton had to invent a new concept of mathematics; it's called calculus.'

'And what will you be doing, Spaulding, that you think will have Milton crowning you a genius?' I said.

Spaulding smiled. 'Don't distress yourself. We are not in competition here. It will, as ever, be more a case of my writing a paper for him to put his name to. More likely, several papers.'

He rose and stood with his back to the fire, shielding it from the rest of us, still holding his slice of cake. Crumbs dropped onto the floor as he waved his hand to illustrate what he was saying. 'My proposal concerns the calculus of finite differences. For instance, in the series of terms 12, 22, 32, 42, where the xth term is $x2$, the values of x are the series of natural numbers and, of course, $\Delta x = 1$.'

'Of course,' Leo said. 'I wonder where this might lead?'

'Assuming $t = hx$,' I said, 'we have $\Delta t = h\Delta$, from which $\Delta x = 1$.'

Spaulding took on the expression of my neighbour's cat, back in London, the time I wrested a baby mouse from him.

'I appreciate that we are not in competition, but doesn't everyone know that?' I said.

'Evidently,' Spaulding said. 'Thank you for my tea. Now, I had better return to my room, to find another novel topic to pursue.' He stood and walked out of the room. The soles of his shoes squeaked against the polished floor of the corridor as he stepped outside. Perhaps now Leo and I could discuss our research in more detail.

The fire burned low; its glowing coals were just the right level of incandescence for making toast.

'Next time, I must bring muffins. Or teacakes,' I said.

Leo cupped a hand round his ear. 'E flat. 311.127

cycles per second.'

'What is?'

'Was. The note his shoe made. Don't you believe me? I can replicate it using my frequency mechanistic generator.'

I had no wish to repeat the experience of having my eardrums almost split. 'I believe you. There's no need for you to operate your contraption. But you must think of a more winning name for it, should you want it to have a commercial application. Such as, "The Lazarus..."' I tried unsuccessfully to think of a word beginning with L. 'Anyway, I'm not arguing with you, but to me, the shoe sounded more like a squeal than a song.'

He shook his head. 'Yes, but behind it all, there's a note. It's a bit of a curse, really, this perfect pitch. Hearing music everywhere. Even Professor Milton scraping at the board with a fragment of chalk.' He snatched a teaspoon from the table and tapped each of our teacups in turn. He winced. 'Well, perhaps not the Prof. But, do you see? If Spaulding had drunk just a little less tea, these three notes would be an augmented triad.' He picked up the teapot and poured tea into the cup, drop by drop, tapping with the spoon as he poured. 'Ah, that's better. Now, if you would assist.' He passed me a spoon. 'On three, tap your cup.' Taking a spoon in each hand he tapped his two cups. I hit mine. It broke.

I dabbed at the spilt tea with a cloth from the washstand. 'I am so sorry, Leo. I will replace it.'

'Nonsense. It must have been cracked, in fact I am certain that it was, from the sound it made. But, perhaps—if this isn't too presumptuous—you would accompany me to buy a replacement?'

'And, perhaps, some saucers? And plates.'

'Most certainly. I'm afraid my aunt wanted to keep all of those.'

'Then buy some we shall. But only if we can take a cup of tea in a cafe, afterwards.'

'I will hold you to that. Friday, after I have finished with the first-year students. Let's meet outside the lecture theatre at two o'clock.'

As I rose to leave, a flame leapt in the fireplace, illuminating his face. He was smiling.

Broken Six

Leo and I spent the next two days in the laboratory, covering a blackboard in equations. However, I had decided to undertake research of my own. Women could equal, or even outdo men, in baking sweets and fancies. Mother would know a cake recipe. With no time to lose, I sent her a telegram.

Her reply came by the next post. I grabbed it from the porter before he had the chance to put it into my pigeonhole and ripped it open where I stood.

> *'Please send no more telegrams about such matters. I thought that it brought bad news. Nurse Wilkins was most agitated and insisted on dosing me with her vile-tasting heart medicine. May, however, thought that you were engaged to be married so it was bad news for her to find out the truth. She was most downcast, until I told her that you had asked for a recipe, whereupon— she decided that you must at least have met a young man. This brightened her mood. I too am pleased you wish to know more of the housewife's skills. Here is the recipe for that fruit cake of which you are so fond.'*

She continued with an account of life at home. One of the maids had given notice and Mother filled several pages about the difficulty of engaging servants, especially when so many were sick from the fog. She ended by wishing me every success in my studies and said that she hoped to see me very soon.

Perhaps Uncle Jacob was not offering high enough wages. Could it be he could not afford to pay more? Mother did not mention money, but in any case, would she tell me if his financial scheme had run aground? I would have to force myself to go back for a visit one weekend. I put the letter in my pocket and set out for the lecture theatre. Leo would be finished in fifteen minutes.

I entered the theatre and took a seat at the back. Rows of desks and chairs stretched downwards, towards the stage at the front, where Leo stood in front of a blackboard, speaking about conjectures. The students scribbled. I jumped as he banged his board duster onto the table to emphasise a point. The chalk flew off into a cloud, which settled in distinguished-looking grey wings on the dark hair above his ears.

Leo coughed and resumed his lecture. 'Mountain climbing is a beloved metaphor for mathematical research. The comparison is almost inevitable: the frozen world, the cold thin air and the implacable harshness of mountaineering reflect the unforgiving landscape of numbers, formulae and theorems. And just as a climber pits his abilities against an unyielding object—in his case, a sheer wall of stone—a mathematician often finds himself engaged in an individual battle of the human mind against rigid logic.'

The students stopped scribbling. Leo continued. 'In mathematics, the role of these highest peaks is played by the great conjectures—sharply formulated statements most likely true but for which no conclusive proof has been found. These conjectures have deep roots and wide ramifications. The search for their solution guides a large part of mathematics. Eternal fame awaits those who conquer them first.' He looked up and his eyes met mine. He put the duster down and bounded up the steps to my place at the back, opened the door and gestured to me to step outside.

'I'm afraid we started half an hour late, owing to the loquacity of the preceding lecturer. Allowing time for questions, I am unlikely to finish for some forty-five minutes. You know this subject inside out. You won't want to sit through the lecture. I'm afraid we may need to postpone our crockery purchasing.'

At that moment, I could think of nothing more important than looking for crockery, or drinking tea with Leo. 'Oh, no—I'll wait.'

'Very well.' He fumbled in a pocket and pulled out a key. 'Let yourself into my room, make yourself comfortable. I'll meet you there. The shops will still be open when I have finished.'

The cake contraption stood on Leo's table. Mother's recipe instructed to bake the cake for half an hour. There should be plenty of time for the whole process, before Leo came back.

He walked into the study as I placed the cake tin on the table.

'Pheemie! Is something burning? Ah, no, you have been baking. Is there no end to your talents?'

'I fear there might be.' I wiped my forehead with the back of my floury hand. 'I've never made a cake before. It was not as easy as I thought it would be. It is meant to be a fruit cake so as well as using some of your raisins, I have included peaches. I almost severed my hand on that vicious tin opening device.'

'I am sure the results will be delicious. Peaches? It will rival that Melba concoction Spaulding mentioned, I am sure.'

'We shall take him a slice,' I said. 'Make him eat his words about women and cooking.'

I shook the cake tin over a large platter bearing the words 'a present from Blackpool'. Nothing happened. I shook it again. No movement. I put it down.

'Allow me.' Leo picked up the wooden ruler that did service for a knife and ran it round the inside of the tin. 'Didn't you flour it first?' I had not understood, and therefore ignored, the reference to 'a floured tin' in the recipe, and shook my head. 'No matter.' He gave the tin another shake and the contents, about one inch thick, dull grey and studded with scorched peaches landed with a thud I thought would shatter the plate.

We looked at each other for a few seconds. 'Not a recipe I'm familiar with,' Leo said, 'but one I am most anxious to try.' He picked up the ruler. It made not so much as a scratch on the cake. 'You must tell me how you made it.'

'Oh, I can't remember. And I'm sure it's not meant to be like this. Throw it away, Leo. But don't put it out for the birds—they will break their beaks.'

'Nonsense.' He grasped the edge of the cake and snapped off a morsel , his face reddening with the effort. He handed the piece to me, then forced away another for himself. 'There—you have invented a cake for which no knife is needed.' He put his piece into his mouth and chewed.

I did the same. After a few minutes I managed to mash it into a consistency that could be swallowed. Something crunched in my mouth.

'Leo—do you keep nuts with your raisins?' He shook his head. 'Then—please excuse me,' I turned aside and spat out a hard object into my hand 'But, what's this?'

He peered into my outstretched palm. 'I am no expert, but it would appear to be part of a molar.'

I touched a newly-sharp area of mouth with my tongue, poking a cake fragment into the broken tooth. A thousand red hot serrated needles jammed through my jaw. I squealed and clutched my cheek.

'Poor Pheemie,' Leo said. 'I fear our outing must be neither to the china shop nor the tea shop, but to a dentist.'

Leo dashed into the corridor and knocked on a door. After a conversation of which I could not distinguish the words, he came back.

'Parbold recommends Mr Overfinch, who operates from a house in the Banbury Road. We must leave right away.'

'Will he be at work on a Friday afternoon, and will he treat me without an appointment?' I gasped as air hit the broken tooth.

'We must trust that he is, and will.'

Leo flung on a coat. I did the same and, wrapping my scarf round my now-throbbing face, we ran down the stairs into the rainy street.

The laurel bushes bordering the path, leading to the

Overfinch surgery, dripped with rain. The house was built of yellowish brick, with a gabled roof and narrow gothic windows set in frames of ornamental stonework. I knocked at the door, which a woman in her late twenties, wearing a long white apron, opened.

I pointed at my cheek and gave a moan. She took my arm. 'No—don't try to speak, you poor creature. My father will treat you. Please wait in here. I will ask him to see you next. I am Nurse Susan Overfinch.'

Leo gave her my name and she ushered me into a room with dark brown papered walls, hung with daguerreotypes of men in cravats, deerstalker hats or both, all with the same disapproving expression. Leo followed. We sat next to each other on hard wooden chairs. A vase of coloured teasels filled the emptiness of the fireplace. I did not remove my coat.

A table in the middle of the room bore a sheaf of documents dealing with the care of teeth, of gums, of dentures (which I hoped I would not need), the care of toothbrushes, of toothpaste canisters, a list of fees, and several omnibus timetables overprinted in red with 'patients who arrive late or fail to attend will be *fined*. By order.'

An old woman slumped in the chair next to mine extended her head from her many strata of outer garments. 'What you got, dear? Cold in the gums?'

I shook my head and unwrapped the scarf. 'Broken tooth.'

'Best have them all out, dear,' she said. 'Don't let him talk you into having one of them fillings. They rot the teeth, press on the nerves, set the rest off, bleed your gums, make you deaf, twist your eye cords and when that's all done, they drop out.'

I looked away. I could not afford such extensive treatment, even if I wanted it.

'I am sure it will not come to that,' Leo whispered.

'Have them out,' the woman repeated. 'Just make sure you know where the false ones come from. I heard they're snatching bodies in London, just for the teeth.'

She did not seem to be expecting a reply, and got none. We sat. Leo pulled a copy of *Mathematics Today* from his pocket and offered it to me. I shook my head. A square dark wooden clock standing on the mantelpiece chimed. Four o'clock. A man sitting opposite me, wearing an overlarge bowler hat pulled down almost over his eyes, lit a small cigar. He coughed. I jumped. Pages rustled. I sniffed.

'What's wrong?' Leo said. 'Have you taken cold?'

'No. I was wondering if that was the ether I could smell.'

He squeezed my hand. 'Not unless it smells like floor polish mixed with tobacco smoke.'

The bowler hat man glared, and stubbed the cigar out on an old coffee tin lid that had been left for an ashtray.

A door on the other side of the room opened, and Susan stepped through. She called my name. As Leo and I walked into the surgery, my knees appeared to have turned to water. Susan put her arm round my shoulders. 'Don't worry.'

In the corner, a black, box-like contraption, about a yard high, stood on wheeled legs. From one side protruded a crank handle, above several glass dials bearing titles including 'potentiometer' and 'transformer'. An object resembling an intricate glass and coiled chandelier stood on the top of the box, connected by a black rubber tube to a metallic cone-shaped object that dangled down the side. Next to it stood some other piece of equipment covered with a piece of green sheet. In the middle of the room was the chair, black, with metal fittings, a round white sink to one side.

The dentist looked to be in his early sixties, balding and with a straggle of beard like Mr Dickens's, but grey. He wore a stiff-looking, collarless white jacket that buttoned to his chin. 'I am Mr Overfinch,' he said to Leo. 'And what is the patient's name?'

'Father, this is not the eighteenth century. Women can speak for themselves.'

'My name is Euphemia Thorniwork. I have a broken tooth that I hope you will be able to fill.'

'My apologies, Mrs Thorniwork. My daughter is perfectly correct. I defer to her in all things. I am training her in dentistry. By the time I leave this world, she will have been able to attend the university, and qualify. Forty years of close work and open mouths have driven me half mad, let alone hastened the day of my doom.'

'Father, you have decades ahead of you,' Susan said. 'And I've much to learn.'

'It is *Miss* Thorniwork,' I muttered as I sat in the chair, gripping the armrests with damp palms. Susan draped a towel under my chin and stood next to me holding a pencil and a piece of card, showing an outline drawing of a mouthful of teeth. Leo sat on a chair in the corner.

'The ondontological Miss Overfinch. We can but hope,' Overfinch said, raising the chair with a foot-operated pump. He tipped the chair back so that I was facing the ceiling. 'Open wide!' Susan placed five metal tools, ended with different miniature hooks, chisels and spikes, on a small round table at head height to one side. He swivelled a bracket bearing a gas lamp towards my mouth and peered inside.

'Charting, please, Susan,' he said, squirting air onto my teeth from a metal tube fitted with a rubber bulb. I winced. 'One, two, three… sound.' With one of the tools, he tapped at each tooth in my upper jaw as he spoke. Susan annotated the tooth drawing. 'Please remain still, Mrs Thorniwork.' He started on the lower jaw. '…five, six fractured.'

My heart skipped a beat. Sitting up, I grabbed his hand and pulled it out of my mouth. 'Six! Must you remove six teeth?'

'Please calm yourself. This merely means that your sixth tooth, your lower right first molar, is the one that needs treatment. I note your details, so that, should you choose to attend once more, I will know the state of your dentition. Now let us see whether I can clean out the bad from your tooth with a little scraper then cover it with a silver lid.'

I exhaled, leaned back and opened my mouth again.

Susan joined him at peering inside my mouth. 'You have been in London, I perceive?' she said.

'Yes. My accent gives me away?'

'No—you speak very well. As you should, with a name that means "fair speech". I refer to the staining on your teeth. The fog, you know. I can recommend Shenley's tooth polish.'

'Thank you.'

'Do not thank us yet,' Overfinch said. 'I fear that the broken tooth may be beyond preservation. To confirm the position, I will radiograph it. I use Dr Roentgen's latest design. Perfectly safe.' He drew the box-like machine next to the chair.

'Power, please, Susan.'

I looked round. She took a dry cell the size of a house brick from a cupboard and connected it to a wire emerging from the side of the machine. Overfinch picked up a small, flat object about the size of a large postage stamp, put it in my mouth between the broken tooth and my tongue and took my hand. 'Please hold this small photographic plate with the tip of your finger. Now, remain still.'

He turned and rotated the crank on the side of the machine. A ticking began. He grasped the cone on the top of the chandelier fitting and placed it against my cheek. From the corner of my eye, I saw a light glowing on the machine. The ticking stopped and the light went out. Susan removed the photographic plate and disappeared through another door.

Someone knocked on the front door. 'Please excuse me,' Overfinch said. 'I must attend to this, while Susan is in the darkroom.' He strode into the hall. I snapped my mouth shut.

Leo spoke up from the corner. 'I wonder if he uses ether, or chloroform? I read that, when giving birth to Prince Leopold—that's how I remember it—Her Majesty pronounced chloroform a blessed relief.'

'You are not helping,' I squeaked. 'I am not giving birth. I don't care what he uses—if he does, which of course is not certain—as long as I'm asleep. Perhaps he can fill the tooth. Do you think he can? It wasn't that badly damaged, was it? Only a small piece fell off.'

Overfinch came back into the surgery. Susan came out of the darkroom holding the image. She held it up to the light and they studied it.

'Well? What is it? What does it show?' I said, heart pounding.

'I'm afraid I will have to lift the tooth out,' Overfinch said.

Susan nodded. 'But we will give you an anaesthetic. *"He that sleeps feels not the tooth-ache"*'.

'Cymbeline,' Overfinch said.

'I haven't heard of that. Is it better than chloroform? Will it make me sleep soundly?'

'I am sure that Mr Shakespeare would hate me to answer in the affirmative,' Overfinch said. In my mind's eye, Mother tutted. 'But I don't use chloroform, or ether. I administer the latest gaseous anaesthetic. Nitrous oxide. It is very popular with our friends in America.'

'You may have heard it called laughing gas,' Susan said.

'Not that it's a laughing matter. It is highly scientific.' Overfinch removed the green sheet, revealing a machine comprising different coloured gas cylinders, glass jars, and rubber tubes. 'This is how I do it. The anaesthetic is stored here.' He pointed to a cylinder leading to a tube, on the end of which was a mask. 'Nothing to fear. I'll show you.'

There was a faint hiss of compressed gas as his hand whirled round opening valves. I smelled roses. Pearl's favourite. A lump grew in my throat.

'This reservoir is intended for ether, but I don't need that for a quick dental procedure, so I fill it with perfume. Oh, don't cry—you won't feel a thing. I will also polish the fog stain away, while you are asleep.' He placed the rubber mask over my nose and mouth. 'Now blow that tooth of yours into this rubber bag. Nice and sleepy. Nice and sleepy.' My vision sparkled around the edges. My eyelids fell shut. From a long way in the distance, I heard Overfinch say 'Mason's gag please, Susan.'

I stood on a deserted, rocky shoreline. The sun had all but sunk below the horizon. Ahead, a lighthouse, constructed of pink bricks, rose into the grey sky. '341' was painted in black halfway up the side. At the top, the light turned, illuminating the shingle in front of me every twenty seconds. Each time the glow passed me, I heard a voice: 'Pheemie. Come to the light.' Pearl's voice. I ran through the open door at the base of the lighthouse. Above, a staircase spiralled. I climbed.

I stepped into the lamphouse. A figure stood, back towards me, looking out to sea, wearing a hooded black cloak. 'I know my Pheemie.' A woman. A voice I half-recognised. 'You'll have counted the stairs.'

'There are three hundred and forty-one.'

'Yes. That is what you need. Three hundred and forty-one.' She turned round, face still concealed. She grasped her hood and slipped it back. 'Three-'

'You've been very good,' Susan whispered, holding my head over the spittoon next to the dental chair. 'It is all over now. Just spit into the basin. All finished.'

'Pearl?' I said. 'Three hundred and forty-one what?'

'It's all done,' Susan said.

I tottered outside, Leo holding onto one arm and Susan the other. At least the rain had stopped.

'Best take a cab home, Mr Thorniwork,' Susan said.

'My name is Lazarus,' Leo said.

'So you and *Miss* Thorniwork?' Susan raised her eyebrows.

'We are partners in research,' I mumbled as best I could, moving my jaw as little as possible.

Susan shone the full radiance of her smile on Leo, revealing both her upper and lower gums so that her mouth that resembled a post box edged with perfect white teeth. 'We can always accommodate new patients,' she said. 'You, sir, must return for an examination—though you appear to have perfect dentition. But return you shall, and I insist that when you do, you tell me all about your research.' If she had held a fan, she would have tapped him on the arm.

Leo stared at Susan, in the manner of a rabbit transfixed by a lamp, counting under his breath.

'When he has a dental problem, he will be sure to do so,' I said. I grabbed his arm. 'Hurry—there's a cab coming down the street.'

From the house, Overfinch called Susan. She stepped in and closed the door.

'I see no cab,' Leo said.

'I must have made a mistake. Blame the laughing gas.' It seemed the natural thing to do, to slip my arm through his. 'Let's walk. The air will clear my head.'

We wandered along the road, past houses where autumn's remnants of sodden chrysanthemums, dahlias and zinnias drooped in the flowerbeds on the lawn.

'An interesting young lady,' Leo said. 'And all her own teeth. But too many, so it appeared. I lost count. *How doth the little crocodile.* A little disturbing.'

'What nonsense you speak.'

'But she was highly intelligent, nevertheless.'

I kicked at a pebble on the pavement. 'Really? She couldn't even get your name right. She called you Thorniwork.'

'That, I did not find disturbing,' Leo said.

Disturbing. Three hundred and forty-one, again. But what did it mean? What did any of it mean?

Twin Prime Numbers

On Thursday morning, I plodded up the wooden stairs to the first floor tutorial room where Leo and I were to meet. I opened the creaking door. The room was not often used and contained only four scarred wooden tables in rows of two, rickety chairs, and a blackboard covering most of one wall.

The grey skies outside had matched my mood as I trudged through the last of the dead leaves. Another letter from mother had arrived as I was about to leave, and I made the mistake of opening it there and then. In her previous letter, she had said it was helpful that Nurse Wilkinson was there and hoped we would be able to employ her for a considerable time.

I had replied asking if there was a problem meeting Nurse Wilkinson's salary, but in this letter she did not answer. She did, however, ask me to come back for the weekend. Did she have something she wished to tell me? Could my time at Huxley College be about to end? If I were a man, I could find gainful employment, but *I* would have to return home. Uncle Jacob would insist on my marrying and probably have a supply of candidates considered not up to May's standards, but good enough for me.

I recalled an argument with Mother. 'I don't plan to

marry,' I told her. 'There is no reason why I should have to change my ways and wishes to suit someone else.'

'But you will want to do it. Their ways and wishes will become yours. When you meet the right person, you'll understand.'

'All I understand is that the odds against that happening are a million to one, and of finding someone whose ways and wishes are mine, two million.'

She'd thrown her hands up in despair and left me alone.

I had brought a valise with me to the tutorial room, packed and ready for my stay at home. As I stood, smelling a mixture of floor polish and chalk, my chest felt tight and I gasped. I felt dizzy and rummaged in my Gladstone bag for smelling salts but found none. I staggered across the room, knocking a chair and banging my hip on a table. I flung the window open, leaned out, closed my eyes and took slow, deep breaths.

'Pheemie! Be careful! Do not lean too far!' Leo called from the quadrangle.

I opened my eyes. He gazed up at me, brow furrowed. He held a heavy-looking bag of books.

'I wasn't throwing myself out, if that's what you think.'

'Of course not. Nevertheless, please return inside.' He hurried into the building entrance. His footsteps beat a tattoo up the stairs. He walked in, removed his coat and hat, flung them onto a table and joined me at the blackboard.

'What is the matter? You seem uneasy. I trust your tooth, or rather its former location, isn't troublesome.'

Ignoring Susan Overfinch's instructions, I poked the tip of my tongue into the socket, now plugged with a blood clot. 'The gum is sound, and no more painful than one might anticipate,' I said. 'The reason for my despondency is that I must go back to London this evening. To stay with my family. Until *Sunday*.'

'I too am headed back this evening. Let us take the same train. I suggest the five o'clock.'

Having company on the journey might distract me from the ordeal to come. 'Isn't there a later one? I want to spend as little time there as possible.'

'I'm afraid not. Had you not heard? The five o'clock is the last one—it arrives in London before the worst of the fog. Any later and it clogs the engines.'

From his bag Leo took six weighty books, concerned with the twin prime conjecture, and spread them across a table. 'I trust we shall find inspiration here. If, as Gauss stated, number theory is the Queen of Mathematics, then the primes are the jewels in the crown.'

'Perhaps. But wouldn't it be preferable to work on something new? But perhaps not magnetism. We can return to that later, once we have published this.'

He wrinkled his brow. 'You are right. Then perhaps— dare I say it—we should dive into the bottomless sea that is Riemann's Hypothesis?

I clasped my hands. 'I've been thinking the same,' I said, trying to eject from my mind an image of Leo in a striped bathing costume. 'It's an article of faith that the primes behave as Riemann's predicts. The person who proves the hypothesis will have made it possible to fill in the gaps in thousands of other theorems that rely on it being true. Our Lazarus-Thorniwork solution will be world-renowned.'

'You forget that Professor Milton will insist on his

name taking pride of place. But I will insist that yours comes next.'

Chalk scratched across the board until, two hours later, we had filled all the available space on it. I leaned against the wall.

Leo dropped into a chair and reclined, elbows bent, arms across the top of the seat back. 'It looks over-complicated.'

I peered at it, tipping my head from side to side. 'I wonder—have we asked the right question?'

He jumped up and seized the board duster. 'We have not!'

'Leo—no!' I grabbed his sleeve. He pulled out of my grasp.

We started again.

We worked on, covering the board with equations, some written round the edges, some linked by arrows to others. A faraway church clock chimed three. My stomach rumbled, as did Leo's, as though they were attempting to communicate.

'Should we find something to eat? It might aid our thinking to get outside into the air.'

'We daren't! Remember that business with Clatworthy's work and the cleaner?'

I shuddered. 'The Thorniwork Hypothesis about that incident is that in reality a competitor erased it. But you are right. I wouldn't want someone to come in and steal our work to pass off as his own. We ought to copy it onto paper ready to submit.' I rummaged in my Gladstone bag. 'I seem to have brought two pencils, but no paper.'

'Leave it to me.' Leo put on his hat and coat and

dashed out, leaving the door open. Approaching footsteps told me I had better shut the door. As I did, Spaulding strode along the corridor. He glanced at the door but did not stop.

I peered out of the window. Leo sprinted across the quadrangle, stopping in his tracks to tip his hat to the young wife of the Associate Professor of Poetry as she emerged from the Old Library, wearing a bright green gown over-burdened with flounces. She simpered in reply. Leo ran on.

I brushed a patch of dust from my skirt, acquired either from the wall, from Leo's enthusiastic board dusting, or both, although it was barely possible to distinguish it from the colour of the dull, stuffy fabric. A bow tied at the neck of my blouse might add a certain something. Brown, perhaps, to match my eyes. Or mauve, which was said to be one of Her Majesty's favourite colours, though of course she wore black.

I stopped. A May-like fugue would not help the development of our proposals. I returned to the board, picked up the chalk and made one or two amendments, finishing the last one with a flourish.

Some half an hour later Leo returned with a roll of paper under his arm, two saucerless cups suspended from the index finger of his left hand and a vacuum flask in his right. After placing all of these on the table and pouring tea from the flask, he pulled a bunched-up handkerchief from his jacket pocket. He undid the knot and held out his hand—the bundle contained two hard boiled eggs without their shells. I took one. It was still tepid— whether because it was recently made or heated by the place in which it had been carried, I did not care to consider.

I sipped tea. 'Just what I needed. Now, let us return to our research. I think we are finished.' I unrolled the paper and removed a sheet. 'I'll write it down. We must be careful not to spill tea on it.' I handed another sheet, and my second pencil, to Leo. 'You copy down what is on the board. We need not include it in the submission, but we must not forget it—the foundations of our research.'

After I had finished, we both signed the paper. Leo looked at it, held his chin in his hand and frowned.

'What's wrong? Is there a mistake?'

'No, but I think we need to give the work a title. One more arresting than Thorniwork-Lazarus. Something that will distinguish ours from other proposals. That will hook Professor Milton, like a fish.'

'You're right. I think this might reel him in. What about *Primes and Perfection: repositioning Riemann's hypothesis through a critical lens*? That will land our Professor.'

'I can think of no more fishing analogies, but let's hope that the title doesn't baffle his brain instead. In any event, we need to hand it in as soon as we can.' He stood.

Movement outside the door caught my eye. Spaulding peered through the window in the door and the handle moved. I ran and snatched the door open, stepped into the corridor, slammed it shut and stood with my back to it.

'Can I help you, Spaulding?'

'I merely wanted to tell you that I, Parbold and in fact all of our fellow researchers have handed in our proposals to the Prof. All but you two. Have you finished?' He tried to peer round me, through the window.

'We have. We were on our way to submit ours.'

'Well, I must tell you that when I reached his study, the Prof wasn't there, so I had to leave mine on his desk. According to Standish, he's gone to Bath for the weekend. Which gives him two fewer days to consider our work.' He turned and strode away.

I stepped back into the room. 'Let's hurry,' Leo said. 'After we have made our submission, I must return to my room to pack a bag. We do not want to miss our train.'

'No, but before we go, the board must be cleared.'

'Very well, for the sake of tidiness, but what difference would it make to us now, if anyone should see our ideas?' Leo said, dusting once more.

'You are too trusting. In the Prof's absence, they could withdraw their proposals and make changes in the light of our work.'

Leo rolled his eyes but cleared the board.

Professor Milton's office was locked. I rattled the handle a few times, as though that might have some magical effect. 'I will ask the porter for the key,' Leo said. 'I shall tell him we have *this* to hand in.' He waved our proposal above his head.

'Give that to me. You might drop it. Someone might take it. A spark from a passing smoker might set it alight.'

'If it will make you happy, take it.'

I waited for Leo outside the door, pacing. Where was he? Had the porter refused his request? I turned and paced in the opposite direction.

'Come along!' Leo called from the other end of the corridor. 'This is no time to go for a walk!' My pounding heart slowed a little.

The proposals sat in a pile on the desk. The top one was Spaulding's, entitled 'Some problems in number theory.' I relaxed—that would not catch a minnow.

Leo put ours on the bottom of the pile. 'Come, come,' I said, 'That is taking fairness a little too far.'

'I am sure he will read all of them,' Leo said. 'But he may start from the bottom.'

I moved ours to the middle.

Leo looked at his watch. 'The train leaves in an hour. It will take half an hour to get to the station—I doubt we can get a cab at this time.'

'I will return the key. Return to your room for your luggage. I will meet you at the station.'

'Very well—whoever is there first should board the train and save a seat for the other.'

I entered the lodge. The porter opened the hatch and stuck out his head. 'Ah, Miss Thorniwork. I have a message for you, from Professor Milton.' He handed me a note. The Professor wished to meet me outside the old lecture hall. No time stated.

'When did he give this to you?'

'At about two o'clock.'

I threw the key down on the counter and ran, clutching my bag. The clock on the front of Wagstaffe hall, on the other side of the road from Huxley, chimed the first quarter. Past four, if the next train was at five? I had no watch with me.

It was growing dark, as I approached the lecture hall. No Professor Milton. Not by the front entrance. Was there a back one? The hall was part of a terrace, if I walked all the way around to find out, I might miss him. And the train. I must not miss it. I must find out whether our research was about to come to grief.

I turned up the collar of my coat. Perhaps the Professor had decided to go inside the hall, to get out of the cold. I pushed at the door. It was not locked. I stepped inside. Gas lamps flickered, casting long shadows that loomed towards me. Stairs led down to the front, where a lecturer would stand. No Professor. I looked around—he was not standing by a wall. I suppressed an urge to run outside and, legs shaking, staggered down the stairs. On the lectern was a piece of folded paper, bearing my name on the outside. I opened it.

> *'Miss Thorniwork—I waited until three o'clock. I wished to enquire about the progress of the work you and Lazarus propose. I must, instead, wait until I read your submission. I am now leaving for an extended weekend. R Milton.'*

I stuffed the note into my bag and dashed outside. The clock chimed the third quarter.

The quadrangle was deserted. I dashed towards the door leading into Broad Street. Across the way, the clock chimed. I looked up. A quarter to five. That was the clock Spaulding said was always five minutes fast. Or had he said, slow?

A cab clattered towards me. I waved my arms and shouted. It stopped, the driver helped me inside, slammed the door and we rattled our way through the dark streets to the station.

Two Lemmas

'All stations to London! Ready to depart!' The Station Master stood beside the train, whistle in hand.

I dashed down the platform, clutching my Gladstone bag. The Station Master raised his green flag. Train doors slammed.

'Pheemie!' Leo leaned out of an open carriage door about twenty feet away. I hurled myself towards him. He reached down and, grabbing my hand, pulled me inside the train. He slammed the door behind me, the whistle blew, and we moved.

I collapsed into a seat and waited for my heart to stop pounding.

'Come along!' A man chivvied a woman and a gaggle of children along the corridor, barking orders as though they were common soldiers and he the sergeant. 'Do keep up, woman!'

Leo took my bag and lifted it. I snatched it from him and stowed it in the luggage rack myself. He sat opposite me. We were alone in the carriage. I wondered whether people might find ironic my having nearly burst a lung in desperation to catch a train to a place I did not want to go.

We sat in silence. I looked out of the window at the anonymous fields and trees passing, as we drew ever closer to London. Ever farther from Oxford. There would be no more companionship after I arrived, and—with May's incessant prattle—certainly no more silence, until Leo and I met to take the train back. Three whole days. The rough seat cover dug into my legs through my skirt.

The wheels clanked along the rails, squealing as we rounded bends. A clang and a clatter filled my ears, louder than the background rattle.

'You look distressed,' Leo said. 'Do not be worried by this sound, it's just the effect of irregularities in the metallic structure of the rails.'

'Thank you, but I'm not upset about the noise. I'm sorry for my sour face. It's the thought of spending an entire weekend with my family. Two days with Professor Milton would be preferable than one afternoon in their company.'

'Ah, yes, if only we could pick our relatives.'

We entered a tunnel and I heard a low frequency hum. I put my hands over my ears.

Leo mouthed something. We shot out of the tunnel and I lowered my hands.

'That,' Leo said, 'was caused by the vibration of the track transmitted as sound by vibration of the tunnel walls.'

The noise changed to a lower pitched rumble. Pressure grew in my ears so that I felt more than I heard. My brain rattled and shuddered against my skull.

'And here, the vibration of the track is transmitted through the ground,' he said. 'Sound levels vary depending on the circumstances—for example, open countryside allows it to travel further than do hills, frost makes the ground hard so it can't absorb noise.'

'Really? I had not considered that.'

He nodded and leaned towards me. 'But think of this.

In the fog, noise is prevented from dispersing into the sky. It causes something I think of as a wall of sound.'

I wondered whether he discussed this with his aunt. I imagined her saying to her friends, 'My nephew—dear Leopold—so clever.' But I feared it was more likely to be a matter of '…but so boring.'

He continued. 'The mathematics is interesting. I wrote a paper about it following a journey to Scotland I made by rail last year.'

'I don't remember reading it.'

'Nor would you have done. Professor Milton felt that the subject was not worth pursuing. I have a draft somewhere in my rooms. I'll look for it when we get back.'

I pulled a copy of *Journal of Mathematics* from my bag.

'You'll find Professor Milton and Parbold's latest findings in there,' Leo said. 'Something they're calling the Milton Lemma. Which term means, of course, that it is only the first step in a longer piece of work.'

'Of course, the Professor has named it after himself.'

Leo smiled. 'I doubt Parbold had much option but to agree.'

I sniffed. 'On the contrary, I'll wager he was all toadying encouragement.'

I flicked through the pages until I came to the article. I pictured Parbold's smirking face, the gaslight in his study reflected on his balding head. Not only had he found a research topic the Professor agreed to supervise, but he had also managed to get something into print. 'Parbold's place is secured. At least for another year. He may no further along than the first stage, but it's more than can be said for you and me.'

Leo frowned. 'Don't worry. As soon as we can discuss

our proposals on prime numbers with the Professor, I am sure he will be champing at the bit.'

I imagined Professor Milton bridled like an old spavined horse, harnessed to a cart with Leo holding the reins. I smiled.

'That's better,' Leo said. 'May I see?'

I passed the *Journal* to him, and our fingertips touched. His felt warm.

'Your tiny hand is frozen,' he said.

'I'm sorry. In my haste to catch the train, I forgot my gloves.'

'No, you don't understand. *Che gelida manina.*'

I shrugged.

'*La Bohème*? Puccini?'

I shook my head. He sang some operatic aria in a strangulated tenor. As he attempted to hit the high notes, and missed, his face reddened.

'Do stop that,' I said when he paused to take a gulp of breath.

'Don't you like music?'

'Oh, is that what it was?'

He coughed. 'Oh, very droll. A comment worthy of Professor Milton.'

'Actually, I don't know much about music. I find harmonies in mathematics.'

'Oh, come-come. I find that too, of course, but where would we be without music to soothe the savage beast? Or is it… savage breast?'

I pursed my lips. 'Now you're being silly. I still don't know what you are talking about.'

'I am sorry for speaking out of turn. Or perhaps I should say, for lowering the tone—pardon, another melodic joke. But yours must be a dull household, that has no music in it.'

'I didn't say there wasn't—it's just not a thing I know about. There is music, or at least that's what they call it. My cousin May plays the piano. I suppose the family could be said to have talents in that direction. Pearl had a lovely singing voice. Also, my mother is very fond of opera, when she is well enough to leave the house.'

Mother's last such outing must have been six months ago, not long after the fog arrived. It enveloped her as she was returning, and she staggered into the house ashen faced and choking. Perhaps, with Nurse Wilkins present, she would be able to attend again.

I gazed out of the window. A scarecrow stood in the middle of a rutted field, a grin cut into its turnip face. One arm extended towards London, as though the creature thought I needed a reminder. I wished I had some projectile to throw, to knock off its leering head. We left it behind and I looked towards the horizon. The November sky was already darkening, fading from bright cobalt, to pink, to lemon yellow. It reminded me of a trifle, if the cake were tinted blue. I imagined Aunt Emily's squeals and Uncle Jacob's shoving the plate aside, should Cook produce such a paint-box confection.

Leo touched the greasy windowpane and turned to me. 'Apart from that blue, which the artists would call ultramarine, the colours remind me of Italian ice cream. Cassata, I believe it is called. *Tutti Frutti*,' he said, in an unconvincing accent. His stomach rumbled. 'I hope that Aunt Matilda will have left me something. Perhaps fried potato chips, cooling under an inverted plate.'

'If she has not, you must boil an egg,' I said,

remembering how, by means of a thermometer and a lecture on vapour pressure, he had taught me. 'If, of course, you feel well enough to eat when you get home. By the time we arrive, the fog will have set in for the night. I have a handkerchief to cover my mouth and nose—I hope you too have some protection.'

'I have this.' Leo dragged a yellowing rag from his pocket and wiped the muck from the window from his fingertip. 'There is little point in washing it, I find.'

'As long as nobody else sees it. I am not offended, but others might feel differently.'

He rolled it into a ball and shoved it back into his pocket. 'I suppose that is true. However, I have a few ideas for how one might improve its filtering properties, to enable free perambulation after dark. I will show you the designs, on our return. Now, have you any plans for the weekend?'

I would be unlikely to leave the house until it was time to head back to the station, on Sunday evening. Time to escape into the light of Oxford. My heart sank. 'No. We will probably spend many hours sitting in the parlour while May plays and sings, perhaps accompanied by Uncle Jacob on the violin.' I grimaced. 'It is a regular Saturday evening phenomenon. Last time, mother had an attack of wheezing and the nurse and I had to escort her to her room, where she made a recovery little short of miraculous. But otherwise, we will sit there, pretending to like this cats' choir.'

'I'm not surprised you're not looking forward to it. Do you share your mother's liking for opera?'

'I don't know much about it, although Mother has explained the stories behind her favourites. They all seem to be miserable things about a wronged woman, a child who dies, or some sort of pagan god. Mother is much taken with Wagner.'

'Oh.' His eyes narrowed.

Perhaps Leo did not share Mother's appreciation. I had no wish to have to listen to more lectures about characters with names like Schwertleite or Grimgerde, which sounded like the hawking of someone who had been too long in the fog.

He shook his head. 'We never listen to his music.'

'We?'

'My family.'

'You prefer Puccini?'

'That has nothing to do with it. It is because we are Jews. He has published vile and unfounded opinions on our role in music. And on us in general.'

'I'm sorry.' Mother had mentioned this, and I cursed my lack of tact. I was about to remark on yet another problem caused by religion, but that was not the right assessment. More a matter of those who disapproved of the religion of others.

'Don't be,' Leo said. 'You were not to know.'

I put my cold hand over his clenched fist, hot and still holding the *Journal*.

'No, it was insensitive of me.'

'I could not expect you to understand that, whatever you do, there are those by whom you will never be accepted.'

I knew how it was to feel out of step. I wanted to tell him I too had met discrimination, because I was a woman, because I was different. But I held my tongue. I did not want, by speaking of myself or my experiences, to appear to dismiss Leo's. He might think me one of those people for whom every discussion centres on themselves. 'I will try to understand.'

'You have the intelligence to do so. Now, take the *Journal* back before I crush it into unreadability.'

I prised it from his fingers and he pulled his hand back. He turned away and stretched his legs, catching me on the ankle with his scuffed brown leather boot. Apologising, he leaned his head against the window and closed his eyes. His face reflected in the glass made it appear that there were two of him. As though there could ever be another.

I flicked through the pages, but the *Journal* had lost its charm. I dropped it onto the seat next to me. Leo and I made a dreary pair.

'I wish you could have met Pearl. She was the only person I could bear to hear talk about religion without losing my temper at the blinkered nature of the opinions held. Which made it all the more distressing at her funeral. People milling about afterwards, telling me it was God's will.'

Leo opened his eyes and turned back from the window. 'At least there's a clear sign that a Jewish funeral is finished, and that people must leave. We wash our hands.'

'Symbolic of a fresh beginning?'

'No, I don't think that's the reason.' His brow furrowed. 'I must find out why we do it.'

'Not that you will have time, once Professor Milton agrees to our research proposal. If he does.'

'Not if, but when. This is gloomy talk.' He grinned. 'Now, I have just the remedy. I hope I do not over-step the boundaries of friendship, but I detect that you don't find your family very congenial company.'

'I don't, although their wide circle of friends suggests that not all would agree with me.' I felt, somehow, that Leo would share my view.

'I have a suggestion. My aunt Matilda is holding an evening of music on Saturday. I should be delighted if you would attend.'

'I really don't think that is for me.'

'Please—come as my research partner. Call it educational, if you like. I'm going to exhibit my tone generator. Aunt Matilda's friend Mrs Levitt is to demonstrate the harmonograph.'

'Is this meant to make me change my mind? What is it—some instrument?'

'No, a device that represents the vibrations of sound in a diagram. A visual representation of the mathematics of music. A little like what we were discussing earlier. With each variation in pitch, it is fascinating to devise equations pertaining to each one—'

'I'll come.'

'And I shall call on you at seven in the evening, which will allow us plenty of time to get there on the omnibus by eight.'

My heart sank. 'Oh no—I couldn't possibly expect you to come all that way.'

'You look horrified. But let me assure you it would be no effort at all.'

'No, I'm sure it wouldn't be. But, please don't. My family—'

He sat bolt upright. 'Then I must assume that you are you ashamed to be associated with me.'

'Certainly not! Look, Leo, it isn't that—'

He patted my hand. 'I'm teasing. I know full well you are an independent woman who can find her own way in the world, or at the very least to Islington.'

'Thank you.'

'But, you must allow me to meet you at the omnibus stop.'

'But it is a mere hundred yards from our house.' And May was capable of following me all the way there.

'I mean, at our end. I shall meet you at seven forty-five sharp. It should take no more than ten minutes to walk to our house.'

I considered how I would dress for the evening of music with Leo. And his Aunt Matilda, Mrs Levitt and the rest of the guests, of course. What would Pearl have worn? I wished I could have asked her. I remembered her standing at the front door of her house not long after her twenty-third birthday, on her way to a party to which I had not been invited. She had turned to wave goodbye, in a cloud of 'Mille Fleurs' perfume, my birthday gift. She wore a shimmering dark blue dress and, tilted over one eye a hat, all drooping veils and marabou stork feathers, with a stuffed bird on one side. I had no perfume, but I did have a dark dress. I could wear my daytime hat, which had been created without slaughtering the entire contents of an aviary. In my imagination, Pearl nodded her approval.

At the back of my mind was a niggling feeling that the friendship between me and Leo had changed in some almost imperceptible way. Could it be a type of lemma? An initial step towards something more? I leaned back in my seat and smiled.

Just Three Drops

Before I opened the front door, I brushed dead leaves and shreds of newspaper from the hem of my skirt, which I must have tramped through in the fog on the way back from the station. I needed to think of a way to ask Uncle Jacob about our investments. I closed the front door.

Mother called me from the dining room, to come and join them. Even if the odour had not made it obvious, I would have known fish was being served, as it was every Thursday. Was Leo, at this moment, sitting in his aunt's kitchen eating crispy, golden potato chips from a bone china plate? I stepped inside.

'We've set a place for you next to me,' May said, patting the seat as though she thought I might not know what she meant. 'You're just in time for dinner.'

I sat. Even the napkins under the bread rolls on each side plate were coloured the same beige as the food. Uncle Jacob muttered a hurried grace. May reached into serving dishes on the table and spooned cod in white sauce, and boiled potatoes onto my plate.

'Mrs Upshaw has prepared something a little bit special. Jerusalem artichoke and celeriac puree.' May raised her eyebrows and paused, spoon halfway between plate and tureen.

I shook my head. For the sake of everyone, I hoped

Nurse Wilkins would be able to dispense a suitable remedy for the wind.

Uncle Jacob shovelled food into his mouth as though he were a fireman on an engine's footplate. Mother poked at her food, taking occasional nibbles. 'How is your cake-baking, Euphemia?'

I poked my tongue into the gap between my teeth as I dabbed my mouth with my napkin. 'I have resolved not to try it again.'

Mother frowned. 'That is a pity. But, how goes your research?'

'Early days. I have been assigned a research partner. We have agreed to work on...'

'I am sure we would not understand it,' Aunt Emily said.

'Yes, it's so dry, isn't it?' agreed May. 'Why can you not study something from the natural world?'

'Galileo said that the book of nature is written in mathematical language,' I said.

'Italian, wasn't he?' Aunt Emily said. 'Then, I'm not surprised—they have always been fond of speaking nonsense.'

Silence, save the ticking of the long case clock, the hissing of the gas lamps and the clatter of cutlery against plate. The long-case clock in the corner chimed eight. Its face showed a white circle with a woman's face, peering from behind clouds above the hands. Pearl and I had made up stories about her, about Betty the Moon.

'Delicious,' Uncle Jacob said, from the other side of the table.

'Perhaps you should invest in an artichoke plantation, Father,' May said.

I leaned forward. 'How are our investments progressing?'

As I finished speaking, he jumped to his feet. 'No, May! Where are your table manners? You don't cut a bread roll. You must break it with your hands.'

'No Father, that is no longer good etiquette,' May said. 'One must cut it. But only with a small butter knife. I saw it in *The Englishwoman's Domestic Magazine*.'

'But that can't be right,' Uncle Jacob said, sitting again. 'You'd get crumbs in the butter. Let us ask Euphemia, for the casting vote. How is it done in Oxford, at high table?'

I remembered hearing about Spaulding throwing a roll from one end of the table to the other, to get Parbold's attention. 'I don't think I've ever been told. Except for about one chap, who uses a spoon. I can't remember whether that's a large or small one.'

'Ridiculous,' Uncle Jacob said. 'The whole lot of them have their heads in the clouds, too much concerned with things that are of no use.' He resumed eating.

'I have made an arrangement for myself, May and you tomorrow evening, Euphemia,' Aunt Emily said.

My heart sank. 'What is it?'

She shook her head. 'It will be a pleasant evening, that you will find interesting. But you must wait until tomorrow. I will not tell you now, as you will most likely cast scorn on it. I will give you time to contemplate your manners.'

I was certain I could wait for the secret to be revealed.

'I am sure that you would not be so rude,' Mother said. 'What will you do for the rest of the weekend? Study?'

'Actually, no. I have been invited to an evening of music on Saturday. At the house of my friend's aunt.'

May turned in her seat, a fork laden with a mixture of fish and potato halfway between her plate and her mouth. 'Really? Tell me about it. Who will be there?' A boiled potato fell onto the tablecloth. Aunt Emily, on May's other side, fussed with a napkin.

'I haven't seen the guest list,' I said, 'But I was told they're friends of this aunt. It's just an informal gathering—I believe she does not know how many people will attend.'

'Then I am sure,' May said, 'that there will be room for one more. What will there be—singing? Instruments? Perhaps even dancing?'

I shrugged. 'One of the ladies is to demonstrate a principle of the science behind music.'

May gave a snort. 'Another old bluestocking, I don't doubt! You must take someone young with you, to lighten the mood.'

After the meal was over, I wandered into the parlour, where mother sat alone. I took a seat next to her. My head ached, stabbing needles into my temples.

'I am, of course, always pleased to see you,' she said, 'But what brings you back to London? It isn't Christmas, or even the end of term.'

'You asked me to come. I wanted to see you. Also, I'm worried. What did you mean in your letter about uncertainty in Uncle Jacob's investments?'

'I asked you because I wanted your company. I don't think the investments are a matter for worry, not exactly. But Uncle Jacob does concern me, in his flitting from one scheme to another. He has moved some of the funds invested in the earlier "Shares in prosperity" scheme but will not tell me into what.'

My throat tightened. 'That is quite wrong of him. It is our money too.'

May came in, sat next to the fire and picked up her embroidery frame from a small table to the side. She looked at her work with her head tilted one way, then the other. 'What do you think of this? Pretty, isn't it?'

I examined a piece of bright pink, shiny fabric, on which she had worked an image of what appeared to be some sort of medusa. Below it, embroidered letters stated *Fog on the hill brings water to the mill.*

'What is it?' I said.

'A picture, silly. It's the mill in the proverb. It's nearly finished. I shall frame it and hang it on my bedroom wall. That's what I was talking about before—the natural world. Not all this numbers tarradiddle.'

'Remember what Galileo said.'

She pouted. 'If he really did say that, then he was a—' she looked left and right '—and I'm sure you, unlike Mother, wouldn't be offended by my saying this, Aunt Agnes—he was a *silly ass.* I say, Euphemia, would you like me to make a picture for you? To take back to Oxford?'

'That's very kind, but I must decline. Unless you can think of a rhyme for "fog fills the street".'

She frowned. '*Watch where you put your feet?* No, I can't. I'm not very good at writing verse. Music is more my forte. What sort of singing will there be at the evening? I am accomplished in bel canto.' She paused, but after receiving no comment, began poking at the embroidery with her needle as though trying to provoke it. 'I shall make a picture for you, Aunt Agnes. I have in mind something to illustrate the text "Candlemas shine, winter behind". It nearly rhymes.'

'That's called an assonance, dear,' Mother said, with a wheeze. 'Thank you, I am sure the picture will be lovely.'

'Look, Mother,' I said, desperation banishing any care I might have had about May overhearing, 'Forget pictures. Won't Uncle Jacob tell you anything? Are we to end up in the workhouse?'

'I have tried to worm it out of him, but—' she coughed, unable to speak further.

Nurse Wilkins bustled in. 'Oh dear, Mrs Thorniwork. You must take a dose of paregoric.' She scuttled out of the room.

'I will ask Uncle Jacob again, myself,' I said.

I returned to the dining room, but he was not there. I hurried back into the hall. Nurse Wilkins came out of the scullery. I asked if she knew where he was. She told me he was in his room. I started to climb the stairs.

'Perhaps it would be better if you did not disturb Mr Pratincole,' she said. 'He told me he wished to retire early and asked for a sleeping draught.'

I held my throbbing forehead.

'If it is not speaking out of turn, you seem to be a little peaky,' Nurse Wilkins said. 'May I suggest that you also take a draught?'

'If it's laudanum you offer, then no.'

'My dear Miss Thorniwork, that's not for aiding sleep. No, I administered chloral hydrate to Mr Pratincole. Please follow me.'

She led me into the scullery and took a small brown bottle from a cabinet on the wall. She took up a wine glass draining by the sink and filled it with water before opening the bottle and drawing a clear liquid into the dropper set inside its lid. 'Now—one, two, three drops. That's it.' She passed me the glass.

The draught tasted vile, catching in the back of my throat, but I managed to get it down, and keep it there.

'That's the way,' Nurse Wilkins said. 'They do say a foul taste means an efficacious medicine. That's what I tell your mother. Now, if you will excuse me, I must prepare her medication.'

She turned from me and I retreated to my room.

Forgotten Number

'Euphemia! Wake up!'

I opened my eyes and sat up. 'Oh, my God! Take it away!' A candle-lit oval loomed over me, green and scaly. Beneath each eye that stared from it, a white trail ran down. For a moment I thought I was still asleep, dreaming. Nightmaring. I tried to run but my legs caught in the bedclothes.

'You were shouting in your sleep,' May said. 'I came in to see what was wrong.' She put her candlestick down on my bedside table and reached for my hand.

I leaned as far away from her as I could. 'What have you done to your face?'

'Oh, this?' she asked, touching a cheek. Flakes fell away onto the counterpane. She brushed them off onto the floor. More work for the maid. 'A paste of lard and beef marrow. If you bothered with skin care, you'd know it was the best thing for the complexion if left on overnight.'

The stench of stale fat made my stomach churn, and I was glad it had been some hours since I last ate. 'Ought it to be green?'

'I don't think so.' She touched one of the rivulets coming from her eyes with the tip of a finger. 'Oh, bother. Those Belladonna eye drops have washed some of it away.'

'I'm sure it is most… efficacious. But what do you want,

May? At this hour.' I sat up and looked towards the window. It was still dark. Tendrils of fog writhed outside, about half way up the pane. They were no longer advancing, so it must be after midnight. They were not yet retreating, so some time before five o'clock.

'You were having a nightmare,' May said.

'I am sorry if I disturbed you. But as you've woken me from it, we should go back to sleep. I don't want to keep you up.'

'Nonsense. Tell me about the dream.'

'It was nothing. Completely trivial.'

'No—tell me. All the latest thinking says that's the best thing to do.'

I wondered when *Ladies' Journal* had begun to include articles written by doctors of the mind, among their usual ones about scouring powder and primping.

'No, I would rather forget it.' I yawned. 'Would you mind closing that gap in the curtains on your way out?'

May folded her arms. 'I'm not leaving until you tell me.'

'I don't see why I should.'

She shook her head. 'You must tell someone, but only a person who can help unravel the dream. Not someone like Aunt Agnes, I mean.'

'Why not Mother? Should I not speak to her of it?'

'If you want, but I'm sure she isn't versed in dream analysis. If you don't talk about it, you'll forget most of it, but bits will come back to you all through the next few days. And that will spoil the lovely musical evening you're going to tomorrow.'

It was clear I would not be allowed to sleep without telling her. 'Very well, but do move away.' I waved my hand in front of my nose. 'Your face reminds me of an Oedipus mask.'

'I've seen that name before, but I can't think where. Does it help with blemishes?'

I shook my head, too weary to explain. 'I am only going to tell you this once, and don't ask me questions while I'm doing it.' I plumped up my pillow and leaned back. 'I dreamed I was in a hotel. The walls were panelled with oak, varnished dark brown and hung with crimson flocked paper. Gas lamps cast pools of light over the carpets, which were thick and russet. They had patterns that swirled as I moved towards them.'

'What patterns?'

'Didn't you hear me? No questions. But, if you must know, they looked rather like cows' faces—and *don't* ask me what breed. I was looking for Pearl, but I could not find her room. I walked up and down corridors, up and down stairs repeatedly, but I could not find it. I was looking for room number… er…'

'Do you see? Already, details are fading.'

'May!' I slapped the mattress beside me. 'For the last time! But no, the strange thing is that I knew the number at the start of the dream, but then I forgot it. All I could remember was the phrase "Red Heifer", which might have been the name of the hotel, but I could not determine if it was. I tried to find the entrance, to see if anyone could tell me which was Pearl's room. But I could not find the ground floor, nor the place where guests register.' I paused. 'Then a man appeared. That's all. Then I woke up.'

But that had not been the end. In the dream, the man told me that Pearl was dead. That her room had been number 341. I heard a tune played on a violin, repeated over and over.

May leaned closer, blinking massive-pupiled eyes. 'A man? Young, old? Handsome? Did he speak?'

I felt a catch in my throat. 'I can't remember. It doesn't matter, anyway.'

He had said that I had come searching for Pearl in the hotel many times before. But that I always forgotten. Perhaps I had dreamed it many times.

May pursed her lips. 'Very interesting.' She produced a small hairbrush from the pocket of her robe. Perhaps it had some role in whatever mock divination she planned. 'While I consider what it means, shall I brush your hair? Would you like that?'

I backed away, banging against the headboard. 'No thank you. I've told you about the dream, now please go back to your room.'

She put the brush down. 'I'll leave this here. Be sure to brush for twenty minutes when you get up. Had you done so before going to sleep—which I'm sure you didn't—you might have slept better.'

'I'd have achieved that if you hadn't come in. But I'm sorry I woke you.'

She seemed to take that as a cue to resume her analysis. 'Now, what would Dr Freud say?'

'That it is all to do with Mother?'

'Oh no, he is full of new ideas on dreams and their interpretation. Father agreed to buy me his latest book. It's in my room.'

'Really? Uncle Jacob allows you to read that?'

'Well, of course, it is in German. I need someone to translate it.' She leaned forward and grabbed my arm. 'I say! You told me that you were required to read articles in

115

German. Could you do it?'

I sat bolt upright. 'Oh no, I couldn't. Unless, of course, it was filled with mathematical treatises, equations, and the like.'

She frowned. 'Well, I don't *think* it is. I didn't see many numbers in it. It's called,' she cleared her throat, '*Die Traumdeutung.* I think. Anyway, I didn't see the word hotel. Perhaps it's different in German.'

'Probably. I think we should try to go back to sleep.'

She shook her head and drew closer. 'I know what your dream means.'

I closed my eyes, waiting for her to tell me it was all due to my spinster status.

'I couldn't distinguish any words in what you were shouting, but it is a classic anxiety dream. The hotel represents life. You are trying to find your way through it, but you can't. You are lost. You need help.' She folded her arms again.

'Is that it? What about Pearl and the missing number?'

'Oh, I don't think that means anything. You need someone to show you the way so that you don't get lost on your own. To be by your side the whole time. For instance, when you go out to that musical evening.'

I slid down under the bedclothes and turned on my side, away from May. 'Good night.' I closed my eyes.

May sat by my bed. I felt her watch me as I pretended to fall asleep. But there would be little chance of that, while the dream loomed in my mind. Something hovered at the edge of my consciousness, trying to gain entry.

Three Guineas

I managed to spend most of Friday in my room reading; I filled half a notebook with ideas for Leo's and my research. Something concerning prime numbers proved to be the most fruitful. Aunt Emily's idea of an interesting evening was that we were to go out with the with the intention of consulting a medium, something even more ridiculous than I thought her capable of. I decided not to attend.

At approximately five in the afternoon, May knocked on my door and entered without waiting to be asked. 'We will be eating earlier this evening, so that we can be at Madame Galdora's by seven. She starts sitting promptly and won't admit latecomers.'

I imagined a giant hen, incubating crystal balls instead of eggs.

'Why do such people always seem to be women?'

'Ah, you need to ask? We women are so much more sensitive than men. Even you, Euphemia.' She turned to leave but stopped, shook her head and looked at me a second time. 'You're not wearing that old skirt, are you? It's exactly, precisely, the colour of mud.'

I put down my copy of *A treatise on the theory of numbers* Spaulding had lent me. I glanced at the inside cover, where he had written his initial and surname, in florid copperplate. Only three more days until I would be in Oxford, and before that there was Leo's aunt's evening, to take up some time. 'It doesn't matter what *I'm* wearing, I'm not going.'

'But you must! Madame Galdora comes with such great recommendations. She may cause a table to turn. Surely, you wouldn't want to miss that.'

'That is simply explainable by involuntary movement of the muscles of the legs. I expect her name's really Gladys and that she does it all with mirrors and bits of cloth.'

'I am certain none of that is true.'

'Very well—consider this. How likely is it that everyone who has ever died is waiting around to speak to the likes of her? Is the afterlife no more than a railway station ticket office, filled with crowds jostling to get to her counter?'

May put her hands on her hips. 'You don't believe in anything, do you?'

'I pride myself on it, if you mean this sort of nonsense. I include religion in that description.'

May let out a gasp.

'However,' I continued, 'I do believe in mathematics, so if you don't mind, I'll continue reading.'

May waved her hand as though shooing away a fly. 'Then, at least have some respect for royalty. Her Majesty consulted a medium and spoke with Prince Albert. After he died, of course. If it's good enough for her, it's good enough for you. Mother had to pull quite a few strings to get three places for this evening.'

'I'm sure your father would like to attend in my place.'

'No, he wishes to discuss his investments with your

118

mother this evening.'

'I would like to take part in those discussions.'

'He wants to speak to Aunt Agnes alone. Not with you interrupting and asking silly questions.'

I decided I had better attend. Sitting through a few hours' table rapping would be better than having Aunt Emily glowering at me until I left on Sunday.

'Very well. I suppose you think there will be young men there.'

May raised her eyebrows. 'It never occurred to me to wonder.'

'You—who wonders about little else?'

She raised her eyebrows. 'I suppose there might be. Actually, I think that skirt suits you very well. The colour matches your, er...'

'Muddy boots? Very well. I'll come along, as a foil to you.'

May poked out her tongue and left. Her feet thumped the stairs as she bounded down.

I placed the book in my bag. I might snatch a glance at it on the omnibus. Perhaps also during the more preposterous parts of the performance.

Madam Galdora lived some fifteen minutes' ride away, in a red-brick house in the middle of a terrace. As we approached the front door, Aunt Emily stopped, and dipped into her reticule. 'Ah good, I remembered to bring my purse.'

'Must we pay for admission, as though attending a music hall?'

'Do not be vulgar.' Aunt Emily snorted. 'You cannot expect her to share her skills for nothing. A guinea each is a small price.'

'Yes, Madam Galdora must eat,' May said.

'She must eat nothing but caviar.'

'Your scorn is misplaced, Euphemia,' Aunt Emily said. 'Sir Arthur Conan Doyle regards spiritualism as a science, so it should appeal to you. And put that book away.'

I slipped it into my coat pocket and Aunt Emily knocked on the door. We stood for several minutes before it creaked open. An ancient maid, with wisps of grey hair protruding from a white lace cap, stood in the doorway. 'Who shall I say is calling?' she said, in a voice that creaked like the door. Aunt Emily gave our names.

'Should the spirits not already have told Galdora?'

Aunt Emily pursed her lips. 'Of course, but I expect her spirit guide doesn't want to parade his superior knowledge all the time. It could disturb those of a nervous disposition.'

'In fact,' May said, 'I have heard that sometimes he holds his tongue, even when he knows the answer. Such modesty.'

'Then what's the point of our being here?'

The maid took our coats and led us into a room filled with heavy dark furniture and many small tables covered with lace cloths, each groaning under the weight of a host of photographs in silver frames. A large gold framed mirror hung above a fireplace in which a fire burned half-heartedly. Perhaps Galdora would make it burst into life as one of her parlour tricks. The room was lit with what appeared to be hundreds of oil lamps. I found myself counting them under my breath, much as Leo had at the sight of Susan Overfinch's many teeth.

'Do stop muttering, Euphemia,' Aunt Emily said. 'I do

not want people to think I have a simpleton for a niece.'

Four women sat at a round table in the centre of the room. May's mouth turned down at the corners.

'Mrs. Pratincole, Miss Pratincole and Miss Thorniwork,' the maid said, swaying slightly, by the door.

A woman in her forties, dressed entirely in unmatching shades of purple, rose from her seat at the table. 'Ah, come in, come in! I am Madam Galdora. Now we are seven—a very auspicious number, you understand. Now, we can begin.' She gestured towards three unoccupied chairs. We sat, I was opposite a woman about my age, dressed entirely in brown. Her bright, dark eyes, pointed nose and lack of chin gave her a bird-like appearance. I nodded to her and she gave a twitch of her head in reply, which only added to her avian resemblance.

'You are just in time,' Galdora said. 'We are to start with an ancient form of prophecy. It has been in use since the ancient Chinese began infusing leaves. It is Tasseomancy! As the lay person might put it—reading tea leaves.'

May grinned and nodded. 'It always works.'

Galdora called, 'Maggie! The tea, please.' The maid staggered out on bandy legs.

The woman sitting on my left, seemingly in her sixties, turned to me. 'I am Miss Joswig. I will be glad of the tea. So refreshing, after having to walk here in the fog. My throat is quite parched. Was your journey here long?'

'I'm Miss Thorniwork. Fortunately, we did not have far to come. Have you been here before?'

'No, dear. I don't really hold with it all, but mother would keep asking to come.' She patted the hand of her companion, a white-haired old lady wizened like an ancient apple, and raised her voice to the volume of an express train. 'Didn't you, dear?' Dear smiled and recited. 'For all flesh is as grass, and the glory of man like flowers. The grass withers and the flower falls.'

The woman patted her hand again. 'She's very enthusiastic,' she said to me in a stage whisper. 'As for me, I try to keep an open mind, but I really don't think there's anything in it. I suppose it might be amusing, although it is likely that we are the subjects of the joke. A fool and his money.'

Or Aunt Emily's. Which was, in turn, Uncle Jacob's, and ultimately, Mother's and mine.

'There's a lot of nonsense spoken and written about this sort of thing, if you don't mind my saying,' I said. 'All types of charlatans seem to have emerged from hiding, airing their foolish notions.' I told her about the letter I had read in *Progress in Mathematical Physics*, from the man Simpson, about communicating with the dead. 'And they say it is all made easier by the coming millennium despite this being, after all, a number we apply arbitrarily.'

'Your mind is closed,' Aunt Emily said. 'I feel there's something significant about year changes. We divide our lives into years, after all. It makes sense that the turning of a year will coincide with some introspection.'

'We stand on the threshold of a new century,' May said.

'The writer of that letter has a vivid imagination,' Miss Joswig said. 'If I want to read a story, I read Mr. Jerome. At least he is intentionally humorous. Have you read his *Three Men on the Bummel*?' I said that I was not a reader of fiction. She looked disappointed and turned away from me to fuss with her mother's cushions.

Shambling footsteps in the hall announced the maid's

return. She placed a tray on the table before Galdora. It bore a teapot resembling a glossy green cabbage, and an assortment of cups, adorned with pictures of playing cards and signs of the zodiac. None matched the others. They would not have been out of place among Leo's collection.

Galdora poured a stream of black tea, with an aroma of coal tar soap, into each cup. She passed one bearing the word *Knowledge* to Miss Joswig.

'Milk for me, please,' I said, unable to see a jug on the tray.

'Oh no,' she said, handing me a cup adorned with *Mysterious things I see*. 'This is lapsang souchong tea. One would not wish to spoil such a delicate infusion with the addition of something produced by a cow. Also, the leaves are much larger, which aids the interpretation.'

The maid tottered from the room. Aunt Emily, May and I removed our gloves and drank tea in reluctant sips. I looked forward to telling Leo about this novel tea experience—but perhaps such a brew was commonly drunk. I must not appear ignorant.

We drained our cups and replaced them in their saucers.

'Now, pick up your cups and briefly swirl the dregs around,' Galdora commanded. 'Then turn the cup upside down onto the saucer. Move the cup from the left side three times in a circle and then turn it over.'

We did as instructed. All that I could see in my cup was a mass of brown leaves, each the size of a postage stamp.

'The tea leaf symbols closest to the rim are events in the near future. The closer to the bottom of the cup the tea leaves, the farther away the event will be,' Galdora said.

She stood and walked around the table looking into each person's cup. 'A crown,' she said to Miss Joswig's mother. 'I divine that a member of the Royal Family will be mentioned in the newspapers, soon.' She paused behind Aunt Emily, peered over her shoulder and pointed at a lump of leaves in the middle of her cup. 'I see the shape of a coin. That, of course, means money in the future.' She pointed at a larger clump at the edge. 'And here, more money. Oh dear… more now than later.'

Aunt Emily let out a strangled cry.

I squeezed her hand. 'Take no notice, Aunt,'

'No, don't, Mother.' May gazed into the cup. 'I don't think that's what it is. It looks more like a cat. I like cats.'

I picked up the cup. 'Or maybe a sheep. I imagine it refers to our Sunday lunch. I poked at the leaves. 'Perhaps that shape next to it represents a dish of mint sauce.'

Galdora sniffed and called the maid to clear the table. As she piled the crockery onto the tray, she passed a piece of paper to Galdora, who glanced at it and stuffed it into her cuff.

Galdora turned to me. 'I see you have observed Maggie's note, Miss Thorniwork. She is asking for her wages a day early. She considers it too vulgar a matter to speak of aloud. As do I, usually. Now, let us begin with the joining of hands.'

'This puts me in mind of a wedding!' May said as she took my right hand. 'But don't we have to turn the lights down?'

'No,' Galdora said, 'I can penetrate the veil between us and those who have gone before, even in the light.'

'See?' May said. 'She has nothing to hide.'

I held Miss Joswig's hand in my left.

'Ah, now the circle is complete. Come, spirits, one and all.' Galdora said. She closed her eyes, took a deep breath, then snorted through her nose like a horse. 'The spirits are with us. Who has a question?' She opened her eyes.

'If you don't find this too vulgar, spirit,' Aunt Emily said, 'I wonder if you can tell me about our possible—er—reversal of fortune, as seen in the leaves?'

Galdora held her hand behind one ear. 'The spirits tell us that all will be resolved.'

'But… when?' Aunt Emily said.

'Soon.'

Aunt Emily relaxed. I did not have the heart to ask what form that resolution might take.

Galdora furrowed her brow, put her fingers to her temples and looked at Miss Joswig's mother. 'I am getting a message from your husband, John. He tells me that he loved to dance with you.'

Miss Joswig tutted. 'His name was Philip, and he had a wooden leg.'

'He has become reunited with the limb, in heaven, and looks forward to whirling you round in his arms, once again.'

'Charming, I'm sure,' I said. 'But perhaps we should not be so eager to wish your mother gone from this world.'

Galdora looked at May. 'And you, my dear. The spirits tell me that *you* live in north London.'

'Yes, I do!' May squealed.

'Of course you do,' I said. '*This* house is in north London. I have already said that we didn't have far to come.'

'And *you*,' Galdora turned to me and pointed her finger. 'You will soon marry.'

'How splendid,' May said.

'Someone of my apparent age is highly likely to marry soon,' I said, 'but not me.'

Galdora laughed. 'You cannot gainsay the eternal truths the spirits reveal. You will receive a proposal of marriage.' I saw no point in arguing. Galdora closed her eyes again and drew in another deep breath. 'The spirits are telling me that one of you is very interested in mathematics.'

I sat up with a start. May nudged me 'See! How could she have known that?'

Galdora raised a hand. 'Now, don't tell me which of you it is. I will let the spirits name you.' She shut her eyes and rubbed at her temples. 'Spirits, reveal! Yes... I'm getting the name Spaulding. One of you is here in disguise! Is there a Miss Spaulding here? I'm getting a name beginning with J. Jane? Are you here?'

I dropped May's hand and banged on the table. 'Enough of this! I hope your maid replaced my book in my coat pocket. Everything else has been done by high probability guesses. In that way, it *is* mathematical. I could do the same, picking up on signals from people's replies as to whether my guesses are in the right direction or not.'

Galdora sat rigidly in her chair. Her eyes rolled up, as though in apoplexy. Aunt Emily reached across May and slapped at my hand. 'See what you have done! She is mortified by your cruelty.'

May pulled a small brown glass bottle from her bag, removed the cork and passed it to me. 'Give her these smelling salts! Where is the maid?'

Galdora's mouth fell open. A gruff, male voice emerged. Her lips did not move. 'Simpson. We need more subjects. The fog comes from the body, spills out and over the sides. Tanyard Lane. Sound interferes.' She let out a bubbling cough. I had not revealed the name of the writer of the letter to Miss Joswig, and nor had the letter mentioned the fog. Then came the voice of a young woman. 'And he that was dead came forth, bound hand and foot with graveclothes: and his face was bound about with a napkin.' At this, Galdora's mouth shut and her head lolled forwards.

Miss Joswig called for the maid, who shambled in and took hold of one of Galdora's hands, slapping at the back. Galdora opened her eyes. 'I apologise, but sleep supervened. Communication beyond the veil is exhausting. I must close the proceedings, now.'

The maid helped her to her feet and, putting her arm around her shoulders, led her out of the room.

We arose, made awkward goodbyes and left, Mrs Joswig's mother repeating, 'He was called Philip *John*, you know.'

'That's in the Bible, what the spirit guide said,' May said as we headed back to the omnibus stop.

'Yes, I know.' I remembered a passage Pearl had read to me. 'A man also or woman that hath a familiar spirit, or that is a wizard, shall surely be put to death.'

'No, silly, not that,' May said. 'I mean, what she said, about a dead body coming forth. That was from the story of Lazarus. That's your friend's name, isn't it? The one who's holding the musical evening tomorrow? So, you see, she was clairvoyant.'

'She was certainly very adept at imitating voices,' I said. I had not the heart to tell Aunt Emily that I imagined we could have heard as much at the music hall and at considerably less cost.

'May is a most musical young lady,' Aunt Emily said. 'And she has no arrangements for tomorrow evening.'

Three is a Crowd

The next afternoon, Mother and I sat in the parlour, reading. As I was engrossed in *Journal of Modern Mathematics* May entered, bounded up like a puppy who has heard the word 'walk', leaned over me and shouted my name from point blank range. I put the *Journal* down.

She put her hands on her hips. 'Surely you're not going to your musical evening dressed like that. Can't you find something more elegant than that dull grey day dress? You don't want the other ladies thinking you're one of the servants. Tell her, Aunt Agnes.'

'Euphemia is a grown woman,' Mother said, without taking her eyes from *A Study in Scarlet.* 'I have long ago given up trying to tell her what to do.'

I doubted Leo would notice what I was wearing, nor that he owned a 'best' outfit, but it did seem people judge others on their appearance, particularly if one is a woman. Why not look my best? 'I've got hours,' I said. 'I'll find something later.'

May sank into the chair next to mine and sighed. I picked up the *Journal* again and read: '*But if θ is not commensurable with 2 π, then, by a proper choice of p, the amplitude—*'

May plucked at my sleeve. 'You won't know anyone there, will you?'

I lowered the *Journal*. 'Only my friend. Now, if you please…' I picked up the *Journal* again: '*the amplitude p θ can be made to differ from an integral multiple --*'

'And your friend might talk to others and leave you alone.'

I felt my throat tighten as I marked my place with a fingertip and looked at her. 'That will not matter. I shall listen to the music.' I looked down at the page and resumed reading: '*…the amplitude p θ can be made to differ from an integral multiple—*'

May stood in front of me. 'Euphemia.' She pulled the *Journal* out of my hands and held it behind her back.

I lunged for it. She dodged. 'You shan't have that arithmetic magazine,' she said. 'You can look at it another time.'

'Do you promise to let me?'

She flicked through the pages. 'How boring.' She dropped the *Journal* on the table next to my chair. 'Can't you think of more useful things to do with your time? What a shame you have not learned to embroider. Shall we teach her, Aunt Agnes?'

Mother closed her eyes. 'I refer you to my earlier reply.'

'I see no use for embroidery.'

'And what is the use of your numbers?' May moved around the room, plucking at the curtains and tweaking the chair cushions. 'Embroidery makes beautiful anything to which it is applied. I've just finished the last of my pillowcases. I think I'll start on the curtains in here.'

I thought of May's bedroom, the curtains, sheets, bedcovers, towels, chair covers, and every other piece of fabric crammed with hard, scratchy knots and flowers in lurid coloured threads, resembling Kew as envisioned by a

130

colour-blind gardener. 'They must be very uncomfortable to sleep on. You will have flowers embossed into your face in the morning.'

'I haven't tried yet, but I'm sure they won't be. They might give me dreams of flowers. You really should try it, after that horrid dream you had.'

'And what does Dr Freud say about dreams of flowers?'

'I expect he approves,' she said, apparently unaware of the connection between flowers and plant reproduction. Were Leo here, he would have launched into an explanation. I decided against doing the same and, instead, reached out for the *Journal*. May snatched it away, wagging a finger, and threw it onto the sofa on the other side of the room. 'I said no. But before you go to get changed, listen to this idea I've just had. It might be considered rude to arrive at the musical evening empty-handed.'

First 'your' musical evening, now 'the'. Next would come 'our'. I began to feel like a stalked animal.

She continued. 'I think it would be nice to embroider a little gift for your friend. I will make a little bookmark, with her name on. What is it?'

'The hostess is Mrs Matilda Lazarus. I am sure you will not have time to embroider so many letters before I go out.' Since it appeared I was not to be allowed a further opportunity of finding out about $p\ \theta$, I stood up. 'Very well. You have won. I will go and look in my wardrobe.'

'I'll come up in a moment and help you. Make sure whatever you choose doesn't clash with my pink dress with the embroidered orchid pattern in green and yellow.'

'You need have no concerns about that. And besides, it wouldn't matter. Once I leave the house, and you remain here, nobody will see us together.' I hurried upstairs to my bedroom.

I shut the door behind me and leaned against it. I would have to make it clear May could not join me, although that ran the risk of her running, crying, to her parents, who would, while not forbidding me to leave the house, make life uncomfortable for the rest of the weekend. Only one more day to endure, though, before I could return to Oxford. My own room, and belongings, nobody barging in, space to think. When I saw Leo—in only a few hours' time—I must remember to ask him on which train he would be travelling back.

I took a black satin skirt and a white, high-necked blouse out of my wardrobe and laid them on the bed. I pulled out a shoe box, containing the blue leather evening shoes with flat heels, unworn, still wrapped in tissue paper, that I had left behind on my return to Oxford. I turned them this way and that. No scuffing to the soles. I had bought them in anticipation of celebrating Pearl's next birthday.

I looked at the reflection of my face in the glossy uncreased leather. Almost the same shade of blue Leo had called ultramarine. Beyond the sea, from Afghanistan, used by artists. Perhaps we might find it among the paintings in the Ashmolean. I wrapped up the shoes and put them back in the box.

I took out a pair of black leather boots. Much more sensible for walking out of doors on a November evening, with the fog licking round my ankles. I put them on and looked at myself in the cheval mirror in the corner of the room. Leo was, at my estimate, about six inches taller than me.

Mother's unmistakeable footsteps, halting and slow, came up the stairs. She knocked on the door and came in. I took her elbow and helped her into the chair in front of the dressing table.

'I have a headache. I am going to lie down.' She looked at the clothes on the bed. 'You will look pleasant enough in that ensemble. Be sure to take your boots off before you change your skirt, so that you don't tear the hem. You don't want to look like a sloven.' That was a word Professor Milton might use, complaining about the standard of his students' writing. It set my teeth on edge.

'I will take care,' I snapped. Mother frowned, and I wished that I had kept silent. At least *she* was trying to give me wise advice. I apologised for my impoliteness.

She took a breath. 'I am sure you will enjoy yourself. I know you're looking forward to the musical evening you are to attend, with this friend of yours from Oxford. It was almost the first thing you mentioned, when you arrived yesterday.'

'I think it will be interesting. If you'll excuse me, I must make a start.' I offered her my arm. 'I'll help you to your room.'

Mother kept her hands in her lap. 'Euphemia. I want you to be kind to May.'

I sat on the bed. 'I have been, in not strangling her today. She has prevented my reading. I did not sleep well and thought to rest this afternoon.'

'About this evening. May has spoken of nothing else since you told us about it.'

'You know, Mother,' I gabbled, 'It's possible that the word sloven is some sort of slight on the natives of Slovenia. Did you know that it is part of Austro-

Hungary? Do you think they are particularly untidy?'

Mother raised a hand. 'May has told her parents, and me, that she wishes to go with you. She is afraid you will say no. She loves music. And I thought to do us all a favour and ask you to take her with you. She wants to meet your friends. Where is the harm?'

'But it is too late to ask Mrs Lazarus's permission to bring an additional guest.'

Mother pursed her lips. 'You said it was an informal gathering and that your hostess did not know how many would attend. One more will make no matter. I shall tell May you said yes.' She began to cough. Nurse Wilkins, who must have been waiting outside, came in without knocking, rushed to Mother and grabbed her wrist. She looked up at me and glared. 'Such a weak pulse! Miss Euphemia, you should be ashamed of yourself for upsetting my patient in this way.'

Yet another person telling me how to behave. 'And how would you like her to be upset?' Nurse Wilkins gasped. 'And—your patient? *My* mother.'

'All the more reason for you not to distress her.'

She led Mother away. I shut the door after her, harder than I intended, and it slammed.

'Absolute simpleton!' I shouted at the shut door.

No response came. And had there been, what could I have said that would not have upset Mother further? I sank into a chair and held my head in my hands.

I lay on my bed and tried to sleep. After an hour's lack of success, I got up and went to look at the bookshelf next to the window. I took out *Harmonic functions*, *Theory and functions of a complex variable*, *Studies on the Harmonograph*, *The Combinatorial Lemma in Topology* and

134

Introduction to Quaternions. I was fairly certain that would be enough but, just to be sure, I hauled the three-inch thick tome, *Trilinear Coordinates*, off the shelf as well, and hefted the pile downstairs to the parlour where I put them down on the table with a thud.

Mother had come back downstairs. May was sitting at the piano with her back to Mother, babbling about the evening to come.

Mother turned to me. 'Euphemia, you should not have spoken to Nurse Wilkins as you did. She has a difficult enough life as it is.'

I saw that she was right. On the one hand Wilkins was not a servant, but on the other, not on the same social level as the family. It was bad enough staying in the house for a weekend, as I was, but she was obliged to live here permanently, or at least until her services were no longer required. There were two reasons why that might be the case, three if Uncle Jacob's investment scheme ended in disaster. 'I see that her position is awkward.'

'She is deserving of respect,' Mother said. 'As are all human beings.'

'It was wrong of me. I will apologise to her.'

'No, it is too late now. You should have done so at the time. Her memory is as short as a pin.'

'Apologising is all very well,' May said, in a mealy-mouthed tone, 'But I always feel that it's better for a person to avoid saying unkind things in the first place. Anyway, let's not talk about that. I've been thinking about what to play at the party. I shall sing them a pretty song. Not one of those music hall ones, though. Something refined. Perhaps this one.' She raised her hands above the piano keys.

'Stop, May,' I said. She turned and looked at me.

'Oh, you haven't even got changed yet. And we must be leaving soon.'

'Exactly!' I said. I picked up the *Journal* I had been reading earlier and put it on the top of the pile of books on the table. It would form the icing on this particular mathematical cake. 'You have work to do, May. The other guests are mathematicians, and indeed Mrs Lazarus herself is well versed in numbers. As you know, it is considered very unfashionable not to be able to converse on the hostess's subject of special interest. If you do not want to appear empty-headed, you must read around it, so that you can hold your side of the conversation. That was what I was trying to do, earlier. These books will be a good foundation.'

May jumped up from the piano stool. 'I can't possibly read all of *those*. You should have told me before.'

'But I didn't know you wanted to go with me. You never said.'

She picked up *Quaternions*.

'Excellent choice, as a starter. Quaternions give mathematicians a way to describe rotations in space.'

She opened it. 'I can't understand what it says. It might as well be in German, like *my* book.'

I took it from her. 'Then let me read it to you.' I opened the book at a random page. '*It is often convenient to take a vector of the length of the unit, and to express the vector under consideration as a numerical multiple of this unit.* Do you see?'

'No.'

'Oh dear. It should be simple enough to comprehend if you remember that it is not necessary that the unit should have any specified value.'

'Isn't it?' May whispered.

'No, of course not. Remember that. You don't want to appear a ninny.'

'But what of the music? Can I not speak of that, instead?'

'What indeed? These texts are germane to the subject. We are to discuss the mathematics of sound, with particular regard to musical notes.'

'Can't I just perform?'

'Perform what?' I clapped my hand to my forehead. 'Oh, wait—you didn't think there would be *playing*? Or *singing*? Certainly not. The guests would never countenance such frivolity, not at their advanced ages. Here's a numerical fact about the guests, which you will find interesting. If you added all their ages together, you would get an answer of nearly one thousand.'

Out of the corner of my eye, I could see mother's shoulders shaking. She stood up, pressing a handkerchief to her mouth and left the room, holding onto the chair backs for support.

'You have made Aunt Agnes choke, with all this dry talk,' May said, pulling her handkerchief out of the cuff of her dress. 'And I think I have taken cold. I must stay at home this evening. I will see whether Cook has some mustard for a bath.' She walked away, towards the kitchen.

As I sat on the sofa flicking through the pages of the *Journal* yet again, Mother came back and sat next to me, in a cloud of lavender water.

'Put your journal down for a moment. About this evening.' I held my breath. Who was she going to suggest I took now? Nurse Wilkins, as recompense? 'Don't look so worried. I want to know about this friend of yours, who invited you. You are clearly very fond of him.'

'I have not met Mrs Lazarus yet, but I am sure *she* is perfectly amiable.'

'Don't insult my intelligence, Euphemia. Whatever Nurse Wilkins may think about the effects of your behaviour on me, my brain is not addled. I recall the feelings of a young woman.'

'You are not so old, mother. In fact, only the other day someone remarked on your youthful complexion. You haven't been putting lard and bone marrow on your face, have you?'

She put her hand on my arm. 'Hush. I will not be diverted. Now, I have a mystery to solve. What would Mr Sherlock Holmes do?' She ticked off points against her fingers. 'Question One. Why are you so keen to go to the party? You, who has never expressed any interest in music?'

'I do like music. Just not May's singing. Or Wagner.'

'I did not know you had listened to his work long enough to form an opinion. I do not consider you a lover of music. Name one composer, one song.'

'Here is one of which I do not know the name, but it goes like this.' I began to hum the tune I had heard played on the violin in my dream about Pearl and the hotel.

Mother shook her head. 'I have never heard that in my life. I believe you have made it up just now, but you will not put me off the scent that way. Question Two: Why are you so keen to go to the party alone? I am sure none of those books of yours had anything to do with music.'

'One did. But as for the others… I fear poor May will have developed a horror of reading. She will be afraid to pick up a book again. Little change from the usual.'

Mother tapped the back of my hand. 'I told you, be kind. I repeat, why do you want to go alone?'

'Well… I do not want to have to listen to May prattling all evening.'

'That won't do, either. She will be sure to leave your side, and prattle all evening, as you put it, to the first man she sees under the age of sixty. But if May is your only reason, then perhaps Uncle Jacob will escort you in her place. Shall I ask him? No, I thought not.' She paused for breath. I felt as though a net was closing over me. I stood and walked to the window. I twitched the curtain and looked outside.

'Question Three: You were invited by a friend, studying with you at Oxford. Are there any other women students besides you?'

'There may be. Studying Arts.'

'*Euphemia*. Do not try to wriggle away. I meant studying *with* you, and you know it.'

I felt my face grow warm. 'Mother, I think you know the answer. Which is also the answer to the other questions.'

'The game's afoot,' she said, with a smile. We embraced. 'I hope *he* is worthy of you, this nameless young man,' she said, unwrapping my arms. 'Or, is it an older man? Your professor, perhaps? A mature and respectable professional man would make an eminently suitable match for an intelligent young woman. What a feather in my cap that would be.'

I shuddered. 'A grey, bedraggled feather, missing many plumes? No, I would rather take the veil. Besides, Professor Milton is too old and too married, although I imagine his wife would be grateful for the respite were he to find another. No, my friend was twenty-eight on his last birthday. October 2nd.'

'You know much about him already.'

'I find him interesting.'

'There'd be little future for the two of you, if you did not. I hope he's worth all this Machiavellian plotting of yours.'

I held mother's gaze. 'We are merely friends.'

'It is perfectly acceptable not to be certain, at this stage. All I have to add is that I have long looked forward to this day, that every time I hear of May and her devotees, I think how much more admirable you are, to the right person. Perhaps, in the fullness of time, you will allow us to meet.'

'Us?' I imagined the scene. Leo arriving at the front door, tripping over his boots as he climbed the front steps. May, announcing to all I had a young man who was beginning to lose his hair. I, trying to defuse the situation by saying that on the contrary, we were colleagues, working together on something called the Thorniwork-Lazarus Lemma. Uncle Jacob asking whether Lazarus was an English name.

Mother's raised eyebrows told me more than words. 'This will be our secret. Meeting the rest of the family is not something to be undergone without full preparation on the part of—what is his name?'

'Leopold. His friends call him Leo.'

I thought of the evening, and it glowed.

A Thousand Paces

At six o'clock I set out for the omnibus. To my left walked May, who had sufficiently recovered from her cold to accompany me. 'Just in case your friend decides to meet you there, instead of at the other end.' To my right, Uncle Jacob carried a lantern. He would escort May home again.

The fog stole out of the ground, tendrils creeping and circling as though alive. Like hydras or blind snakes determining where to strike, they oozed across the toes of my boots and snatched at my ankles.

'Father, will you not lend the lantern to Euphemia?' May asked.

'And how will you and I find our way home, if I do? I expect her friend will have one.'

We reached the crowded stop. 'Uncle, thank you for escorting me. It is cold—you need not wait.'

'If you are sure.'

I nodded.

'But criminal gangs are everywhere!' May said. 'Why, I read in the newspaper only last week of a lady set upon by a gang. And remember, Jack the Ripper was never apprehended.'

'That will suffice, May,' Uncle Jacob said. 'Euphemia need fear nothing, while these stout citizens and honest housewives also wait at the stop. You must leave it for another day before you meet Euphemia's friend.' He led her away.

The omnibus arrived. I climbed inside and sank into the last vacant seat, at the front. A fluttering, empty feeling in my stomach reminded me that I had merely picked at my earlier meal. Aunt Emily had asked whether I felt unwell, while Mother smiled and patted my hand. In my mind I urged the omnibus on.

As we approached the stop where I was to alight, I saw Leo pacing, next to a queue of people waiting to get on. No lantern. He paused and looked at his watch. I was not late—was I? I stood and jumped off as soon as the omnibus stopped.

He smiled as he saw me approaching. 'Ah! A friendly face in a crowd of strangers. Is it not interesting, the way we each look different, one from the other? There's a man down the road whose name, from his expression, must be Mr Lemon Eater.'

I gave no reply and we set off along the street. Although the omnibus journey had taken no more than fifteen minutes, it seemed darker as we walked away and the raw, swirling fog reached my shins.

We crossed the road and Leo led me towards an alley. Houses towered on either side. We had discovered a shared taste for walking in pleasant surroundings, but this felt like creeping along a tunnel.

'I apologise,' Leo said, 'But this is the most direct route. We should spend as little time as possible in the fog.'

I missed my footing as I picked my way round the greasy puddles and scraps of filth-covered rags, putting one hand up against a wall to steady myself. It felt rough through my thin glove. A dog, snuffling at a pile of rubbish, started at our approach and ran away. The smell of rotting refuse and animal waste vied with the fog to choke me.

The alley opened into a sloping street. We walked downhill into a patch of fog so dense I could not see. It was as though it had wrapped everything in a dirty yellow blanket, reeking of sulphur. It reached above our heads. People walked past coughing, remarking to each other what a foul night it was. 'I cannot orientate myself,' Leo said. 'It's as though the fog has lifted everything and put it back in the wrong place.'

I hit something solid and fell back. An enormous figure loomed in front of me, a man, who helped me to my feet and asked directions to Sebastopol Terrace. 'I'm afraid I do not know,' I replied.

'Can you help, Leo?' No reply. 'Leo?' I could not see him.

I found the edge of the pavement and stepped along it. Water gurgled under a grating in the kerb, heading for the sewers. The man walked beside me. I could not see his face, only a blurred bulk. I heard his voice, spluttering and hawking. 'Which way are you going? May I walk with you? The fog has collected in this valley and it is like being blind. I have no lantern.'

'I am not going your way,' I said. 'I'm going…' I realised I did not know the address of Leo's aunt. I fumbled my way along the road, through the thickening fog. It was like walking towards a wall that retreated as I advanced, one that threw back the light from the streetlamps. My feet and hands began to freeze. The man left my side and stood in front of me, forcing me to stop. 'I'll wager you can show me the way.' His breath, warm after the chill of the fog, smelled of fish. I staggered backwards.

Someone grabbed my arm, stopping me from falling. My mouth dried as I tried to scream but it came out as a high-pitched wail. The fog in front of my face thinned and I saw Leo. 'Thank goodness!' I gasped. I realised that I had been holding my breath.

'I thought I'd never find you,' he said, with a cough.

I held my hand out in front of me. It vanished into the cloud of yellow. The man let out a bubbling snort.

'Has this fellow been troubling you?' Leo asked, dropping my arm and turning towards him, hands balled into fists.

'No, no!' The man backed away until he was, once more, a shapeless hulk in the fog. 'I am looking for Sebastopol Terrace.'

'You have passed it, my friend,' Leo snarled. 'Turn round and retrace your steps. It is the third on your right.' The man disappeared into the swirling chaos.

'Are you all right, Pheemie?' I heard Leo's voice. I could not see him.

'Yes. I'm very relieved to find you, but I have no need of a champion to fight for me. Now please, let's hurry.'

He took my arm again. 'We will reach a crossroads in another twenty yards or so, then we must walk about five hundred yards. We will pass a church.'

'Will we be able to see it?'

'Possibly not. I wish I had brought a lantern. Fortunately, there's a stone wall along that stretch, we can grasp it. Then, when we have passed a lone poplar tree, my aunt's house will be opposite. It will take us no more than ten minutes.'

Disembodied footsteps passed, figures manifested at

close range and disappeared. A scream of laughter from one. A cough from another. The fog danced and writhed. Someone collided with Leo, knocking my arm from his. I reached out, but nobody was there.

'Leo?' No reply. 'Leo! Where are you?' No reply. I called him again and again, my voice growing higher and louder until it felt like I must scream. The fog cleared in front of my face. I ran out of breath and stopped shouting. The fog returned. I remembered what May had said but told myself not to be foolish, that it had been eleven years since the last Whitechapel murder. But what else might be done under cover of fog?

I must try to find the house on my own. I shuffled along, feeling for the edge of the kerb through the soles of my boots. Leo said there was a wall. I reached out a hand and felt firm stone. Five hundred yards. A thousand paces, in my skirt and footwear? I counted. Twenty-five, thirty... the wall came to an end. It could not be the one of which Leo had spoken. Where was he? I tripped and fell again. My hands flew out in front of me to cushion the fall. I fell headlong, banging my cheek on the pavement and knocking the wind from my lungs. I scrabbled for my hat, and, wheezing, hauled myself to my feet. The front of my skirt was spattered with mud, my gloves in tatters. I would look a fright when I arrived, if I ever did.

I had lost count, but should I not have reached the crossroads? Had I already passed them? A journey of ten minutes felt as though it had taken half an hour. I quickened my steps, and stumbled off the edge of the kerb into the road. I crossed it, and found myself walking into a clump of trees. Poplars? The fog did not permit my identifying the shape. But Leo had said there was only one tree. I took off my glove to get my handkerchief from my bag, and my hand froze before I could replace the glove. I dragged it on, held the handkerchief over my nose and mouth and walked.

From a long way off, I heard Leo call my name. I stumbled towards the sound, feeling as though I was stepping into an abyss. Nothing. I stopped where I was, and turned my head this way and that, trying to locate him. Leo had mentioned that the fog seemed to move buildings, but it also seemed to do the same to sound and I heard his voice whisper, as though from behind me. I flinched, swung round and listened intently. Nothing but a hissing in my ears. I must have imagined Leo's voice. I would have to stay in the street till the fog lifted. What would happen if I breathed it in all night? I called Leo's name again, on a rising pitch. With each shout, the mist in front of my face shimmered and formed patterns. Now an X shape. Then impenetrability, as I drew breath. Now concentric circles, on top of clear air. I stopped calling. Back to thick haze. I shouted again. Now honeycomb. I could not see Leo.

'Pheemie!' he called, almost on top of me.

I dropped the handkerchief and turned, coughing. 'An interesting phenomenon! The fog… different patterns, when I changed the pitch of my voice.'

'I called and called,' he gasped. 'For twenty minutes. I knew I'd find you.' He wrapped his arms round me and smiled. That smile.

I stood inside his arms, smiling back. Tears ran down my cheeks.

'Don't cry! We have found each other,' Leo said.

'I am not crying; the fog is irritant to the eyes.' I

146

sniffed. 'And the nose. And I've torn my gloves.'

He lowered his arm and squeezed my fingers. 'That tiny hand's frozen, again. And you have something on your face.' He reached out a thumb and rubbed. 'There, that's better. Now, we are bound to find the house soon. Let us be sure not to separate again.' He gripped my hand. A fine, penetrating rain began to fall.

Across the street, the front door of a house opened. A blur of light melted the vapour enough for me to see raindrops glistening in Leo's hair. He put his arms round me again, and I wrapped mine around his waist. I closed my eyes.

'Leopold!' a voice shouted from the open front door.

'Aunt Matilda!' He flinched and let go of me.

'Of course it's me!' the voice shouted. 'Now, do come along.'

We crossed the street.

Mrs Lazarus stepped onto the pavement and peered out from the grey shawl wrapped round her head, looking like an inquisitive mouse.

'At last! I thought you were never coming back.' She wafted her hand in front of her face. 'All the other guests have been here for some time. In fact, we have resumed without you.' She turned to me and put an arm round my shoulder. 'Dear Leopold never did have a decent sense of direction, Miss… Er. Vieni! t'affretta! MacBeth. Do you like Verdi?'

'It means "Come on, hurry up,"' Leo said from behind me, before I could answer. 'And that is capital advice.'

'Quite,' Mrs Lazarus said. 'What vile weather you have had to contend with, Miss… Er. You must be frozen.'

'Do not worry,' I said. 'I am enjoying myself.'

I looked down, to be sure of my footing. Through the fog, through the rain, the pavement gleamed like silver.

One in the Gallery

Mrs Lazarus shut the front door behind us. She hung her shawl on a carved wooden stand, next to a hollowed-out elephant's foot containing a furled parasol with a brass duck's head for a handle, a gnarled wooden walking stick with a solar topi dangling from a protrusion on the end and what, from the look of the haft, might have been a rapier. She appeared to be aged in her seventies, her grey hair scraped into an elaborate concoction of curls on the top of her head, in the style of the Princess of Wales. She wore a black silk dress embellished with a froth of flounces and frills.

'I am so sorry for my appearance,' I said. 'I was lost, I fell…' I stuffed the remains of my gloves into my bag and Leo and I hung up our hats and coats. The three of us stood, looking at each other.

'I believe you are studying with Leopold,' she said, after some seconds.

I nudged Leo with my elbow. 'What is it?' he hissed.

'Manners, Leopold,' she said, with a frown.

I shook my head and sighed. 'May I introduce myself?' I said, stretching out my hand. 'I am Euphemia Thorniwork and, yes, we are researching together.'

She shook my hand. 'Matilda Lazarus. Euphemia—what a delightful name! It means fair speech—did you know?'

'Yes, I've been told. How do you do?'

'Very well, thank you,' she said. 'And you must call me Matilda, for I am certain that we shall be good friends.' She held my face in her hands. 'Large brown eyes. Prominent features. Yes, an *intelligent* physiognomy… 'But—' she took a handkerchief out of her sleeve '—a little grubby.' She dabbed at my cheekbone. 'That's better.' Would the entire Lazarus family take turns in cleaning my face? 'And the mud will brush off your skirt, once it has dried. Now, come along, before Leopold does anything else that casts aspersions on his upbringing.' She led us along a wide hallway past dark wooden doors until we came to one that was half open, and ushered us inside.

The room had a high ceiling. The walls were white, with mouldings in the shape of musical instruments entwined with flowers and bunches of grapes. At the far end a fire blazed, set in tiles depicting Romans, playing drums and cymbals. I felt as though I were an actress who had walked onto the wrong stage set—one crammed with two rooms' worth of furniture, and Leo's tone generator that I had seen in his study. He had found a way of connecting it to a dry cell, for power.

Matilda introduced us to two elderly men, Mr Szekely and Mr Ginsberg, seated with musical instrument cases on the floor in front of them. Next, a woman of about Mother's age, Mrs Levitt, and her daughter Minnie, who looked about ten years old.

Leo and I sat next to each other, underneath a crossed cello and its bow, wrapped around with honeysuckle. 'I see you admire my swags, Euphemia,' Matilda said. 'When my late husband and I came to live here, I simply had to make this our music room. And after Leopold joined us, he would climb up and try to play the instruments. He has stopped now, of course.'

Out of the corner of my eye, I saw Leo's face redden. I kept my gaze ahead, at what looked like a clarinet engulfed by some kind of predatory daffodil. 'Now, you have missed Mr Szekely's performance of a Hungarian tune on the cymbalom, and Mr Ginsberg's rendition of, er, something on the accordion. You have missed Leopold's exhibition of his tone generator and Mrs Levitt's demonstration of the harmonograph. But you are just in time to hear little Minnie sing.'

'I have another intriguing device to demonstrate later,' Mrs Levitt said. 'But now Minnie's going to perform a poem by George MacDonald, set to music by her sister Julia.' She and Matilda smiled at each other.

The other guests murmured approval. Matilda turned to me. 'Julia is such a musical young woman. So talented.' She stood. 'I shall be sorry to miss the song, but I must see to the refreshments. The maid's visiting her sick mother. The fog, you know.'

Minnie strutted across the room and clambered onto a small round table in the middle. Her mother pursed her lips and shook her head. Minnie climbed down and clasped her hands, opened her mouth wide enough for me to see her tonsils, and sang, unaccompanied, in a quavering voice. 'Where did you come from, baby dear? Out of the everywhere into the here. Where did you get those eyes so blue? Out of the sky as I came through.' The tune seemed to comprise two notes only, but whether this was the composition or its execution was impossible to tell.

Minnie sang, 'But how did you come to us, you dear? God thought about you, and so I am here.' She fell silent and took a bow. Her mother smiled broadly. Everyone applauded.

'Encore!' Mr Ginsberg shouted.

Minnie drew breath and opened her mouth again.

Having no wish to receive further instruction on where babies came from, I stood and headed for the kitchen. Matilda looked up as I came in. 'Let me lend a hand,' I said. 'Shall I make the tea?'

'Thank you, that would be most helpful. The kettle has just boiled.'

I washed my hands at the sink, took the lid off the silver teapot on the table and scooped tea out of the caddy next to it, remembering too late I should have warmed the pot first. Matilda, engaged in placing miniature cakes into cut glass dishes, did not seem to have noticed.

'Cut up that lemon over there, please, and put it on this plate.' I did as she instructed. 'No, not that plate. It is silver, and the lemon juice will tarnish it. Use the little Wedgwood dish. I mean that blue one, with the white pattern.'

She stopped what she was doing, a minuscule cake in her hand. 'Listen to Minnie sing. Her sister has such a prestigious musical talent, she could have sung in the opera, but prefers to be a home-maker.'

I bent to pick up a slice of lemon that had fallen onto the floor.

'Her mother is one of my oldest friends. I have seen Julia grow into a beautiful young woman, with the voice of a nightingale.'

'That must be pleasant, for her mother.'

'Julia and Leopold were such friends, as children. They used to love to walk in the park, hand in hand.'

I put the plate onto a tray. 'Leo and I have taken a number of strolls together, around Oxford. I was going to suggest to him that we walked on Shotover—'

'Oh, I don't think he'd like to do *that*, dear.' Before I could ask why not, she continued. 'Julia's mother feels it is time Julia married, and I concur. Do you have a sweetheart?'

'No. And I have no desire to marry.'

I waited for her to tell me I would change my mind when I met the right man. Instead, she told me that it had been Leo's late parents dearest wish that he marry within their faith. 'And he will abide by that.'

'Is it not his own decision? He is a grown man.'

'It is his wish too,' Matilda said, looking over her shoulder as though she expected to find Leo looking back. 'I think Minnie has finished singing. Please take the tea glasses into the music room.'

Lemon tea was drunk. Cake eaten. After sending Minnie to bed, Mrs Levitt took a device from a box next to her chair. 'I will now demonstrate a way to make sound visible,' she said. She took out a violin bow and a crystal jar with a perforated silver lid, filled with white powder. These she put on the table in the centre of the room, followed by a device consisting of a square metal plate mounted, by a pole in its centre, on a stand.

'Now,' she said. 'We've heard this evening that sound can be high or low, loud or soft.' She looked at Mr Ginsberg. 'And pleasant or unpleasant. Sound has been compared to a wave in the water. We can show how it moves through materials.' She picked up the glass jar. 'If I scatter salt over this square plate, we can see it falls evenly. But see what happens when I activate the plate.'

She picked up the bow and stroked the plate in the middle of one edge. There was a sound a little like a dull violin. The grains of salt danced, and formed a pattern of a large letter X covering the plate. 'These are called Chladni patterns. I am playing the plate's fundamental tone. Its natural frequency. Sound moves through the metal. Any rigid plate has a possible natural frequency at which it wants to move, each corresponding to a particular note, a particular frequency of sound. I will now replace the plate with one made from a different metal.'

'No, leave it,' I said. 'What if you were to bow faster, or harder? What would happen then? Would it make a different note? Would the pattern change?'

She frowned. 'I expect it that would make a louder sound. Perhaps a larger X shape. Let's see.'

She did as I had suggested, producing, rather than a louder tone, a higher one. This created a more detailed pattern, with fewer open spaces. As the notes grew higher in pitch, the patterns became increasingly complex. Now like flowers, now like honeycomb.

'That's what I tried to tell you about earlier. I saw that in the fog,' I whispered to Leo. 'Those swirling patterns. When I shouted to you.'

'It is a brilliant demonstration of the science of sound, Mrs Levitt,' he said. 'Of the way that it moves through materials. Where there is no vibration, there the salt collects.'

'Let us not speak of science,' she said. 'All materials are made by God, ultimately. This shows us that His brilliance surpasses any of our own.'

Mr Ginsberg yawned. 'Talking of God...' He began discussing funerals, the numbers attending one, compared with another. I shivered, despite the heat of the room.

'Does anyone know why we wash our hands before we leave the grounds?' Leo said.

'Well, cleanliness is laudable,' Mrs Lazarus said. 'After all, it is next to godliness.'

'It is nothing to do with that,' Mr Szekely said. 'It is concerned with ritual purity. The mourners will have been in proximity to a dead body. From a ritual perspective, that is the most impure thing, as it is no longer animated and therefore farthest from God.'

I remembered the passage in Pearl's Bible, saying that whoever touched a corpse would be unclean for seven days. 'Numbers chapter 19,' I said. 'That's where you can find all the instructions about purification.'

'You seem quite the Biblical scholar, Euphemia.' Matilda said.

I shook my head. 'Not me, but my cousin Pearl. I often listened when she read from the Bible. She did so every day. Until she died.'

'I'm sure hers was a *lovely* funeral,' Mr Ginsberg said.

I felt a sudden urge to shout at this kindly man. What could he know of Pearl?

'Afterwards, her body was stolen, as was her mother's, my aunt's. The latter was recovered, and reburied.'

'Two of your dear ones! What a dreadful thing,' Mrs Levitt filled an awkward silence. 'There have been no accounts of body snatching in the newspapers for some time. Let us hope that these terrible people have ceased their ghastly work.'

'I wish that were true,' Mr Ginsberg said. 'Her Majesty

attempted to prevent it being reported, but she only succeeded in silencing the quality press. There's plenty if you look for it. In fact, only the other day in *The Star...* I have a cutting somewhere.' He rummaged in a jacket pocket.

Mr Szekely hushed him and reminded him that there were ladies present. He turned to me. 'Our custom is that someone watches over the departed until the burial, so there would be no chance of a body being stolen. But, once the funeral has taken place, what can you do?' He tutted and shook his head.

Matilda clapped her hands. 'What ghouls we are. Look at all the solemn faces! We are here for pleasure and entertainment. Now, shall we hear a song from Euphemia?'

'Oh, no, I couldn't possibly. I don't know any.'

'Do not be modest,' Matilda said. 'I am sure you can carry a tune, at least.'

Leo cleared his throat, and I wondered whether he was about to offer to sing in my place. Perhaps he expected us to sing a duet. He sniffed and pulled the fog-stained handkerchief out of his pocket.

'Leopold!' Matilda hissed. 'Laundry!'

He retrieved a clean one and, with a noise like a trumpeting elephant, blew his nose.

'I'm reminded of a song that my cousin used to sing,' I said, looking at Leo. 'But I can only remember one verse, and the chorus.'

Old Mr Ginsberg rubbed his hands. 'I'm sure it will be charming.'

I stood. I hoped I would remember the tune correctly.

'Now, if I were a Duchess and had a lot of money,
I'd give it to the boy that's going to marry me.
But I haven't got a penny, so we'll live on love and kisses,
And be just as happy as the birds on the tree.
The boy I love is up in the gallery,
The boy I love is looking now at me…'

I remembered Pearl, singing the song as she sewed a ribbon onto a new hat. My voice grew husky.

'There he is, can't you see, waving his handkerchief,
As merry as a robin that sings on a tree.'

My face reddened as I flopped into my chair. The men, and Mrs Levitt, clapped.

Matilda joined in as they finished. 'Well, it rhymes "tree" with "tree", but I can see how it might be considered moving.'

'Marie Lloyd herself could have done no better,' Mr Ginsberg said. 'You must sing another.'

'Later—we must take turns,' Matilda said. 'Now, I shall sing a piece that requires an unusually high note. It's from *The Magic Flute*. You may know it as "The Queen of the Night's Aria". Its proper name is "*Der hölle Rache*".'

Leo whispered in my ear, 'Which means "The Vengeance of Hell".'

I gripped the edges of my seat.

After the applause, and the ringing in my ears, subsided. I tugged Leo's arm. 'I fear it grows late.' I turned to Matilda. 'Thank you. This has been a most pleasant evening, but I must leave if I'm to catch the omnibus.'

Leo looked at his watch. 'Perhaps it's an apposite time. I have read that the best performers leave their audience wanting more.'

Matilda told Leo to come back quickly and closed the front door behind us. The fog had receded so that it only reached waist height. As we trudged along the road past the wall of the churchyard, I felt as though I were wading in the sea.

'I am afraid I will be unable to travel back to Oxford with you tomorrow,' Leo said. 'I won't know which train I will take until the last moment. But we will meet at Professor Milton's, on Monday.'

'Mrs Levitt and Minnie are staying at your Aunt Matilda's,' I said. 'Will the other daughter be joining them?'

He shrugged. 'Julia? I shouldn't think so, tonight.'

I shoved my hands into my pockets and looked at the ground. 'Yes, it's probably too late for her to come all the way from her lovely home.'

'I've no idea whether she's even invited.'

I kicked a pebble out of the way. 'She is certain to have been.'

'Do you know her?'

'I almost feel as though I do.'

'I don't think I've seen her since she beat me at hopscotch when we were about nine years old. By all accounts, though, she is a nice, homely girl.'

A gust of wind blew a clearing in the fog. I waited, jaw clenched, for Leo to say that he was sure she and I would be good friends. Instead, he stopped walking and grabbed my arm. 'A funeral? At night-time?'

I followed his gaze over the wall. At the edge of the churchyard stood three men wearing dark overcoats, hats pulled down and scarves wrapped round their faces so that only their eyes were visible. At first, it looked like some private interment—but surely that would not be permitted after dark. The fog cleared further, and I saw the gravestone already placed at the head of the tomb. I found it hard to breathe.

A hole had been dug at the end of the grave and the coffin was part way out. The blood pounded in my ears and my hands shook. I felt as though I were looking through a distorting lens. I could not look away. One of the men threw a sack over the top of the coffin. He raised a sledge-hammer. With a crack, the lid smashed. The other two reached inside.

Leo gave a shout. The men looked up. The scarf slipped from the face of one. I drew closer. He was aged about fifty with black mutton chop whiskers, moustache. Dark eyes. Thick eyebrows. They turned and ran, leaving a wooden spade leaning against the wall.

At One in the Morning

Leo craned his neck and peered into the fog. 'A beat policeman can't be far away. We must report this.' We stood for some five minutes. Nobody came. 'Very well, we will go to them.' He picked up the abandoned spade.

I stepped back. 'What are you doing? You surely don't think to... re-inter that unfortunate?'

'No. This may be helpful to the police.' He explained a phenomenon I had not heard of, called fingerprints. Each unique to a person. 'They will want to test it. And perhaps they already have a record, an identity, for the prints on it, which will lead them to at least one of the criminal gang. Come along.' He crossed the road and headed down a street on the left.

I quickened my step to keep up. 'Shouldn't you have worn gloves? Surely your marks will now have obscured theirs.'

'I am sure there is room for both.' He frowned and strode ahead.

We trudged through the fog, which hung like a pall on all sides. Muffled sounds came at me: a skittering on the pavement, as though beyond my vision, rats ran.

The faint blue glow of the police station lamp flickered as we approached through the gloom. A soot-stained building, metal bars across the windows. We climbed the steps and pushed open the door.

People who must either have braved the fog or been hauled in from it, crammed the space in front of the counter. A shoeless man dressed in rags sprawled on a chair in the corner, tattered bundles around him. From a doorway off the main area, an officer dragged out a man and woman, arms flailing, trying to punch each other, failing to connect.

The booking officer surveyed the chaos from the counter behind which he sat; a massive black ledger open in front of him. Leo and I stood behind a man enquiring about a lost dog. 'Black mongrel, about knee height when seated. Answers to the name of Jess. Likes minced beef, as long as it is well cooked.'

My throat tightened. 'By the time it's our turn, the body snatchers will be long gone.'

Leo drew closer to me as an officer shoved past, supporting a woman who appeared to be covered in blood.

'Enjoys a long walk but not in the rain. Will beg for small pieces of cheddar cheese.' The lost dog man finished, turned and left. The officer beckoned to us.

Leo thumped the spade onto the floor sending clods of earth to join the filth already there, then put it on the counter. He explained what we had seen, while the officer wrote in the ledger in slow unjoined letters. Leo stopped speaking and the officer looked up. 'And that is all, is it? Very well. We may need to discuss this with you again.'

'I don't see how,' I said. 'You haven't asked for our names or addresses. How will it be if you find these men but cannot locate the witnesses?'

He sighed and shook his head. 'Proceed.' We gave him the information, including addresses in both London and Oxford. The tip of his tongue protruded from the corner of his mouth as he wrote our names, while we spelled them out. 'Whatever happened to people called Smith or Jones? But thank you. I've all the information I need. You may leave and take your shovel with you. We will investigate, in due course. I bid you good night.'

Leo left the spade where it was. 'You must send someone now, or there will be nothing to see,' he said.

'Yes, you must hurry,' I said. 'Before the sexton fills in the grave.'

The officer put his pen down. 'Don't tell me how to do my job, madam. If we cannot actually catch these men in the act, there is little point in attending. And *I* told *you* to move that mucky shovel.' He pushed the spade off the counter onto the floor.

Leo picked it up. 'This *spade* is vital evidence of a crime. I brought it so that you can look for fingerprints.'

'I know,' the officer said. 'I'll go to Huxley College Oxford and do whatever it is you do there, shall I? Seeing as how you're trying to do my job.'

'We're doing no such thing,' I said, standing on tiptoe so I could lean forward. 'You don't seem to appreciate the urgency of the situation.'

The officer smiled. 'Look, Miss. I am sure you have had a most distressing experience. Best you go home and have a nice cup of tea. It is Saturday night and we are at our busiest. You can see that we are occupied. We will place an *Apprehensions Sought* advertisement in the *Police Gazette*.'

'Perhaps there has already been such an advertisement,' I said. 'Could it be that other stations have information that will help?'

The officer shrugged. 'I can't tell, without looking through them all.' He opened a cupboard behind him, stuffed with magazines. 'Would you care to try?'

We stood in the street outside. 'I'd have expected him to take us to the Inspector's office,' I said. 'But he didn't seem interested.'

'More preoccupied with that fight that broke out in the corner. And these are the people who are meant to protect us from criminals.'

'They seem to regard crime like rat catchers regard rats, a nuisance to be kept down but not altogether abolished.'

Leo looked at his watch. 'It's nearly two o'clock in the morning. You must get home, but it is so late. The last omnibus will have left hours ago.'

A cab clattered along the street. Leo waved, but it kept moving, the driver probably unable to see him in the fog. Leo inserted an index finger into each corner of his mouth and gave a piercing whistle.

'I'd never have imagined you could to that,' I said. The cab stopped. 'But you cannot mean to take it all the way to Highgate. The expense! I do not mind walking. Besides, I read that, in the fog, a cab drove into the Serpentine, on the way to Knightsbridge. We can't be too careful.'

'You should not believe all that you read in the newspapers. Besides, that's nowhere near here, so there is nothing to worry about.' He took my elbow and urged me to climb in. Taking a seat next to me, he gave the driver my address. Nothing to worry about, except for the reaction of those of my family whom I would wake by coming in.

The cab rattled along the road, the horses in front of us scarcely visible through the fog. 'I noticed that when I shouted to you, it had some kind of effect on the fog,' I said. 'It was similar to Mrs Levitt's achievement with the bow. I tried to tell you before.'

'I didn't notice that result from my own shouting. I have usually found that fog deadens sound or creates uncertainty as to its direction. Fog particles have no effect on sound waves themselves.'

'I'm talking about the effects of sound on fog, not the other way around. My voice is higher pitched than yours, and the patterns changed the higher I cried out, like with Mrs Levitt and the bow.'

'Under other circumstances I would suggest we perform an experiment. But on Monday Professor Milton will approve our research proposals, I know. In which case we will have no time to spare.'

'I hope that you are right.'

Leo frowned. 'So do I.'

The lamp beside my front door was lit. Perhaps the family were still awake. Leo and I stepped out of the cab.

'I'm afraid I only have my omnibus fare, but please take it.'

'I would not dream of it.' He rummaged in his jacket pocket and pulled out a few coins he dropped into to the driver's open palm. The driver kept his hand out. Leo dipped into his other pocket, but his hand came out empty. He tried three more pockets, retrieving an oddment of coins that sufficed. Leo waved the cab away.

'Didn't you want to take the cab back to your Aunt's?'

'It would be remiss of me not to come in and apologise to your family for keeping you out so late. That might take time, I fear, and I cannot afford to pay the driver to wait. I will walk. It will be bracing.'

'I am deeply sorry that you had to spend your last penny on me.'

'There's no better cause. Now, let's go inside. I trust your family will be adequately sympathetic.'

'Your trust is misplaced.' I pulled my key out of my bag. My voice cracked. 'I must face this ordeal alone.'

'But surely I could reassure them about what we saw, that we are in no danger.'

'Leo, no. I mean it!' I realised I was shouting. I stopped, held my breath, waiting for the sound of an upstairs window opening. None came. 'Please,' I whispered.

Leo raised his eyebrows. 'If you insist. I'll see you at Professor Milton's office door at noon on Monday. Which is in fact tomorrow!'

We said our goodbyes and Leo disappeared into the fog.

I slipped inside the house and closed the door. It made no more than a click. The hallway was in darkness. If pressed, I would merely say I had had to walk home. The rest would upset Mother. I pictured Uncle Jacob's horror. 'The police, Euphemia? You bring shame on the family.' I shook my head. It would remain a secret, and I would have to hope the police would come to Oxford to interview me further.

The long case clock in the hall struck two. As if waiting for a cue, the door to the kitchen opened and the scent of carbolic soap that always preceded Nurse Wilkins filled the hall. She approached, holding a lit candle in one hand and a poker in the other. 'Oh, it's you, Miss Thorniwork.' She lowered the weapon. 'You did give me a scare.'

'I apologise for disturbing you.'

'You didn't. I had to get up to administer your mother a sedative draught. She could not settle, because you had not yet returned. She's sleeping now.'

'Poor mother. I regret having caused her such anxiety. I missed the last omnibus. I had to walk home.'

'It's fortunate that your poor mother was unaware of that. But I told her that you had returned, that I heard you go into your room. You must go to bed now. You look unwell—you're trembling.' She reached out and touched the back of her hand to my forehead. 'You seem a little feverish. A sudden change of temperature, such as from coming into a warm house from the street, can cause one to take cold. You too must take a sedative.'

I declined, assured her I felt quite well, and stole up to my room.

Mother, Uncle Jacob, Aunt Emily and I sat at the luncheon table. Uncle Jacob tucked his napkin into the front of his collar and scanned the dishes. He drew in a noisy breath, as though there was a dead rabbit lying there by way of cold meat. 'Emily! Where is the roast mutton? The roast potatoes?'

'There is no need to shout,' Aunt Emily said. 'Mrs Upshaw has gone out. She has left us this cold collation. It is perfectly adequate.'

He shook his head. 'Things have come to a pretty pass if a fellow cannot have a hot luncheon on a Sunday.'

'There, there, dear.' Aunt Emily patted his hand. 'I see we have a cornflour shape for pudding. You like them. And you shall have a hot dinner this evening.'

He helped himself to a large portion of cold sliced ham

and passed the platter along the table to May. I sat, pushing pieces food around my plate. Perhaps if I hid my meat under a slice of bread, nobody would notice.

'Euphemia, what has happened to your appetite?' Mother said, helping herself to a hard-boiled egg. 'You have not touched a single bite. You look upset.'

'Yes,' Uncle Jacob said. 'You look as though you would benefit from a dose of Epsom salts. Cleanse your blood. Beetroot, please, May.'

'I'm not ill. Merely tired. I missed the last omnibus and had to walk.'

Aunt Emily dropped her knife, put her hand to her throat and gasped. 'Alone?'

'My friend accompanied me.'

May pouted at me. 'And we missed her. Or—can it be true—*him*? What a pity.'

Nurse Wilkins came in, bearing Mother's medicine.

'Euphemia,' May said, 'you should ask Nurse for a glass of coca wine. Keeping such late hours has tired you. What time did you return? It must have been long after we all went to bed. You had not returned when I heard the clock strike twelve.'

'I crept inside. And you probably miscounted, the problem being that you only have ten fingers.'

Nurse Wilkins opened a bottle and poured a brown concoction into the water in Mother's glass. 'Miss Thorniwork arrived at about eleven o'clock.' She told Mother to swallow the medicine after she had finished eating, then left the room.

I stood. 'I will speak to Nurse. About the wine.' I followed her into the corridor.

'Thank you for that,' I whispered. 'You have been a

friend to me today.'

'My duty is to my patient, even if I must lie to meet that duty. And I know I speak out of turn, but I will not have her upset by the idea that her daughter was out with who knows who, who knows where, for half the night.' She strutted back into the kitchen.

I returned to the dining room and resumed my place at the table.

'When will you return to Oxford?' Mother asked. 'Surely, you won't leave until after we have eaten dinner. Mrs Upshaw would be so offended.'

The thought of another dreary family Sunday evening meal, when I had not yet finished luncheon, made my stomach lurch. A change of subject might help. 'Uncle Jacob,' I said, 'How do your investments fare?'

He heaped tough-looking lettuce leaves onto his plate. 'I am glad you asked me that, Euphemia. There has been a most interesting development.' He pushed a fork, loaded with potato salad, into his mouth.

'That is not a subject fit for discussion on Sunday,' Aunt Emily said.

'Not in detail,' Uncle Jacob said, 'But perhaps I may be allowed to tell you that I have hopes of diversification— which is, after all, the key to successful investment. I have hopes.' He wagged an index finger in time with each word. 'All founded on not putting my eggs in one financial basket.'

'Oh, Father,' May said. 'Do you intend to raise chickens?'

'Don't be silly, May,' Aunt Emily said. 'It is merely a figure of speech. And, Jacob, didn't you hear what I said about Sundays? Let us discuss the vicar's sermon.' She looked at me. 'Or, at least, let those of us who heard it do so.'

It appeared that the Vicar had included many lengthy quotations from obscure parts of the Bible, and that most of them concerned the Day of Judgment. I let the discussion wash over me. 'Please excuse me,' I said, and withdrew to the parlour, in the hope of finding something distracting to read.

On the table next to the sofa lay Mother's *Study in Scarlet*, the latest *Bradshaw's Train Guide*, and my *Journal of Modern Mathematics*. I took the *Journal* and sat on the sofa in front of the fire, opened a random page and flicked through until I came to the start of an article. I read the first paragraph, but it made little sense. I began again. As I reached the end of my third reading, Mother came in and shut the door. She sat next to me. I put the *Journal* down.

'I'm sorry to interrupt you,' she said.

'It doesn't matter. I can't concentrate today.'

Mother's brow furrowed. 'That's unfortunate. I'm worried about you. You seem upset.'

'There's no cause for concern. I'm merely tired.'

'And small wonder, considering when you came home. No,' she raised a hand, 'the fog has not softened my brain, despite Nurse Wilkins's opinion to the contrary. Not only can I tell the time, but I can also count. But I'm not asking you about that.' She took my hand. 'Has your friend—has *Leopold*—offended you?'

'No, Mother. He is the perfect gentleman. He paid for a cab to bring me home.'

'Ah, you did not walk. Then, what is the matter?' She looked into my eyes. 'I'm your mother. I hope you will confide in me. All we have is each other, after all.'

I looked away. 'That's not strictly true, Mother. We also have Uncle and Aunt. And May.'

'And I can hardly imagine your sharing your woes with them. So, please. Perhaps I can help.' My memories of the night before welled up inside my head, like a series of pictures, one following the other, unbidden. Unstoppable. 'There is a body of opinion that favours the cleansing effect of discussing our troubles,' Mother said.

I drew breath. 'Well, I have been worried about Uncle Jacob's handling of our money. But there's something else. It is horrific—'

May flung the door open and bounded in. 'Did I hear my name mentioned?'

'What, "Horrific"? You can only have heard it if you were listening at the door.'

'That's wicked. I happened to walk past. But, don't stop, what happened to you last night?'

I dropped Mother's hand. 'Oh, nothing much. Only that I had to sing at the party. It was embarrassing.'

May pouted. 'You told me that there would be no opportunity to perform. I'd have come if you'd told me the truth. Do you know, I didn't have a cold after all?'

'I am pleased for you,' I said. 'The evening was not as I expected it to be.'

Mother shook her head and picked her copy of *A Study in Scarlet*. 'I believe Dr Doyle to be a better storyteller than others closer to home.'

'What did you sing?' May said.

I shrugged. 'Merely a verse or two of some music hall song that Pearl liked.'

May threw up her hands. 'Oh! I would not have

expected that from you. I imagine it tired you.'

Mother looked up from her book. 'And I imagine it upset you, to remember Pearl singing. But you do look unwell. When you return to Oxford, take a cold bath and a long walk.'

Oxford. I felt the greyness clear from my mind. A walk—perhaps Leo and I would finally be able to visit Shotover Hill. Since he would be travelling back on his own, it made no matter when I did. I leaned across to the table and picked up *Bradshaw*. There was a train in an hour and a half. I would catch it, even if I had to run all the way to Paddington. I picked up the *Journal* and dashed upstairs to pack my bag.

Ninety-nine Stairs

On Monday morning, Leo and I met outside Professor Milton's office. Leo stuffed his hands in his pockets and whistled some cacophony. I put my hand to my stomach and winced. I had not been able to eat breakfast.

'Did the police call on you yesterday? They didn't visit me.'

He shook his head. 'We should have done better had we tried to catch the men ourselves.'

'If that's how they conducted the investigation into the Whitechapel murders, it gives me no surprise that they never caught the Ripper.' I shuddered. Any confidence I might have felt about our meeting with the Professor had evaporated.

'Take courage. Let us think of other things. The Riemann Hypothesis is now the keystone of number theory. The Professor will have been most impressed by our proposal.'

'Let's hope so. In any event, the twin prime conjecture has, until now, been unsolved.'

The clock in the college chapel tower chimed nine. I clenched my fist and banged on the door. No reply.

Leo blinked; his brow furrowed into his receding hairline. 'I am sure that he is so engrossed in our idea, finds it so fascinating a concept, that he did not hear your knock.' I tried to smile, but only succeeded in baring my teeth. Leo looked at his watch. 'I feel as though I am in school, waiting to see the headmaster. We will not endear ourselves if he thinks we are late.' He tapped on the door with his knuckle.

A shout came from inside the room. 'COME, I said.'

Leo opened the door and we stepped inside at the same time, trampling on each other's feet. The Professor looked up from his document-cluttered desk. 'Oh. You two.'

We stood together. 'Sit down, sit down,' Professor Milton said, nodding at a couple of battered schoolroom chairs' in front of his desk. 'You make the place look untidy.'

We did as told, the chairs creaking in protest. Professor Milton threw the papers he was holding, covered with comments in red ink, onto the desk. 'This, *idea* of yours. I hesitate to call it a proposal. It just won't do.'

My mouth fell open. 'Won't do?' Leo said.

'There is no need to play the parrot, Lazarus. No, it will not do.' He turned to me. 'Miss Thorniwork, as this is your first year here, you represent an unknown quantity. Others suggested that mathematical research was beyond you.'

My heart raced. After the events of Saturday evening, this was too much to bear. 'What others? If that is what they really said, perhaps I ought to challenge them to produce evidence.'

'Challenge? That would be most impolite. But, in any case, I was foolish enough to give you the benefit of the doubt. I think it possible that my faith was misplaced.'

I felt my face grow hot. 'It was not,' I said. 'We will demonstrate a new way of organising mathematical

173

truths. You cannot have read the entire proposal.'

'I *beg* your pardon, Madam?' Professor Milton raised his eyebrows.

I continued. 'We intend to show how concepts from geometry, algebra and analysis could be brought together by a common link to prime numbers. You are being unreasonable.' My hands shook as I worked the fabric at the waistline of my skirt into tiny pleats.

He leaned across the desk, towards me. 'You are the rudest young woman that I have had the misfortune to meet. Such a display of hysteria does you no credit. Any repeat of it will result in your rustication.' He turned to Leo. 'I would have expected more of you, Lazarus. To date you have admirably applied your people's skills with money to mathematics.'

Leo's face tightened, and his mouth set into a thin line.

Perhaps there was something we could rewrite. 'Where is the fault in our proposal?' I said.

'Everywhere. The hypothesis. The methodology.' The professor stood. 'However, I am prepared to give you one last chance. Today is November 17th. You have a month to produce a sensible research proposal. That, I feel, is more than generous.'

I jumped up, knocking my chair over in the process. 'And what is sensible, according to your definition?'

'That is for me to know, and for you to find out.'

'What would you have us do first?' I said. 'Solve this riddle, or propose new research? Make up your mind.'

'*Pheemie. No,*' Leo hissed through the corner of his mouth, as he tried to stand my chair up.

Professor Milton pursed his lips. 'Can you not keep her quiet, Lazarus?' He stood and leaned across the table towards us. 'Do you know why I paired the two of you for research?' I shook my head. Leo stood fiddling with his tie. 'I did it to prevent any of the other students having to work with you. You are both, for different reasons, inherently unsuitable. Others within the college are obsessed by liberalism. By your failure you will prove what I have been telling my colleagues all along.'

My throat tightened. 'You can't—'

He wagged a finger. 'Oh, but I can.'

I turned and strode into the corridor, pulling Leo after me by his sleeve. I slammed the door. Leo wandered away, looking down at the floor. I ran after him and stood in front of him, blocking his path.

'Why didn't you say anything? How dare he speak like that? Especially given your publication history. Why, he's no better than Wagner.'

He shook his head. 'Do not distress yourself. I have heard it before. But, I have only published one paper, and that as third author.'

'But, the way he spoke to us. About us. I could have struck him.'

'And be arrested? Or sent down? How would that have helped? Although, considering it's a matter of "publish or perish", that is what is likely to happen anyway.'

'Nonsense. We will think of something else.'

Leo's shoulders drooped. 'And Professor Milton will find fault with that, also.'

He turned to walk away again. 'I will return to my room. We should meet again, perhaps in a week or two. We may grub up an idea meanwhile. I will contact you in due course.'

Fourteen days, or more? 'I think we can do better than

sulk,' I said. 'Let's go for a walk. The fresh air is bound to aid in the process of devising a new proposal.' I thought of the books I had used to repel May. 'What about quaternions?'

'What about them?' His mouth turned down. 'I will walk with you, if you insist. Where would you like to go?'

I shrugged. 'Anywhere, as long as it's not here.'

We wandered out into the crisp November air, across the quadrangle. The buildings towering on either side were the standard Oxford colour of pale biscuit, but the flagstones beneath our feet were of some blue-hued stone whose identity had been lost in time. We walked round the octagonal raised lawn in the centre. 'I wonder what would happen to anyone who tramped across it?' I asked. 'Probably some ancient charter means they would be made to black Professor Milton's boots for a month. Which do you think would be worse—if he took them off beforehand, or still wore them?' Leo did not reply. 'He is old enough to be named in the most antiquated college documents.'

Leo kicked at a pebble.

'Would it not be funny if that stone was the Professor's head?' I said. No reply.

We walked past the Porter's lodge, through the arched gateway into The Broad. Leo stopped. 'Please excuse me if I do not find this as amusing as you seem to.'

'I? On the contrary. Even my uncle and aunt don't speak to me so rudely. But, it is a minor setback. Do cheer up.'

He reached out as though to take my arm but seemed to think better of it and replaced his hand in his pocket. His shoulders hunched, and he sighed. 'You don't understand. This is the first time—correct me if I'm wrong—that you have received what bitter experience has led me to think of as the "Milton Rebuff"'.

I nodded.

'Whereas I have received many. In fact, he has declined all my original research ideas. I despair of ever finding anything to suit.'

'Oh, but—'

He reached out again and patted my arm. 'I appreciate your attempts to raise my mood. But I fear that is impossible. Let us continue in silence.'

We walked along the pavement, crowded with sightseers, students and people weighed with purchases. Puddles left behind by an earlier rainstorm forced me into a game of hopscotch across the pavement. I slipped my arm through Leo's. He did not remove it.

As we passed the Bodleian Library, the heel of my shoe caught in a crack in the pavement and I was obliged to stop. As I did, a man came out of the library carrying a bag that looked as though it was filled with books. He looked at me. Black mutton chop whiskers, moustache, aged about fifty, dark eyes. Thick eyebrows. He looked away and scurried down the street. Where had I seen him before?

'That man!' Leo shouted, over horses clattering along the roadway. 'He was—'

I let go of his arm. I remembered. 'In the cemetery! We must stop him.'

We ran down the street after him.

The man turned his head, saw us and darted into Turl Street. As we reached the junction he ran into Market Street, where he slipped on the wet pavement, turned his ankle and fell. We were nearly upon him when he hauled himself to his feet and staggered away, across the street. I reached out and grabbed his sleeve. He swung round. His punch caught my arm, knocking me off balance. As he reached the other side, a cyclist came around the corner. The man dropped the bag of books, reached out and grabbed the handlebars, pulling the bicycle and its rider into the road across our path. He ran on.

'Fool! Damn his eyes.' The cyclist sat up in the road, the bicycle lying beside him, wheels spinning. Leo helped him to his feet and he hobbled to the kerb. I righted the bicycle and picked up the bag. I rubbed my arm.

The cyclist took the bicycle from me. 'I am much obliged, Madam. Sir. Do allow me to buy you both a cup of tea.'

'Thank you, but we have no time,' I said. Our quarry was on the move, limping as he ran.

'Let me tackle him,' Leo said, as we took up the chase once more.

The man disappeared into Cornmarket Street but, but by the time we were halfway down I could no longer see him. He was nowhere to be seen among the crowds pushing out of St Aldate's, by Carfax Tower.

'Damn!' Leo gasped, as we stood red in the face, panting for breath. 'Are you all right, Pheemie?'

I looked down at the muddy edge to the hem of my skirt. 'It appears neither of us is accustomed to this sort of exercise, but yes. How are you?'

Sighing, Leo straightened his dishevelled collar and tie. 'He got away. Yet another thing I could not do right.'

'Leo, don't be silly. We did our best.'

'Which is clearly not good enough.' He pressed his lips together.

I took the books out of the bag. There were four, all the property of the library, bound in heavy dark brown leather with gold lettering on the spine. Precisely the sort of peculiar tome you would have to come all the way from London, to the Bodleian, to read. *The Other World and This*, *On the Threshold of the Unseen*, *The Scientific Basis of Spiritualism* and *The Vital Message*. That last one was by Dr Conan Doyle, although when I looked inside, it did not seem the sort of book in which Mother would be interested.

'We must return these stolen books to the Bod,' I said. 'That man would not be so foolish as to try to steal them again. We would gain nothing from waiting to try to catch him.'

'If he is London-based, we may find him in the British Museum Reading Room.'

'And how often will we be there? Please let us forget him, Leo. I don't want to be reminded of Saturday evening's events. We need to be in Oxford, to think about our research.'

Leo looked at his watch. 'Very well. Now, I think I have had sufficient exercise. I will return to my room and see whether I am capable of devising a better research topic. Or, rather, one that is less inferior.' He turned away.

I looked around. Two women walked out of the Tower. 'Wait—the door to the tower is open,' I said. 'I believe there is a spiral staircase. Have you ever climbed to the top?'

He turned back and shook his head. 'No, but I've heard that the view over the town is superlative. Have you seen it?'

'No. I would love to, but—' I cast my eyes down, '…no,

you'll poke fun at me.'

He raised his eyebrows. 'I hope that I am enough of a friend that you know I shall not. But, what?'

'Well, please don't laugh, but I am afraid of heights. Terrified.'

'That doesn't sound like you.'

'Because I never speak of it. It is my shame, and my terror. I long to climb the tower.' I sighed. 'But I don't suppose I ever will.'

He wrinkled his brow. The clock on the tower chimed the hour. I dabbed at my eyes with my handkerchief. I looked at the doorway, then at him, then back at the door.

He raised a finger. 'I have an idea. Would it lend you courage if I accompanied you to the top?'

I clapped. 'Oh, would you? Oh, how can I ever thank you? Let me pay for myself, at least.' I dipped into my bag and took out my purse.

'Put that away,' he said, 'and follow me.' He went through the door, paid for us both, and we headed up the winding staircase.

There were ninety-nine stairs to the top. The staircase was only wide enough for one person, but nobody needed to pass the other way. We reached the top and stepped out, blinking, into the light. We were alone.

'You were right,' I said, as my heart rate slowed. 'I did manage it. With you. True teamwork.'

He frowned. 'Which is more than you can say about our research.'

'Let's look at the view.' I stepped over to the raised wall. 'You can see so far. Come over here.'

He joined me. We looked out over the domes and spires of Oxford, and onwards towards the countryside, misty in the distance. 'You know,' I said, 'I do think the view from St Mary's is more comprehensive.'

'You've been there?'

'Yes, several times. Well worth the effort.' I clapped my hand over my mouth.

He smiled.

'Look,' I said. 'Such ancient buildings all around us. People talk about dreaming spires, but I think they're awake, and watching us little people, who come and go. Waiting for us to do the truly memorable thing, to mark our fleeting stay in this world. They were here long before our grandparents were born, and I hope they will stand long after we have gone.' I looked down, along the High Street. 'So many people. All leading their own lives and knowing nothing of ours. All finding a way to go on. All in their own little bubbles in time.'

He leaned over the wall. 'In "that great city, wherein are more than six score thousand persons that cannot discern between their right hand and their left hand; and also much cattle".'

'That is a bit severe, if you mean the townsfolk. Some of the students, however...'

He laughed. 'It's a quote, the end of the Book of Jonah. It's God, talking about Nineveh.'

I turned my back to the view, against a blast of cold wind. 'My cousin Pearl would have understood that. I wish you could have met her.'

He took my hand. 'You miss her very much.'

'Yes. Seeing that man reminded me. Her body... stolen.' He squeezed my hand. 'Lately, I've been dreaming about her. So strange. Full of numbers.'

'You must tell me about them. According to the

Talmud, a dream which is not interpreted is like a letter which is not read.'

I shuddered. 'I've had more interpretation than I want, already. And I find there's little more boring than hearing about other people's dreams. You don't want to hear mine.'

'There is nothing that you could do that would bore me.' He put his arms round my waist. 'Pheemie. We are a team.' I felt his warm breath as he drew close. I closed my eyes.

'Well, really!' We jumped apart as an elderly woman in black, wearing pince-nez, emerged from the staircase and onto the roof accompanied by a gaggle of small schoolboys. The children sniggered, and she stood in front of them. 'Class, come to order. There is nothing to see *here*. Go and look at the buildings. Make a list of each that you can identify.' She shooed them away like so many chickens. 'If you have quite finished, *Madam*,' she said to me, 'you may as well leave. There is little enough room for people who *do* want to see the view.'

I led Leo back down.

We returned to Leo's staircase. He unlocked his door and turned to me. 'We will research together. I will think of something and let you know. We will discuss it. Very soon.' Doors opened and closed on the floor below us. Dust motes hung in the air. Very soon? 'Tomorrow,' he said. 'Nine o'clock. Let's meet in the reading room. What could be more fitting than the place where we first met?'

I exhaled. 'That was Blackwell's bookshop, actually. But let's not work on quaternions.'

'No. Something new. Something Milton cannot gainsay. Goodbye, for now.' He turned towards his door.

I tapped him on the shoulder. He turned around. I threw an arm round his neck, pulled his face towards mine and kissed his lips. It was meant to be the briefest touch, but his arms went around me, and we stayed like that for some time, while fellow occupants of the staircase shuffled round us. All I could think of was Leo and me. In our own space, our own bubble in time.

Words and Numbers

Our arms dropped to our sides. Leo looked at me and smiled.

'Oh dear—I should have asked your permission,' I said.

'Consider it granted, retrospectively. Now, I hope you have no objections if we repeat it.'

I smiled my consent. He put his hand on the small of my back and drew me towards him.

The door of Parbold's room, next to Leo's, opened for a split second before slamming shut. We jolted apart; the door opened again, and Spaulding stepped out.

'Perhaps we should go somewhere less crowded,' I said.

Leo looked at his own door. 'Would that be seemly?'

My face grew warm. 'That is not what I meant.' I was by no means certain what 'that' was, but I must not make Leo think badly of me. 'I must speak with you further; about the patterns I saw in the fog when I was lost. When I cried out for you.'

He took my hand. 'And I called back. I'm so glad I found you.'

'As am I. But I speak of the same phenomenon Mrs Levitt demonstrated.' I bit my lip—now was not the time to remind Leo of Julia, even if only of her mother. 'When you called me—did your voice cause any changes to the fog?'

'Not that I noticed.' He looked away; brow furrowed. 'What's wrong?'

He turned towards me again. 'Euphemia. Pheemie. You will recall that the gematria of our names was the same. I am not one for superstition, but there may be a deeper meaning.'

'Words? Numbers? Does it signify that the ancient Hebrew sages would approve of our working together?'

'You mock me. But I must tell you that I have always esteemed you. And now…' He fell silent.

'I esteem you too,' I said, after a few seconds.

He opened and closed his mouth like a fish. Should I knock on Parbold's door and ask for some sal volatile? 'Leo, are you well?'

He coughed and spoke in his normal pitch. 'Yes, thank you, I am quite well. As I was saying, I have always esteemed you.' He paused. 'But now, I must tell you that my feelings—'

The door of the next room flew open yet again and Parbold jumped out into the corridor, as though propelled by Spaulding's foot. 'What did Professor Milton say about your research proposals? He approved of mine.'

'We must make some changes,' I said.

'Fairly fundamental ones, in fact,' Leo said.

Parbold raised his eyebrows.

'Really? Didn't he like yours?'

'We had planned to work on what is, arguably, the most important and notorious unsolved problem in all of mathematics,' Leo said. 'But Milton took a different view.'

Parbold leaned in, eyes bright. I looked at Leo, put my finger to my lips and shook my head. Spaulding stepped into the corridor and clutched Parbold by the sleeve.

'Come back inside. Have you not heard the mathematical proverb "two's company, three is none?"'

Leo and I were alone once more.

'There was something you wanted to tell me?'

'Yes, indeed there is, but it must keep.' Leo looked at his watch. 'I must return to London. I should make the next train if I hurry. It leaves in half an hour.'

'Why must you leave?'

'I realise there is something I must do there, in person. I am afraid we must postpone our visit to the Reading Room, but I will return as soon as I can tomorrow, to discuss proposals. Please excuse me for not escorting you to your room, but I have no time to lose.'

I took his hand. 'Leo, I too... be careful in the fog.'

He strode away along the corridor. I heard his footsteps on the stairs, the sound dying as the distance between us grew.

I returned to my study and sat at my desk, trying to think of ideas for new research proposals now Professor Milton had thrown the idea of Riemann's Hypothesis back in our faces. Could there be merit in researching the phenomenon I had observed in the fog? Something to do with the mathematics of sound. Might it have a practical application?

My thoughts were as hard to gather as corks bobbing along on a lake. I stood and walked to the window, looking out in the direction Leo would have headed. What would he be doing? Surely, we had been apart for hours. I glanced across the street at the Wagstaffe Hall clock. He would not yet have disembarked from the train. The clock must be wrong.

I gazed through the gap between Wagstaffe Hall and

Freedon College, towards the rooftops in the distance and the chimney pots of Oxford. Such an array—some jar-shaped, some like faceted columns. As varied as a crowd in the street. Leo had been fascinated by how each person looked different, one from the other.

Something Leo had to do in London. But what? When he came back, he would discuss our proposals. Research proposals? For what? Was he going to London to propose to Julia, having learned the art of kissing? 'I must return to London,' he had said. 'There is something I must do there. In person.' 'I will return tomorrow' Bringing Julia with him? To announce their engagement? What would Pearl do if she were me? Would she snap her fingers in Leo's face and say, 'It is you who will be the poorer for this'?

I acknowledged what I had only suspected. Something I had tried to ignore. My feelings for Leo. But what were his for me? Relations had been so congenial. But that was *before*. From now on, it would be the world of *after*. Now it would be complicated. My thoughts whirled. I paced. This was meant to be wonderful, but it felt otherwise. I remembered a few words from *Daisy Bell,* a favourite of Pearl's: 'I'm half crazy…' I felt as I had once in the sea at Brighton when a wave dashed my feet from under me. But worse—now I was being propelled by a force I could not withstand.

I went to bed where I lay, unable to keep my eyes closed. I had never imagined Leo's lips could be so soft. His warm arms around me, secure, the beat of his heart. Unable to sleep, I found the bottle of valerian tablets Nurse Wilkinson had given me. I opened the top and a smell like unwashed feet burst out. Nurse had said to take two tablets. I held my nose, swallowed four, and climbed back into bed.

I dreamed I stood in front of a closed window curtained with heavy crimson velvet, in a ballroom with a high vaulted ceiling and gold mouldings. Couples crowded the floor, the women in shimmering taffeta dresses, each a different colour. Beside me, Professor Milton said, 'This is one of Wagner's best known waltz tunes. And not a Jew in the orchestra—even in the string section.' I spotted Leo in the distance, wearing gleaming black leather shoes, whirling his aunt around the floor. She wore an unflattering shade of acid green that reflected its colour onto her face. Behind me came a banging at the outside of the window. I shoved the curtain to one side. It was Pearl. I managed to raise the window a few inches. Pearl said, 'Gematria, the sound of gematria.' Inside a bell rang, louder and louder, drowning my voice, asking Pearl what she meant. I woke. The Wagstaffe clock was sounding six.

It was still dark. I stretched, turned over and closed my eyes. Then, with a feeling like a punch to the stomach, I remembered. It was all my fault. I was wrong to see Leo so often. We could have researched separately and met occasionally to compare progress. I wished that it could be as it was, a friendship between two like-minded people. It would have been better that I had joined someone like Parbold instead: calm, boring research sessions with no emotional complications. But then, I would not know Leo.

I rose, dressed, and tried to read *A History of the Mathematical Theory of Probability*, a text that would normally have drawn me to dive into its depths. But I could not force my eyes down the page. After trying for some five hours I left my room and strolled the quadrangle towards the gate. The porter came out of his lodge and called my name. He handed me a telegram.

My heart turned over. What was wrong at home? My hands shook. I dropped the telegram. Was it from Mother? I picked it up and looked at the end of the page. One name: Leo. Just Leo, not Leo and Julia. Was it usual for a man to throw a woman over by telegram or to use one to tell her that his proposal of marriage had been accepted? Couldn't it have waited until he got back? Perhaps he was not coming back. I forced myself to read from the beginning.

It might be possible to decompose arbitrary signals into combinations of simple harmonic waves. Stop. I have found a most interesting book in the British Museum. Stop. Please join me. Stop. I will meet you at Euston station at 3pm today. Stop. Take the 12.00 train to London.

As I hurried the station, I felt the fog lift from my mind. My thoughts were clear, bright, and knife-sharp, severing forever the barrier between before and now. I spared no time to think how long I would be in London, where I'd stay if I needed to. As I crossed Walton Street my hat blew off. I retrieved it and jammed it, half-crooked, back onto my head. I must have looked a fright. 'I'm half crazy, all for... *esteem* of you.' No, Daisy Bell. People told me my name meant 'fair speech' Now, I would provide an example. 'I love you, Leo,' I shouted. Let people stare—I had said it. Perhaps it did not count, as Leo hadn't heard. But now I had said it once, I could again. *Not only can, but must*, as Leo often told me.

One is Odd

I stood in Praed Street outside Paddington Station, wondering how best to get to Gower Street. A queue stretched from each of the many omnibus stops along the road, not that I could tell which would take me there. How like Leo, who knew the train timetable by heart, to omit how to complete the last stage of my journey. I tried to find a familiar place as I wove around the bustling crowds.

I stopped to look at a street name, colliding with a man striding towards me, head down. I apologised and asked if he knew the way to Gower Street. He shook his head and hurried on. I crossed the road and wandered down a side street, turned right and right again, walked a little further and found myself back on Praed Street once more. I had walked in an ellipse. I looked across the street—there was Paddington Underground station. I would take a train to Gower Street. I crossed back and followed a crowd of people streaming inside. There was still ample time before I had to meet Leo. Would he already be waiting for me? Was he looking at the passers-by and giving them his own jocular names?

As I arrived on the platform, a train was disappearing into the tunnel to the left, causing a great gush of air that made the gas lamps hanging from the high, arched ceiling sway among swirling grey-black clouds. The air smelled of soot. A timetable on the wall told me I had fifteen minutes to wait until the next train. Only another three stations to pass through. Edgware Road, Baker Street, Portland Road. Then, Leo.

Their feet clattering on wood and stone, more people poured onto the platform. What would happen if it filled before the next train arrived? I stood as far away from the edge as I could. Would there be space for me inside the carriages? No wonder some called it the 'sardine box railway'.

A frowning, elderly woman with pursed lips took her place beside me on the platform. With her was a boy aged about five, dancing from one foot to another. 'Nan! Is the train here yet? Is this the train?' She grasped his hand. 'For heaven's sake, Gerald, don't keep asking me. You can see that it isn't. Now stand still, do. I can't abide fidgeting.' She leaned over him. 'Look—you've soiled your cuffs.' She straightened. 'Concentrated fog down here.' Unsure whether she had been addressing me, I nodded. How would Leo be with his children? I would not know how to converse with one. Perhaps it would be different for a child you had borne.

The train, lighted carriages full of people, clanged into the station, all hissing steam and rushing air. The windows were tiny, but what would there be to see in a tunnel? The doors opened, people spilled out, and those waiting shoved forward as though hearing a starting pistol, propelling me, Gerald and Nan with them.

I squeezed into a carriage and dropped into one of the few empty seats, clutching my bag. It was best to sit in a corner with your back to the engine as there would be the least chance of getting a face full of smoke and ash. This seat was not it, but I was grateful for any. Nan sat opposite me and dragged Gerald onto her lap, where he lolled with his feet dangling. 'Stop kicking me and keep a-hold of my hand.'

Leo had never held my hand. In my mind's eye, I saw his. Smooth and sinewy, but firm—not a soft little, short-fingered paw like Parbold's. Clean, trimmed nails each with a white half-moon, not like Spaulding's, bitten to the quick, although working with Professor Milton was enough to make anyone do that. The guard slammed the carriage door shut, interrupting my reverie before I could consider the appearance of the Professor's hands. The engine moved on, jerking the carriages after it. We rattled into the tunnel and towards Leo.

The man sitting next to me pulled a copy of *The Daily Telegraph* from his pocket, shook it open and spread his arms, forcing me against the carriage wall. Without having to turn my head, I saw the headline: 'Fog spreading further from London'. Lower down the page: 'Return of the body snatchers.' I began reading. Perhaps the police had finally decided to do something about what we reported.

As I was reading that it had been a case in a different part of London, the man closed the paper. 'Madam, this is a train, not a library. Buy your own copy.' Why could I not be brave enough to ask whether he thought I would wear it out by looking, as Pearl might have? I turned to the window, watching the tunnel walls speed past.

The train slowed. 'Baker Street!' the Guard shouted. He opened the door and four young men wearing white coats pushed past him and burst into the carriage. They looked to be in their early twenties, each with a painted-on moustache and glasses. One wore a circular mirror strapped to his forehead and held a giant brown glass bottle under his arm. The second carried a massive mallet, painted black but incompletely applied so that I could see it was papier mâché made from newspapers. A third, hair filled with some white paste so it stood on end, carried a life-size human dummy, its face and body spattered with red paint, a bandage wrapped round its head, one arm in a sling. A sign hung round its neck read 'St Mary's Medical School Rag Week'. The three took their seats. 'Ladies and gentlemen!' The one with the mallet shouted. 'We have given our patient laudanum, so that he will sleep on his journey. But now, to examine him. Awake, blast your eyes!' He stood and clouted the dummy on its knee. 'Needs urgent treatment!' he shouted, sitting. The one with the mirror tipped the bottle against the dummy's mouth. It slid off its seat onto the floor. 'We must procure better medicine!' he shouted as he gathered it up again.

The fourth student had a skeleton's arm protruding from one of the pockets in his coat. He worked his way sideways like a crab along the row of passengers opposite, rattling a tin cup in the face of each one, shouting 'Help Mary's!' from point blank range. Some waved him away while others found an overwhelming urge to sleep. I fished in my bag and found a penny, which I dropped into the cup. 'Thank you, ma'am.' The collector pulled the arm from his pocket and saluted with it. He replaced it and resumed his sideways shuffle along the carriage.

'You there!' Nan called to the guard. 'You should not allow such mafficking about on your train. It won't do, disturbing decent people and scaring the children. Every time I take a train, there they are.' She hoisted the now sleeping Gerald, drooping like a dead weight, into a more comfortable position.

The guard shrugged. 'It's merely youthful high spirits.' He pulled the door shut and the train started again.

'Well said, that man,' the mallet carrier said. 'One day any us may be in need of the hospital's care.'

'Drat your insolence,' Nan said. She looked along the carriage. 'Saints preserve us, there are more of them along at the end. I am certain that I saw them yesterday, as well.'

From the far end of the carriage, two men moved towards us, propelling another dummy between them, its feet dragging along the dusty floor. They sat next to the first group but made no sound other than letting out a frequent bubbling cough. Droplets of sweat beaded their pallid brows. The first group did not acknowledge their presence and this new pair, for their part, stared straight ahead.

These two had made up their dummy in an even more grotesque caricature of illness. Its face was tinged purple, and they had taken the trouble to insert glassy eyes into its head, held stiffly upright. The first group continued to shake their tin mugs in front of the faces of the passengers, but this duo merely sat.

The train slowed for Portland Road station. The larking young men remained on board, but the second two stood, hoisting their dummy upright. As they headed for the door, they drew closer to me. One put up his hand to cough, and the dummy pivoted forward so that its head swung inches from mine. An unblinking, unbreathing face of human skin.

I recoiled as far as my seat would allow, but as the

group dragged towards the door, one hand brushed against mine. Stiff. Cold. Flakes of skin dropped away and floated to the floor. My heart thudded and my hands shook. My vision distorted, as if I were looking through the end of a bottle, sparkling round the edges. I pawed through the contents of my bag for a bottle of smelling salts but found none. The men dragged the thing through the door and onto the platform, where I lost sight of them among the waiting passengers.

I stumbled out of the station into Gower Street, struggling for breath. Leo stood at the kerb opposite the doorway. He strode to me and took my hand. 'I'm so pleased to see you. It feels like many days since we were together. I've missed you.'

His hand felt like I had imagined, but warm. 'I have thought about you many times,' I said.

We wandered from the station, in the direction of the British Museum I supposed. We passed a small public garden. 'Let us sit for a moment,' he said.

'Aren't we going to the reading room?'

'Indeed, we are, but I have something I wish to give you first.'

We sat on a bench. 'You seem uneasy. Forgive my not asking after your journey.'

'The train from Oxford was uneventful, but the Underground…' I shuddered.

'Are you cold? I am sorry—we must hurry on.'

'No, I am quite warm. It's just, there was a passenger on the Underground who troubled me.'

'The boor. Had I been there, I should have struck him. I blame myself for your distress. I should have told you which omnibus to take.' He began an explanation involving routes and numbers. I looked away at the leafless plane tree in the centre of the garden, its bark flaking like the waxy skin of the thing in the train carriage.

'Pheemie,' Leo said, squeezing my hand. 'I am sorry to bore you.'

'I apologise, you are not. It's just that, sitting opposite me—'

'Please don't forget what you were going to say, but *I* need to say something to *you*. It is, please pardon me, very important.' He released my hand and fumbled in his pocket.

'I suppose you have made notes from the book in the library, about the effects of sound. But I have something I must tell you first. Please.'

Leo took a deep breath. 'Pheemie. When I said I missed you, I ought to have said I had been longing for you.' He paused.

'Leo, I too. But now we are together, and I must tell you about the Underground.'

Leo touched a fingertip to my lips. 'The Underground will not disappear in the next few minutes. Please allow me to speak.' He took out a small box made of black leather from his pocket and placed it on the palm of his hand. Was he about to perform some conjuring trick? 'My father gave this to my mother.'

'I am certain that he was a very generous man. But please stop talking. I must finish. In the carriage, two people manhandled something into a seat and sat on either side. It sat there unmoving, looked so inhuman, so eerie. At first I thought it must be a dummy—a waxwork.'

Leo shrugged. 'Well, Madam Tussaud's is in Baker

196

Street.' He replaced the box in his pocket and took my hand again. 'Your tiny hand is frozen, once more, and all a-quiver. I haven't seen you so distressed.'

'I have never seen such a dummy as this. But as I looked, I thought rather that it was a man, who had been given a sleeping draught. Its… his… hand brushed mine as they disembarked at Portland Road. I know the reason for my feelings of revulsion. I think it was a man,' I forced the words out of my dry throat, 'and I think he was dead.'

Repeat Three Times

'Dead?' Leo took my hand again. 'Was some poor passenger struck down where he stood? Could it have been his heart?'

'I don't know.' I explained about the medical students. 'But, as they stood to leave, the cold, grey-green hand brushed mine, and I couldn't help but see the mottled, flaking skin.' I rubbed the back of my hand against my skirt.

Leo put his arm around me. I clutched my hat in my hand and we sat stiffly for a moment. He drew nearer to me and I rested my head on his shoulder, inhaling the faint scent of coconut from his hair pomade.

'What a thing to happen on the Underground,' I said. 'I've never seen a dead body before. My poor father died ten years ago but before, when he was in his final sickness, I went into his room and sat by his bed. From his looks, I thought he had already passed away—his face had shrivelled to no more than skin stretched over his skull, his mouth was open but without seeming to breathe. I took his hand—and he turned to look at me.' I gave a shudder, ashamed that the memory of my own father should induce such horror. 'But after he died, the family thought it was better I did not see him. I had that image in my mind, of the way he last looked, for a long time.'

'Poor Pheemie.' He kissed the top of my head. 'I suppose I might have seen my parents after they died, but I was too young to remember. Besides, the funeral would have taken place on the same day so there was hardly time. Although, after I lost my Uncle Felix, when I was twelve, Aunt Matilda took me in to see him. I was fearful, but he looked as though he was asleep.'

I stroked his hand. 'And poor Leo.'

He sat up and dug in his coat pocket, pulling out a notebook. 'This is what I have found in the book in the Library.'

I peered at a page of notes, all in Leo's impeccable copperplate, and graphs showing some sort of wave. 'Do you see?' he said, pointing at an equation combining Greek letters with Hebrew. 'This builds on our earlier work but it is new. My idea, to use Hebrew letters in addition. This one here is called ayin.' He touched one that looked like a figure eight with the top removed.

'Really? And what is its gematria?'

He smiled. 'It's seventy, but I simply liked the shape.

'We must call this the Lazarus Thorniwork Equation. Then we can at least tell Spaulding and Parbold that we have an equation named after us.'

'Perhaps it should be called Thorniwork-Lazarus,' Leo said.

'Either way, we should enjoy the notion while we can. Professor Milton is certain to claim it as his own.'

Leo looked into the distance. 'Sound and mathematics. Everything seems connected, as though nature plays its own music with numbers instead of notes.' He turned his face away. 'Or does that seem foolish?'

'No, not at all. It's just how you would feel. Oh, Leo, I

love you.'

He caught his breath.

I must already have said too much, but I no longer cared. 'I love you. And you love me too, don't you?'

'Of course I love you! You mean the world to me. Not that I want the world, of course. I want you.'

From a kiss to something more (or so it seemed, although I did not know what that something was), so quickly. What should I think? What must I do? He edged closer and put both arms round me 'Not now!' I said. 'Someone may see us.'

'I don't care.'

After kissing until I felt breathless, we separated. Leo took the leather box out of his pocket again and fiddled with the clasp, but it would not open. 'Damn, this was always difficult.' As he wrenched at the lid, an elderly man plodded past our bench, leading a fat bulldog that gasped as it waddled along to keep up with him. The man's square face, flat nose and lack of hair resembled the features of the dog, or perhaps it was the other way around. They both appeared to be without a neck, and both wheezed as they breathed. Perhaps owners and their dogs eventually breathed in the same way, as well as looking alike.

The man walked a few yards, turned, came back to our bench, and sat next to Leo, dropping the dog's leash. The dog wandered to a nearby patch of grass, squatted and relieved itself, scratching about afterwards in some instinctive attempt to bury the result.

The man burst into a paroxysm of wet-sounding coughing. 'I do beg your pardon,' he said. 'The fog—' He broke off and coughed again, spitting onto the ground by his feet. He rubbed at the products with the sole of his shoe. 'Destroys the miasma, you know, if you crush it.' He turned to Leo and spoke in the tone of someone imparting a great confidence. 'Have you ever wondered where the fog comes from?' He continued before Leo could answer. 'The Jews. They're behind it. Cringing cowardly worms, spreading their filth.'

I rose and faced the man. 'You and your dog produce the same thing,' I said, 'but from different ends.'

The man's face reddened. 'Only a Jewess would speak such ordure.' He spluttered. 'And you, sir, defile yourself by associating with such a subhuman creature.'

Leo jumped to his feet, a fist raised. The box fell to the ground. 'Do not speak of this lady in such terms.'

I grabbed Leo's arm. 'No, Leo, let us leave. That man is not worth the candle.'

Leo lowered his hand, his mouth set in a line. I picked up the box and put in it my bag. I would return it to Leo when he was calmer. I turned up the collar of my coat, linked my arm through his and we walked out of the garden and along Gower Street.

'I apologise for that crude display,' Leo said.

'You have nothing to regret. What an ignoramus. I hope his dog will bite great chunks from him.'

'One can hope. Let's go to the Library. It's not far from here.'

We wandered along arm in arm, the wind blowing pieces of discarded newspaper around our ankles. I stopped. 'Leo, the mathematics you have shown me is pure beauty, but I cannot set my mind to it. Is there nothing we can do about what I saw on the train? I owe it to Pearl—the same monsters must have stolen her body.'

He squeezed my arm. 'Of course. This is doubly

distressing for you. We must report it to the police. Although given the lack of interest and efficacy on their part last time, I doubt that would help.'

I dropped his arm and turned to face him. 'It's obvious. We must provide them with the evidence. If we can prevent one more person losing their loved one, as I have, it will be worthwhile.'

'I agree. But how?'

'A woman on the train said she had seen them before. We must return to the Underground and repeat my journey. If they are moving one body at a time, they must be making multiple excursions.'

'True. But—listen—I must ask you something,' said Leo.

I shook my head. 'No time to discuss research now. Ask me on the train.'

As we reached the westbound platform a train pulled in. There were fewer passengers than earlier, and we found seats next to each other. I looked up and down the carriage, but the men were not there.

'I suggest that we remain until we have reached at least two stations further than the ones at which they boarded and alighted,' Leo said.

The train rumbled along a tunnel. 'I wonder where the fog does come from, in truth?' I said.

'And is there a way to stop it?'

The train rattled to a stop at Portland Road, where the men had alighted. I leaned forward in my seat, looking to the left and right once more, but saw nobody of interest. It was the same at Baker Street, where they had boarded.

At Paddington, we stepped out of the carriage and

crossed to the eastbound platform to take a train back again.

We repeated our journey. I looked along each platform as the train slowed to enter a station but nobody of interest boarded or left. We stepped out of the train at Gower Street and stood on the platform.

'I fear those men must have found an alternative mode of transport. Perhaps a horse and cart,' Leo said.

'And we can hardly spend our time combing the streets for them. Let us make one, final trip to Paddington and back here. If we are unsuccessful, we must forget them, and go to the Museum.'

'Very well,' Leo said, 'but I do not think the Reading Room will stay open for much longer.'

For the third time, we tramped to the opposite platform at Paddington and waited. Nobody came. After some fifteen minutes, a train rattled into the station. There was scarcely space inside, but Leo boarded, pulling me after him by my hand. This time, there were no available seats but our having to stand in the aisle facilitated my looking at the other passengers, all of whom were alive as far as I could tell.

Leo patted his jacket pockets. 'Oh no... the park... that man...'

'If you're looking for your little box, I have it.' I took it out of my bag and peered at it, turning it around. 'The closure appears to be a standard puzzle mechanism. Just press this, and that, while holding these.' I handed it to him. 'It's yours, you open it.'

'Now would appear to be as good a time as any,' he said. The train slowed in its approach to Baker Street as he clicked the box open. Inside was a ring with three colourless stones in a row, surrounded by clusters of smaller ones. I knew nothing of jewellery, but the stones looked like diamonds. The yellow metal it was made of must surely be gold, to do such stones justice. It was set so that the light shone through the gaps in the polished setting, making the diamonds glitter.

'As I said, my father gave this to my mother.'

'How lovely.'

Leo lowered his voice and spoke into my ear. 'He gave it to her on their engagement. According to Aunt Matilda, they were soulmates. I never thought that I would be lucky enough to find mine. But it's you, Pheemie. Please say that you will marry me. Make me the happiest man alive.'

I bit back an urge to ask which of the two requests he wanted me to grant. But marry? I had never wished for such a thing. Had I?

The train pulled into Portland Street and the guards opened the doors. 'Oh, Leo, I…' Out of the corner of my eye, I glimpsed two men leave the carriage ahead of ours, dragging something grey and immobile between them. 'Look! There!'

'Don't forget what you were going to say.' Leo snapped the box shut, stuffed it into his pocket, grabbed my hand and wrenched me past the people standing by the door, onto the platform and up the stairs at the end.

We thrust our tickets at the collector. He held up a hand, barring our way as he scrutinised them from every angle. The men had reached the exit. I could not see which way they turned. The collector held the tickets up to the light, clipped them, returned them to us, and nodded us on our way.

The pavement outside was packed with pedestrians hurrying along—women with parcels and baskets, men hurrying to some urgent meeting, the roadway crammed with a solid line of carts and buses. The smell of horse dung and smoke choked me. In the distance, a clock struck half past four.

Leo, a head taller than most other pedestrians, craned to look from side to side. 'There!' he pointed to the left. We ran. The pedestrians seemed to part and allow Leo to pass.

We staggered to a standstill at the edge of the kerb, gasping for breath as we waited to cross. 'Look—I'm delaying you,' I said. 'You go ahead. I'll follow you.'

He grabbed my hand, kissed my fingers and was away across the road, weaving between the vehicles. I crossed moments later, as Leo turned into a narrow alley. I ran.

When I reached the alley, I could no longer see him. I stumbled on the uneven cobbles and slowed; my throat stung by each gulp of air. I picked my way along the alley, so narrow the tops of the blackened buildings on either side seemed to lean in towards each other, as though exchanging secrets. Leo appeared at the other end and stepped towards me. 'I lost them in a maze of warehouses. It is growing dark. Soon, the fog will obscure everything.'

'Then we must return tomorrow.'

'I agree. I can remember the route the men took, until I lost them. Let us meet at Portland Street Station as soon as it becomes light and the fog has cleared—at half past seven. Now, I assume you will stay in London. Allow me to escort you to your uncle's house.'

'Oh no, that won't be necessary. It's in completely the opposite direction from your Aunt's.' The idea of my family's reaction to Leo at all, let alone making some sort of premature announcement, was more than I could bear.

'Very well. Take this, for a cab.' He handed me money.

'Oh, no, really… oh, very well.'

He took my hands in his and kissed me. As we parted, he said, 'I do not expect you to reply to my question now, but I must have your answer soon. Please, consider it. I will be on tenterhooks.'

I was tempted to remove Leo from the hooks but recalled Pearl telling me that one should never reply at once to a proposal of marriage. Keeps them keen, she said. To play such games hardly seemed fair, but I knew nothing of the ways of love. 'Yes, Leo, I will consider it. I will give you my answer tomorrow.' I hailed a cab and gave the driver Uncle Jacob's address. I could never think of it as home. And perhaps, now, there was a chance I would no longer need to. Leo's proposal would act as a shield for anything I would have to endure, until we were together again, in eleven hours' time.

The Perfect Fifth

I tiptoed along the landing, my sturdy walking boots in hand, past May's closed bedroom door. It would not do to awaken her—she would likely ask if I was eloping, arousing the entire household in the process.

Mother called out to me as passed her open door. I entered her room. 'I am sorry to have woken you,' I whispered, aware of the thinness of the wall between her and May. I closed the door.

'You didn't. Betty did when she lit my fire, clattering the coal bucket about so. But why so early?'

'I'm going to work in the British Museum Library. I want to spend as long as possible there.' I coughed through a throat parched from the thought of what Leo and I must do.

Mother hauled herself up onto one elbow. 'I do hope you are not affected by the fog.'

'It's nothing.' I lifted her up and thumped her pillow. 'Would you like a cup of tea?'

'No, thank you—Nurse will bring me one later. You must have something to eat before you go, if you intend to be there all day.'

'Very well, Mother. Now, do try to go back to sleep.'

I was not hungry, but a cup of tea might help my dry mouth. I crept downstairs, avoiding the second step, that always set off a squeak fit to raise the dead, or May at the very least.

The maid knelt in front of the range, dabbing at it with some paste on a piece of rag. The soot stains appeared to be coming away with little effort. A comment seemed expected. 'Well… good morning, Betty—' She stopped, dropped the rag into a bucket, stood and faced me. 'Oh no…you needn't stop on my account.'

Betty dropped a curtsey. 'I've finished now.'

We looked at each other.

'I see you have used plenty of elbow grease,' I said. 'The range is gleaming.'

Betty grinned. 'It's this cleaning paste of my mam's.' She nodded towards a jar containing a white substance. 'Made of something she calls hypo, an' washing soda, an' glycerine with a bit of water. Stops the fog stains from coming back, too—I use it on my boots, Miss.'

This was beginning to sound like one of the advertisements in the newspapers May read.

Mrs Upshaw, the cook, waddled into the kitchen. 'Miss Thorniwork doesn't want to hear about *that*, Betty. Haven't you got work to do? I'm sure I have.'

'Thank you, Betty. I'll bear it in mind, should I ever find myself needing to clean soot from, er… something.' Leo and I would have servants.

Betty picked up her bucket and the jar containing the paste and scuttled into the scullery.

Mrs Upshaw tossed a screw of newspaper and pieces of coal onto the previous night's glowing embers in the range. She placed a kettle on the hotplate and turned, pushing a stray lock of greying hair back under her cap. 'I'm sorry, Miss Thorniwork, I should have wished you a good morning. Anyway, I'll make tea.'

'Oh, do let me, Mrs Upshaw. You've got enough to do without me giving you more.' I picked up the kettle.

'Oh, no, Miss—wait for it to boil. Then—'

'I know.' I recited what to do next, just as I had learned from watching Leo.

'You've been having lessons, Miss!'

The kettle boiled, and I made the tea. She declined a cup, wiped her hands on her apron and wobbled to the scullery, calling for Betty. I drank mine standing. We must take it in turns to make the morning tea, Leo and me. Then bring the cups back to the bedroom. The thought left a glow deep inside me.

I stepped outside, closing the door behind me with a mere click of the lock. The sky hung grey, frowning over the street. I walked to the omnibus stop, the receding fog swirling and dancing around my ankles, like a dog seeking attention. At half past six, the street was almost empty save for those with an early start to their work. Or perhaps, those returning from a night's labours, legitimate or otherwise. As I waited at the stop, the street grew busier. A man came towards me, face half hidden in muffler. Next came two old women, shawls over their heads. A clattering told me they wore clogs, but the fog obscured their feet. One hag stopped to cough. I jumped aside to dodge the spray she discharged from her gap-toothed mouth.

Her companion patted her back. 'Get it out, dear. That's the way.' What would any of them say if I told them where I was headed? That I belonged in an asylum, that I must have imagined it all?

I wrapped my scarf tighter round my neck and turned up my collar. The omnibus pulled up, horses stamping, breath steaming. I climbed on board. I had allowed half an hour's travelling time—ample to meet Leo at Portland Street Station.

After twenty minutes' stopping and starting the omnibus halted, although we were between stops. Five minutes later, it had still not moved. Outside in the street, people shouted. I looked out the window. In front of us, a coal cart had overturned. I rose and stepped out onto the pavement. The cart had shed its load and, among the clamour of people trying to pass, a group of feral urchins scrabbled among the coals. The carter grabbed the collar of one wretch holding a few pieces of coal and held him in a ham-like fist. The boy stamped on the man's foot and ran off with his filthy treasure. I made the rest of the journey on foot. striding as far as my skirts would allow.

Leo stood at our meeting place, looking at his watch. The need to be close to him overwhelmed me. I ran to where he stood. 'I'm sorry if I'm late... the omnibus—'

'No, you're right on time.' He replaced the watch in his pocket and took my hand. 'I hope you have prepared yourself. This will take all the fortitude we can muster.'

I reached up and touched his cheek. 'I'm as ready as possible, since we do not know what *this* is.'

Chimney pots belched smoke. The retreating fog revealed a layer of soot that had settled on the ground and the wretched tenement buildings. Leo paused, looking left and right.

'Have you forgotten the way?'

'No—there.' He pointed to where feeble gas lamps

illuminated a passage between two buildings, their grimy windows and doorways barred. It led into an alley. A half-broken sign dangling by one end from the wall read Tanyard Lane.

'I hope the men will be there. Perhaps we should have found torches and returned last night.'

'We have witnessed their working by night and day.' Leo set his mouth.

Tufts of yellowed grass grew between the cobblestones of the alley. Arches across the top every twenty feet or so gave it the appearance of a tunnel. Stone buildings loomed on either side. At the end were four doors. Two hung open. One led to an empty warehouse. The second was packed with rags and bottles.

Leo pushed at the third. It creaked open, revealing rough stone walls. Wooden steps descended into darkness. We picked our way down steps, to find another door. It was daytime, but fog oozed under it. Leo pushed the door. It did not move. He pulled instead and it gave way, as though propelled by the stench that blasted towards us like an exploding bomb. Putrefying meat and ammonia. Rotten eggs and cabbage. Choking garlic. Blocked privies. I recoiled and retched.

Leo clutched my arm. 'Do you wish to reconsider?'

'After all we have endured? We must continue.'

'I'd expect nothing less of you.' Leo coughed. 'But we cannot enter without some sort of protection.'

I took a deep breath, wrapped my scarf around my nose and mouth. Tears streamed from Leo's eyes onto the handkerchief he had tied across his face.

I looked through the door into a dark cellar that appeared to have been carved out of the ground. Patches of grey-green mould made patterns on the walls. My foot slid, as though the rock floor was covered in seaweed. I clutched Leo's sleeve. He put out his hand and touched the wall to stop us falling. 'Take my arm,' he said. 'But not my hand. I don't care to speculate what might cover it now.'

We stepped inside. 'Strike a match, Leo.'

'I dare not. This vile miasma might explode.'

The place was crammed with objects under sheets, as in a furniture store. A pane of filthy glass set into the roof provided a faint glimmer of light. My eyes adjusted to the near darkness. Taking tiny paces, we moved across the space.

I froze mid-step. The cellar was filled with tables, set out like the beds in a hospital ward. On each was what appeared to be a dead body. Fog spilled from each, overflowing onto the floor. To my left lay what had once been a man, covered with a cloth that left his purple-grey face exposed. A mass of black and iridescent green flies shimmered over it. His arm protruded from under the cloth, as though trying to reach the bloated body on the next table. The arm of that one was no longer there— perhaps it had made a meal for the vermin. Maggots swarmed in the place where it had been attached.

I looked away. The one to my right was no more than a skeleton. Next to that, yet another shape, draped with a cloth. I jumped back with a shriek as a rat skittered across the floor and up the leg of the table, to join its squeaking, swarming companions under the cover. Larger maggots squirmed from under the cloth, falling onto the floor. I grimaced but was unable to look away.

'Let us leave,' Leo said in a tight voice, as though trying

not to breathe. 'We have seen enough. This is the body-snatchers' lair. They must be away, about their ghastly business.'

'Wait!' I pointed to the far corner. On a table, a man writhed like one of the maggots.

'It is some poor devil, still alive,' Leo said. 'These vile creatures must be too impatient to wait for people to die.'

'We must help him.'

We dashed through the swirling fog that reached as far as our knees, to his side. His face was grey and covered with beads of perspiration. He raised his head.

'My poor fellow, do not try to rise,' said Leo. 'What have they done to you? We must fetch a physician.'

The man's voice creaked out between parched, blue-tinged lips. 'Simpson—is that you? Wake up. Help me. I do not know what to do. The fog has killed the others. Save the machine, that someone might continue our work, and speak with the dead.'

He lifted his arm and pointed to the table next to his, where a spherical flat-based jar about the size of my head stood, filled with bright orange fluid. An oily globule the size of a hen's egg rose to the top of the liquid, floated a moment then fell back to the bottom like lava. Above it a pair of metal rods were mounted on a dais shaped like a squat cylinder. The rods inclined away from each other in a v-shape.

'Hush, man,' Leo said. 'Save your strength. I fear you are the only survivor of some sort of visitation.' He turned to me. 'You must go for a doctor. I will stay.'

The man let out a wet cough. Dark red matter dribbled down his chin, as though he was rejecting his own lungs.

'No—stay!' the man said. 'If Simpson is dead, you must

learn of our work. We are on the verge of communication with the dead. Nearly, so nearly. Others must take up the torch. Hold it high.' A pulse throbbed at his temple. He flung out an arm, hand clawing.

I staggered backwards.

'We are pioneers. We found that bringing in bodies on the train enhances the post-life force. Some sort of property of the rails. The vibration. The oscillation.'

I remembered Leo's and my conversation on the train to London. I looked at Leo. 'Could it be?'

Leo shook his head. 'Complete gibberish.'

The man coughed again. 'Not so. It is a double-edged sword. Look around you. The bodies... the fog rises from them. We did our best. Male and female subjects. Young and old alike. A young woman here, dead a few months only, she is a promising subject. The fresher, the easier to work with.'

Leo spat out a word that I had not heard in polite company.

'We grew sicker and sicker. Died one by one. I tried to communicate with my dead colleagues. No reply. If we are to achieve communication beyond death, we must prevent the fog it generates. Have you not seen how thick it grows here?' His mouth opened and he let out a wheeze. All movement ceased. There would be no need for a doctor.

'The man was insane,' Leo said. 'The bodies cannot be the cause of the fog; despite the way it spills from them. If they were, this would happen in every mortuary in the country.' He flicked a switch on the machine, from the off to on position. 'Nothing. Madness.' He switched it off.

'He seemed to suggest that it owed to some sort of enhancement they had induced. It does not matter. We must find a policeman.'

I turned to leave. My foot scudded forward on the slimy floor.

'Pheemie!' Leo put his arm around my waist in support.

'Pheemie?' another voice called from behind me.

I turned. The figure on the table behind us, still covered, jerked. 'Pheemie. Help me.'

With trembling hands, I slid the cover away, and there was a face I knew, even though all the colour had departed. Pearl's face. A sickly-sweet smell arose from her. I looked into her eyes, as dead as the catch on the fishmonger's slab and recoiled. Leo stood by my side.

'She speaks. But she's dead,' I whispered. 'I saw her in her coffin. I saw her buried.'

'Don't speak of me as though I wasn't here. Dead? Living? I no longer know the difference. Impurity. Purity.' I took her hand. Cold. No pulse. The fog swirled over her, covering her body like a squirming blanket. 'It is no delusion... so many bodies... such impurity. Only the song of the red heifer can conquer it.'

Once more, the red heifer. I grabbed her shoulders. So cold. 'What do you mean?'

'Listen. This is the sound. The song.' She opened her mouth and chanted a single note. The fog surrounding her shimmered and formed Chladni patterns, honeycombs, shrinking circles, retreating into nothingness.

She stopped. The fog reappeared, wrapping itself around her body. She turned her head towards Leo. 'Red heifer. It is no allegory. Find the Gematria.' Her eyes closed. Her face shrivelled. Dessicated skin stretched over bones.

'Pearl, stay!' I shouted.

The skin melted away. Only a skeleton remained, crumbling into dust. I held my breath. The dust vanished. It was as though she had never existed. I could not cry. I swayed and grasped the edge of the table. My tongue felt thick and cold sweat covered my forehead.

Leo threw his arm around my shoulder. 'Enough. I can stand no more.' He led me outside. We staggered into the street. I leaned on him and would have fallen if he had not held me so tightly. I heard him speak, as though he was under water. Or perhaps, as though I were. Something about the fog.

Locked together, Leo and I sat on a low, soot covered wall at the end of a mean back street with a trench running down the middle, along which foul liquid flowed. A layer of slime along the hem of my skirt weighed it down. I moved it, smeared muck against my boots. I pulled off my hat and, with a shaking hand, swept back the bedraggled strands of hair it had been holding in. I dragged the makeshift mask from my face and threw it to the ground.

Turning from Leo, I vomited. I wiped the back of my filthy hand across my mouth. '*Take up the torch.* The whole place should be burned to the ground.'

Leo gagged. He pulled a handkerchief from his pocket and passed it to me. 'For your face and hands. Keep it.'

I twisted it round and round in my fingers. 'I could not have endured this without you.'

He took out another handkerchief and wiped his hands. 'Nor I without you. You are so brave. No tears, even. But I'm a wretch to have made you take part.'

My throat clogged. I tried to swallow. 'You didn't

compel me. Pearl looked at you. I wish I had told her who you were. She would have loved you. As I do.'

Leo pulled me close and kissed my cheek. 'Wishing, it's always the same. We wish we had spoken out, then they are gone and it's too late.' He reached into the inside pocket of his jacket. 'Here are a pencil and paper. Note what Pearl said to you. In case you forget.'

I shook my head. 'We don't have time. We must go to the police. The remaining bodies must be removed. They are entitled to burial. Besides, I don't think I could erase this from my mind, even if I wished to.'

He took my grimy hand in his even filthier one. 'We will go in a moment. Record it first. You would be surprised what the mind can do. It can soften a memory you wish to retain, or preserve one that causes agony. *Carpe diem.*'

'As you seized the moment on the train. To propose. You didn't have to do it then. I'm not going anywhere.'

'Nor I. I will not leave you. We make up a perfect fifth. The ideal chord. As I demonstrated using my tone generator.'

'Oh Leo, I know you are trying to distract me, but do speak English. We are only two.'

He frowned. 'I demonstrated this in my room, although that seems an age ago. I meant, like the notes C and G.' He sang the first two notes of *Twinkle, Twinkle, Little Star*. 'The frequency ratio between them is three to two.'

Which made five. I sang the higher note. He joined in with the lower. It was pleasing to the ear.

Leo looked down at his slime-covered boots. 'May I tell you that you are my star? My diamond?'

'If you feel you must, but perfect fifth is all we need. And you are the C to my G.'

I smoothed out the paper against my skirt. 'I will record Pearl's last words. At least, now I know of her end. No second funeral for her. And she sang too...' I shuddered and wrote. I put the paper in my bag and gave Leo his pencil. 'There, I've done it, but it makes no sense. What did she mean, the song? She only sang one note. Whatever it was, it affected the fog. Like when we were lost on the way to your Aunt.'

'One note,' Leo repeated. 'F natural.'

'F, for farewell. I have longed to see Pearl again. But not like this.'

Leo put his arm round my shoulder. 'Now I understand why the Jewish custom is to bury the dead very quickly. Purity doesn't come into it. In a hot country, where we originated, it's essential.'

'That men can perform such horrors proves there is no God to intervene. This is as far from any form of goodness as it is possible to be.'

Leo gave a cough and muttered. I could not distinguish the words and nor did I ask him to repeat them. Would the police believe us? Would they think that we were somehow involved? A gust of wind blew my skirt flapping around my ankles. I shivered. Leo took my hands and rubbed them between his. 'Well? It is an important matter. What do you say?'

'Yes, Leo. I'll marry you.'

He let out a gasp. 'I asked you whether you thought the fog might cease, rather than emerging during the day as well as the night. But I like this answer better.' He held me close. He murmured into the hair at the top of my head.

'I left the ring at home, but it is yours now.'

'I'll have to scrub my hands for a week before they would be fit to wear it.'

Leo traced the pattern of a ring around my finger. 'We can pretend it's there already.' He stood. 'Let us leave. As soon as we have finished with the police, we must cleanse ourselves and our clothes thoroughly—or discard them.'

'We must reek. I cannot imagine what my family will say.'

'Yes, your family. There's due process to be followed. Let's give ourselves a day to come back to some sense of calm, but then I must call on your mother. And your uncle. Mr Jacob Pratincole, that's his name?'

My voice quaked. 'Yes.' Uncle Jacob asking about Leo's finances. Aunt Emily asking what church he attended. May looking askance at his unfashionable outfit—not that I could tell whether it was. And Mother—would she look away from him in disappointment? But I was of age. The family could not forbid it. My chin trembled and my face contorted. Pearl would have understood. But she was dead.

My tears flowed and sobs wrenched me as I gave into spasms of grief. I cried for the deluded desire to call the dead back from their rest. For those whose resting place was a stinking charnel house. For my clever, beautiful Pearl. Would I always remember her as I had last seen her?

Leo held me close. Eventually, my tears ran dry.

'It's years since I thought of my parents' funeral,' Leo said. 'But now I recall it. The watcher sitting with the bodies the night before. The chant of the cantor at the graveside. My uncle repeating the mourner's prayer because I was too young to understand.'

I looked up and dabbed my eyes with the last uncontaminated square inch of handkerchief. 'But you did understand.'

'All I could do was wonder what would become of me. But, of course, my uncle and aunt gave me a home. And now I do recite the prayer, every year on the anniversary of my parents' deaths, to show that despite the loss I still praise God.'

'I suppose it must provide comfort, but that will be my role. When you are married, you will need no other source. I will make sure of it. But what will your aunt say, about your marrying outside your faith?'

'But I will not be, for you will convert to Judaism, won't you?'

I gasped, and looked away from him. I, an atheist? But after all that we had endured, Leo and I were one person and would be forever. He made me live. He knew me, believed in me, accepted me. I loved every thought of his, every word.

'I will, Leo.'

One More Matter

We hurried out of the alley. They say that, in London, you are never more than fifteen minutes from a policeman. The same constable that had been on his beat as we entered walked past once more. Leo dashed to him and, in between breathless gasps, described what we had found.

'Are you certain?' the constable said.

I tried to put my hands on my hips, but they slipped in the slime splashed across my skirt. 'Do you think my fiancé and I are trying to trick you about a mere student caper? Of course we are certain.'

'Follow me,' Leo said, running back down the alley. The policeman pursued him. I stayed on the main road. The thought of what lay within the cellar had already set me shaking. I trembled, with an unreal feeling I was watching myself doing so, from the outside.

After minutes, the two of them returned. Much blowing on the police whistle brought others hurrying to join him.

'Send for the photographer,' the first one said.

The officers ran up the alley.

'Do you require statements from us?' Leo called after them.

One officer stopped. 'That is not required, you have done enough. Take the lady home. She has received a nasty shock.'

I took Leo's hand. 'And so have you. How can life return to normal after something like this?'

Leo and I staggered along the opposite side of the road from my house. At this time, the family would be eating in the dining room at the back, but it was possible one of the servants might look outside. Nobody was in sight.

'Goodbye, my love,' I said, touching his cheek. 'Please visit us soon.'

It was not until I had crossed the road and watched him walk away that I realised I did not know when we would next be together.

I closed the front door behind me with the smallest click and crept upstairs. Once in my bedroom, I leaned against the door and exhaled. My teeth chattered and my entire body shook. I took a bolster case from my closet. My clothes would never be rid of the stinking mixture of solids and liquids that clung to them—I doubted that even the maid's soot removing paste would work. In any case, how could I try without questions being asked? I removed my skirt and boots and, tumbling them together, forced them into the pillowcase. This, I knotted at the end and threw from the window. My room was at the back of the house—would anyone in the dining room see it fall? I put my ear to the floor but heard no raised voices from downstairs. I would remove the vile object later and leave it in some alley. The laundry must take the blame for the missing pillowcase. I stayed in my room that evening, pleading a headache.

The next morning, I braved the breakfast table. Mother, as usual, ate in her room.

'Are you recovered?' Aunt Emily asked. She stabbed a fork into a piece of sausage, dipped it in a poached egg and raised the fork to her mouth. Egg yolk dripped onto her plate, viscous as the products of bodily decomposition.

'Yes, thank you.' I looked away.

Uncle Jacob strolled to the sideboard, lifted the cover of a silver dish, and peered inside.

'Ah, scrambled eggs with pigs' brains.' He waved a serving spoon at me. 'Euphemia?'

'No thank you, Uncle. A bread roll will suffice.'

'You should try the brains,' May said, sticking her fork into a pink and yellow mass on her plate. 'They're delicious, and they're very good for the complexion. Of course, you have to eat them, not rub them into your face.'

My tongue thickened and saliva filled my mouth. I clutched my napkin to my mouth and ran from the room.

I lay on my bed, my body frozen, my hands clenched. After an hour, the nausea abated, and I felt stable enough to tackle my next ordeal. I entered Mother's bedroom. She sat on a sofa in the window bay, reading Mr Wilkie Collins' *The New Magdalen*. She inserted a bookmark and put the book by a cut glass bowl holding glossy red apples on a small table next to her.

'Is your book pleasant?'

'It is certainly interesting. It concerns a fallen woman who becomes a nurse.' She looked up at me and her brow furrowed. 'Euphemia—you are pallid. You were not at dinner yesterday. What is the matter? We must ask *our* nurse for a draught for you.'

'I'm not ill. Just tired. But I have something to tell you.'

She raised her eyebrows and patted the seat next to her. I sank onto it with a thump, raising a cloud of dust.

Mother wafted her hand in front of her face. 'We must speak to the maid. But first—what did you wish to say?'

I leaned forward and held my head in my hands.

'Mother... I... I do not know how to tell you this.'

She patted me on the back. 'I am sure it is not so bad a thing. Remember the sentiment May embroidered on the cushion she gave me for my birthday: *The Things that worry you most of all are the Things that never happen, after all*. She rhymed *all* with *all*, but she meant well.'

I sat up again and took a deep breath. 'Very well. You may recall my mentioning my friend, Leopold?'

She nodded. 'And does he—perhaps—wish to become more than a friend? If so, this is a cause for rejoicing. You are deserving of such happiness. If, indeed, you *are* happy with this situation.'

I smiled. 'I am, but matters have progressed beyond the stage of walking out together. He has proposed marriage.' I paused. Mother made no reply. 'And I have accepted.'

Mother gasped. 'Heavens above! This is potentially a most welcome piece of news, but we have not met him. Who is he? Who are his people?'

'His name is Leopold Lazarus. He is twenty-eight, his parents are no longer with us. When he is in London he lives with his aunt. His late uncle was a businessman and left him well provided for—the business thrives under the care of his cousins, and he receives a share of the proceeds.'

'There is nothing wrong with any of that. Why were you so worried? What did you think I'd say?' She smiled.

'There is something else that you should know,' I said, wishing I could run out of the room. 'Leo is Jewish.'

'Oh.' Mother's face fell. 'Of course, my wish is for you

224

to be happy. But, a Jew, Euphemia? This is less than perfect. I am of a broader mind than your uncle and aunt, but I think only of your welfare. Although the Jews treat their own well, you are not one of their people. They are not like us. They have many foreign ways.'

'Leo's family *are* originally from Russia, but they have lived in England for many years. Mother, what is perfection? If you mean completeness, then I have found that.'

'But...' Mother seemed to be casting around for objections. 'They don't eat the same food as us. You will have to exist on a foreign diet.'

'Leo and I love each other. He makes me happy. And, didn't Grandfather initially refuse to consent to your marrying Father? An impoverished teacher, the first in his family to hold a profession? But they learned to value him, you married him anyway, and you were happy.'

Mother sighed. 'I cannot forbid you to do what I did. You have aways ploughed a lone furrow. I cannot say what your father would have thought, but I give you *my* blessing.'

I knelt, flung my arms round her and kissed her cheek. 'Mother,' I said into her hair. 'There is one more matter.'

'What?' She shrieked, holding me at arms' length. 'Your aunt told me that you ran from the breakfast table. You're not... in a delicate condition, are you?'

I stood. 'Of course not! The matter is that I plan to become Jewish.'

She slumped back on the sofa. 'But, Euphemia, this is too much. Surely you can marry in one of their churches without doing that?'

'You can't. And remember, you once told me that when

I met the right person, their ways and wishes would become mine. Leo wishes to marry within his faith. And if they are his people, then I want to be one of them.'

'But you have never been able to believe any of the religious teaching that even your birth faith required you to. How are you to believe someone else's? Can it be that Leopold has shown you the light?'

'Now you are teasing me. People already assume that I am Christian, and I ignore it. Really, it will be a matter of exchanging one outmoded title for another. Besides, I haven't seen Leo be overly observant. Really, religion is a jumble of false assertions, with no basis in reality. The very idea of God is a product of the human imagination.'

'I will not waste what little breath I have arguing with you on that point. What might this change of title, as you put it, involve? Surely there must be more than that.'

I frowned. 'Actually, I don't know. I expect I will have to read a few books. Leo will be able to recommend some.'

'When may we expect to receive the pleasure of meeting your… fiancé?'

'Soon, I hope—he will write to Uncle Jacob. I have not informed the rest of the family yet, so please let this be our secret until then.'

'I do not like secrets. It is too difficult remembering what one must and must not say. But it must be endured—I hope not for long.' She handed me an apple. 'Now, do try to eat. You will need all your strength when you tell the family.'

We sat round the luncheon table. Mrs Upshaw had gone out and had left us a ham and hardboiled egg salad.

'Cold food again,' Uncle Jacob said, helping himself to as much as his plate could hold. The slices of egg resembled the dead eyes of the bodies in the cellar. A procession of images and smells fought their way into my head, moving like unstoppable theatre, from which I could not look away. I struggled to draw breath and my heart pounded. How could I stop the dead actors inside my head? Would the images ever leave me?

'Euphemia!' Aunt Emily, sitting on my left, nudged me. I jumped. She continued. 'I said, when do you plan to return to Oxford? We need to know, so that I can speak to Cook.'

'If she ever returns,' Uncle Jacob, sitting on my right.

'I intend to return next Monday morning,' That was five days hence. By that time Leo should have paid his visit on Uncle Jacob and Mother. How long must I wait until he did? I managed to grasp the water jug in shaking hands. I poured myself a glass.

The maid entered. 'A letter, sir.' My heart leaped. Uncle Jacob put down his fork, took the letter and dismissed her with a nod towards the door. He opened the envelope. I cast my eyes as far to the right as I could, but he shielded the paper with his hand as though a schoolboy afraid of cheating. He passed the letter across the table to Mother, who read it, glanced at me, and handed the letter back.

'Well, well, here is a mystery,' Uncle Jacob said. 'Who is this man—' he picked up the letter again and squinted at it, 'this man Lazarus, and why does he want to call on me and Agnes? He intends to bring his aunt with him, which is a further puzzle. What sort of name is Lazarus, anyway?'

'Oh, that's Euphemia's friend, isn't it?' May said. 'The one who had that dull mathematical musical evening.' She turned to me. 'You know, while it is in order to invite someone to your home after you have visited theirs, it is polite to wait for that invitation, rather than to ask.'

Mother cleared her throat. I held up a hand. 'Please allow me to reply,' I said. 'Thank you, May, for that lesson in etiquette. Yes, he is my friend. Now, Uncle Jacob, to answer your questions.' I ticked them off on my fingers, aware I was answering them in the wrong order. 'One—his name is Leopold Lazarus. Two—it's a Jewish name.' My mouth simultaneously dried and ran away with me. 'And three, he wants to visit and bring his aunt who is his closest relative because we love each other and are to be married.' I drew breath.

Amid the clatter of dropped cutlery, Uncle Jacob choked. Aunt Emily leaned across me and banged his back. May clapped her hands. 'Oh, this is like a fairy story. I will be your bridesmaid! You will let me choose my dress, won't you?'

'Nonsense, May!' Aunt Emily said. 'As though we would permit such a match.'

'We are not asking for your permission,' I said. 'We are both of age.'

Uncle Jacob took a sip of water. 'Let us not be too hasty. A Jew?' he croaked. 'Then, he has money. They all do and are very shrewd in its management.'

'Leo is a student. He and I are researching together in Oxford.'

'Then, do you intend to live in a garret?' Aunt Emily said.

'If that is what is required.'

'A penniless student? But, Euphemia,' May said, 'You can't survive on kisses. Don't you want to live comfortably?'

'Nonsense, Emily. May,' Uncle Jacob said. 'They are all rich.'

'I don't care if they're not. I don't want to be rich. I simply don't want to be poor. But, no, the family are not penniless.' I thought of Matilda's house, with its expensive decorations and silver dishes. 'They live comfortably, in my observation. The family have a prosperous business in non-ferrous metals.'

Uncle Jacob turned to Mother. 'And what have you to say, Agnes? You do not seem surprised to hear that some Jew counter-jumper wishes to marry your daughter.'

'Euphemia informed me, this morning. I wish to see her happy.'

'As do we all,' Aunt Emily said. 'But this is less than perfect,'

Perfect. That word again. A lump constricted my throat 'It's not a matter of finding perfection. In Leo I have found equality of purpose.' I stood and raised my voice. 'Someone with whom I am at last in step.'

Mother tugged at my sleeve. 'Hush, Euphemia. We can't have raised voices at the table. Do sit down.'

I dropped onto my chair. 'Leo will travel with me through everything life presents to us, without submitting.'

'Euphemia's pretty words are all very well, Agnes,' Aunt Emily said, 'but when a woman marries a man, she marries his family as well. These people look after their own. Lazarus's family may be unhappy that she is not of their faith, nor has means. They may shun them both. Then where will they be? They cannot live here.'

'Address your questions to me,' I said, 'I have not left the room. As far as the first potential objection is concerned, I am to take his faith.'

'Faith?' Aunt Emily exploded. 'When you always insisted that you had none? That in fact, there was no God? This Lazarus must be a veritable Svengali to have induced you to change your mind.'

'It is just a matter of title, of description. Like changing the deeds on buying a house. Euphemia Thorniwork—atheist. Euphemia Lazarus—atheist Jew. As to the second objection, Leo has money of his own, inherited from his parents and his uncle.'

Uncle Jacob nodded. 'As I said before, they are all rich.'

'But in any event, we do not want an elaborate wedding. We would elope, if necessary.'

Uncle Jacob raised his eyebrows. 'Let us hope it does not come to that, I could not bear May's disappointment. The fellow has money and seems to want to marry Euphemia, despite her obsession with numbers. We must seize the chance. I will reply to the letter and tell them to call tomorrow. In the early afternoon, so that they may leave before the fog comes. I trust business can be concluded in no more than a few hours.'

'That's very little notice,' Mother said. 'Mrs Lazarus might already be engaged.' My heart jumped at the thought of having to wait longer than a day before I could be with Leo.

Uncle Jacob waved a hand. 'I am certain that for so important a matter, she would alter her arrangements.' He turned to Aunt Emily. 'You must tell Mrs Upshaw to expect company.'

'But tell her not to make a lardy cake,' I said.

'Oh, that's a shame. Mrs Upshaw's lardy cakes are delicious. Why can't we have one?' May asked. I told her what I knew of the Jewish dietary limitations.

'Oh dear—I expect you'll miss bacon. You'd better have some more of this ham too, while you can. And these.' She passed me a dish of sliced tomatoes. 'Have some of these love apples, Mrs Lazarus! So romantic! Even if your story is less *Cinderella* and more *Beauty and the Beast*.'

I frowned. 'Leo is very pleasing to the eye.' His aunt would insist he put on cuffs without rips and darns, and that he polish his boots.

'Did I say he was the Beast? Do you have a picture of him?' May asked. I shook my head.

'What, no secret locket? I despair of you sometimes. Well, we shall see him soon, this man whose handsome face has turned your head. I'm looking forward to it.'

Three Books, One Assegai

Mother and I sat in the parlour waiting for Leo and his Aunt Matilda. I took up a place by the window and tried to read Matteson's *A Collection of Diophantine Problems with Solutions*. Each time I heard feet splashing along the rainy pavement, I rose and peered through the lace curtains. I read the first sentence over and over, until it made no sense. *It is required to find four affirmative integer numbers, such that the sum of every two of them shall be a cube.* I could not think of any such numbers, nor of anything that might require it.

'Do remain calm, Euphemia,' Mother said, after my fourth journey to the window. 'Your nervousness is contagious. My heart flutters. Nurse will be insisting I take to my bed.' She let out an echoing cough.

'Oh no—I'm sorry. Please don't leave.'

'Have no fear, I won't. But what shall we talk to our guests about, besides making the wedding arrangements?' Mother dabbed her lips with her handkerchief. 'I doubt I could carry the weight of a conversation about mathematics.'

'Leo has many other interests. He likes to walk. He is a lover of music. I am certain that you will find a meeting of minds in that. But let's not talk about Wagner.'

'No—I understand that he has made his opinions on

the Jews very well known. But do a composer's views inform his compositions? Surely, one can appreciate the man's art, even if we disagree with his beliefs?'

I stood once more, heart racing. Children dashed past the window. I sank back into my chair. 'It would be no loss if we did not waste our time on Wagner's works,' I said. 'There is so much more music that we can value.'

'Oh?' Mother raised her eyebrows. 'If Mr Lazarus has broadened your knowledge of the arts, then he is to be commended.'

Footsteps on the doorstep. A knock at the door. I jumped and my book fell to the floor. I made to dash from the room. Mother caught hold of my skirt. 'No, sit down. Let the maid do it. Do you want them to think we have no servants?'

I heard voices in the hall and fussing with umbrellas and coats. But whose? If they were anyone's but Leo's and Aunt Matilda's, I would lose my mind. The maid entered. 'Mrs Matilda Lazarus and Mr Leopold Lazarus, Madam.' She stood aside.

Leo carried three books bound in a leather strap. He and Matilda hesitated in the doorway. 'Tell Mr Pratincole that our guests have arrived,' Mother said to the maid, who left the room, closing the door behind her.

I rose. 'Please come in! Mother, may I introduce Mr Leopold Lazarus, and Mrs Matilda Lazarus, his aunt? Leo, Mrs Lazarus, this is my mother, Mrs Thorniwork.' Had I made the introductions the right way round? Leo bowed. His face betrayed no strain. Did he feel as I, not only as though an omnibus had driven across him, but that now we were in a court of law?

'How do you do?' Mother said. 'Please sit.' Leo and

Matilda perched on the edge of a sofa, as though ready to run. It had room for three people, and I longed to sit next to Leo, for him to put an arm around me. I picked up the book I had been reading and sat on the sofa opposite, next to Mother.

Leo smiled at me. 'I have read that book. I was unimpressed. Here are others for you.' He stood and passed the leather-strapped bundle to me. I touched his hand. Yes—he was real. He returned to his seat. He had given me *Studies in Judaism, Judaism and its History*, and *The Jewish Woman and her Home*. I supposed the last one was a version of Mrs Beeton.

'Thank you, Leo. But tell me,' I leaned forward, 'why did you say that about Matteson's *Collection*?'

'Now, Euphemia,' Mother said. 'I am certain that the rest of us have no desire to sit through a discussion about mathematics.' She turned to Matilda. 'I trust that you had no difficulty in finding our home, Mrs Lazarus?'

'No, we did not.'

Silence. The clock in the hall struck four. Matilda cleared her throat. 'I hope that you are well, Mrs Thorniwork?' she said in an unnecessarily loud voice. Perhaps Leo had told her that Mother was deaf.

'As well as can be expected,' Mother said coughing into her handkerchief. Matilda leaned back in her seat. 'Do not concern yourself,' Mother said. 'It is not contagious. The fog, you see.'

'Ah yes,' Matilda said. 'It has caused so much sickness. There seems to be no end. And yet nothing is done. We seem to be expected to live with it.'

Mother looked at the door. 'I am sure my brother and his family will join us presently.'

Nobody replied. I was certain my thumping heart was audible. The clock in the hall struck the quarter hour. Even the chimes seemed to drag, as though the clock were filled with treacle.

Leo drummed his fingers against his lap, as though playing a melody on a piano only he could hear. 'Well, here we are.'

'That is certainly true,' I said. How did one make conversation between people who did not know one another? 'It is very rainy today, is it not?'

'But not so cold,' Leo replied. He resumed tapping and looked away from me. He began to hum a scale. Would he break into song? And, which one?

'Do stop fidgeting, Leopold.' Matilda pulled at his sleeve. 'Every blow of your fingers goes through me. Like one of those African spears... an assegai.'

'It would have to be a blunt assegai to resemble a finger, Aunt,' Leo said. 'And then it could hardly go through anything.'

'Have you been in Africa, Mrs Lazarus?' Mother said, grasping Matilda's extraordinary comparison like a drowning swimmer to a lifebelt.

'Certainly not!' Matilda said. 'However, we do have distant relatives in Johannesburg. Distant in miles, as well as removal,' she added, with a tinkling laugh.

'Have we?' Leo said.

'Yes, Cousin Montague—you must remember him. Cousin Theodore's son.

'Ah yes. A scion of the wet fish Lazaruses.'

I glared at Leo. The conversation must be steered away from *trade*, even at a removal, before Uncle Jacob arrived. 'Oh, how fascinating!' I clasped my hands. 'I trust they would be enjoying better weather in South Africa, at this time.'

Matilda supposed it was possible.

'I believe it is summer there,' Mother said.

No reply.

Leo spread his fingers as though to resume his percussion, but seemed to think better of it and steepled them instead. He looked up at the ceiling, from which he seemed to derive some inspiration. 'Of course, some constellations are visible in South Africa, which we cannot see here.'

'Oh? Which ones?' I had not realised he had an interest in astronomy, about which I knew nothing.

Leo frowned. 'I'm afraid I do not recall.' I would not have to add the subject to the list of subjects I must study.

The door opened, putting a merciful end to the tortured discussion of South African climatology and stargazing. Uncle Jacob, Aunt Emily and May entered. For the first time I could recall, I was pleased to see them.

Mother performed the introductions, we established that everyone did very well and Uncle Jacob, Aunt Emily and May sat opposite Leo and Matilda as though they were the opposing team in some game.

'Good afternoon, *Leo*,' May said, sending such a dazzling smile towards him that I expected him to lift a hand to shield his eyes.

'I believe that you and my niece share an interest in mathematics, Lazarus,' Uncle Jacob said.

'But what is the point of mathematical research?' Aunt Emily said, before Leo could reply. 'We already know how to count. What can it possibly lead to?'

I had heard this many times before. The mood of the

236

afternoon appeared to be becoming one of disagreement, and we had not yet discussed our marriage.

'Oh-ho!' Leo smiled. 'This has been asked before. Mathematical research looks at the myriad problems for which we don't have a method. It's about finding the tools and systems that other subject areas find so useful, in formulating their own work. Sometimes it stumbles across facts and numbers that we have no conceivable use for at the moment but that one day could become vital to the world. Euphemia's and my research may yet do so.'

May spoke up. 'Oh, I don't understand all that. What do you mean?' Her question voiced what her parents' expressions suggested. She gave Leo another blast of the smile. 'Can you perhaps draw me a picture? You are so clever that I am certain you will be able to make it simple.'

'Well,' Leo pulled a notebook and a pencil from his pocket.

'There is no need for that,' I said. 'It simply means that one thing can lead to another.' How to describe a thing that she would understand? 'For example, each musical note has its own mathematical frequency—signature, if you like.'

May raised her eyebrows. 'So, are you telling me that learning mathematics could help one to sing in tune? It doesn't seem to have aided you.'

'Euphemia holds a tune very well,' Leo said.

'Indeed,' Matilda said. 'She entertained us all beautifully at our evening of music.'

May turned to me. 'And what did you perform? Some little Schubert *lieder*, perhaps?'

I muttered a reply.

'Speak up! Don't hide your light under a bushel,' May

said.

'I've already told you what I sang, the day after the music evening. *The Boy I Love is Up In the Gallery*,' I said, eyes downcast. 'It was one of Pearl's favourites.'

Aunt Emily tutted. 'A music hall song.'

'There was no vulgarity in it,' Leo said. 'But we stray from the point. Mathematical theory is often ahead of its time, and the abstract nonsense of yesterday underpins the applied mathematics of today.'

'Which must be of much use to you people in financial matters,' Uncle Jacob said.

Matilda stiffened. Leo sighed. I felt sick.

'Oh, Uncle, *really,*' I said.

'Do not "Oh Uncle, really" me, Euphemia, I meant no offence,' Uncle Jacob said. 'I merely wished to introduce the possibility of discussing, with Mr Lazarus, a financial proposition. A possible investment. Perhaps we can do so this afternoon.'

'Very well,' Leo said. 'But I must impress upon you that I am ignorant of such things.'

'I am sure you do yourself a disservice,' Uncle Jacob said.

'Of course,' May said, 'Numbers can be used to discover hidden meanings in words. You give each number a letter and then add them up. Then you end up with another number. And that can be lucky for you.'

Leo nodded. 'It can be done using Hebrew letters. It's called gematria. For example, the word for alive is composed of two letters adding up to eighteen. This has made eighteen a lucky number among the Jewish people. Donations of money in multiples of eighteen are very popular.'

Uncle Jacob raised his eyebrows and leaned forward. 'And do you believe that?'

As Leo made as though to reply, the maid knocked and entered, carrying a silver tray set with fine china cups, pink with gold edging, a matching teapot, milk jug, sugar basin and tiny plates. A larger platter held small, ordinary-looking cakes. She placed the tray on a low table that stood between our opposing seats.

'Ah, the cup that cheers!' Uncle Jacob rubbed his hands.

Aunt Emily poured a pale-yellow stream into each cup.

May took a sip and replaced her cup. 'Leo—tell, me, what do you call your horse? Someone like you would choose "Destrier" or "Gringolet", I rather fancy.'

'My horse'? Leo frowned. 'I am afraid I have none. We do not keep a carriage.'

'But—are you not a scrap metal merchant?' May said. 'Do you mean to say that you pull your cart yourself? You look strong enough to do so, but it must be such a strain.'

Matilda sniffed. 'Mrs Pratincole, I fear Miss Pratincole takes my nephew for a rag and bone man. Our family is engaged in metal trading. That is not the same at all. We have no need to soil our hands.'

'I receive income from it,' Leo said. 'It funds my research, and it will fund Euphemia's too, once we are married.'

'But surely, she will abandon her studies, then?' Aunt Emily said.

'I most certainly will not,' I said, lightheaded at the thought of no longer having to rely on Uncle Jacob's mishandling of our money. Let him invest in whatever he wished.

'I would countenance nothing else but that we continue together,' Leo said. 'I am quite firm on this matter.'

'You show great resolve, Leo,' May said. 'Stiffness in a gentleman is all.' Leo blinked. 'Stiffness of resolve,' May said.

'Hold your tongue, May,' Uncle Jacob said. 'Find some embroidery to attend to.' He turned to Leo. 'I understand that it is your intention to marry my niece.' Finally. 'I give my consent.'

Matilda raised her palm. 'We need to discuss Euphemia's conversion to Judaism before we consider making wedding arrangements. I believe it takes several years. I fear that theirs will be a long engagement.'

'I do not care,' I said, anxious to join this discussion about me.

'This is the only way that Leopold and Euphemia's children, should they be so blessed, would be considered Jewish,' Matilda said.

'Can they not make up their own minds when older, and do what Euphemia intends to do—convert?' Mother said.

'That is not our way,' Matilda said.

'Well, she has made a start,' Mother said. 'I noticed that Leopold has given her some books.'

'Better than those boring old mathematical tomes,' May said.

Matilda smiled. 'I quite agree. Now, one thing I do know is that the last stage of the conversion is to immerse in the ritual bath. How should you feel about that, Euphemia?'

'Why?' May said. 'Euphemia is as clean as any Jewess.'

'It's not a matter of cleanliness,' Leo said. 'It is concerned with ritual purity.'

'What is that?' Mother asked. 'Do you people believe that Gentiles are impure?'

'No, of course not,' Leo said. 'It marks a rite of passage. But, again, impurity is different from dirt. It's believed to be connected to distance from God.'

I thought better than to comment that I must submerge myself in water to become closer to a fictional entity.

Leo continued. 'You can become ritually impure in many ways. And there are methods for removing it.'

May's eyes opened wide. 'Oh! How is it acquired?'

'First of all,' Leo said, 'you must understand that this is a belief from ancient days, and only its residue is present in some rituals today. My understanding is that many are concerned with dead bodies—because that was viewed as the furthest thing from God. For example, whether our hands are dirty or not, we wash them on leaving a graveyard.'

'Can we *see* the impurity?' May asked. 'Is it some sort of substance? I imagine a funeral cortege, with a cloud surrounding the hearse.'

Leo smiled. 'No, and neither can you feel it like the wind. But the ancients believed it could penetrate down through the ground, and upwards through the ceilings of a building.'

'So, it pervades everything? Like the fog?' May said. 'Maybe it's some sort of force. Like the psychic force to which a medium is sensitive. But what does the impurity actually do?'

'Well… nothing,' Leo said. 'In ancient times, there were things you couldn't do if you were impure. The Talmud—the book of religious law—goes into incredible detail about it.'

'I'm sure that is not a matter for discussion in polite company,' Matilda said.

May raised her eyebrows. 'Imagine if it could… *attack* in some way.' She gave a shudder. 'I'd have to look to you to defend me against this primeval evil, Leo.'

'Don't concern yourself with these ancient superstitions, dear,' Matilda said. 'We have enough to contend with as it is. Self-appointed clairvoyants abound, and there is all manner of nonsense in the cheap papers about the effects of the coming millennium.'

'My daughter has a vivid imagination,' Aunt Emily said, smiling and nodding at May.

'Yes—perhaps I'll pen a novel,' May said.

'May! This is marvellous news. I didn't realise you could write,' I said.

Mother nudged me with a sharp elbow. 'Will Euphemia have to receive instruction, in addition to reading?' she asked.

'That is likely,' Leo said. 'We may be able to find a rabbi in Oxford prepared to do this, although there are few of us there. Perhaps someone might need to be found in London.'

'We will tell you as soon as we know more,' Matilda said.

Uncle Jacob rose. 'Now, if you would accompany me to my study, Mr Lazarus, I have a most interesting proposition. It concerns health, a matter that is of the utmost concern to everyone.' They left the room.

May leaned forward and lowered her voice. 'Mrs Lazarus, is it true that you Jews have a secret name that you are forbidden to divulge?'

Matilda frowned. 'We do have other names, but they are not secret. They're only used for prayer.'

'And what is yours?' May asked.

'I apologise, Mrs Lazarus,' Aunt Emily said. 'May, you are most intrusive.'

'I take no offence,' Matilda said. 'It's gratifying that she shows an interest. The form is a name, son or daughter of the father's name. Mine is Mirel, after my grandmother. Leopold's is Leyb. It means lion.'

'Must Euphemia take one?' May asked.

'Yes, but not until after her conversion,' Matilda said. She furrowed her brow. 'Perhaps Ruth—she took her mother in law's religion—or Esther, as that begins with the letter E.'

'Esther was a very brave woman,' May said. 'She has an entire book of the Bible to herself. And, do you know, that book never mentions God once. Like you, really, Euphemia.'

Leo and Uncle Jacob came back to the parlour. Matilda stood. 'Please excuse us but we must leave now. I fear it will soon grow dark, and foggy.'

Farewells were made. I went into the hall with Leo and Matilda. She whispered in my ear, 'I wish to wash my hands.' I directed her to where she needed to go.

'How are you? I am still upset,' I said to Leo once she had disappeared.

'I'm shocked too. It's very hard not to be able to speak to others of what we endured, to unburden ourselves.'

'Some might say that horror of any kind is best not

spoken of. Then, perhaps we will be able to bury the appalling memory. But tell me, before Aunt Matilda reappears—why did she mention assegais? It wasn't germane to what we were speaking about.'

'We weren't speaking at all, then. My aunt has drastic methods of initiating a conversation. But I admit that it worked.'

'I suppose I must agree with you. What did Uncle Jacob discuss with you?'

'A miraculous treatment for consumption in which he feels I should invest eighteen hundred pounds. Apparently, you cannot obtain it in this country—for which there is probably a good reason—but he intends to be the first person to sell it here.'

'What was your reply?' Surely Leo would not be gulled into one of Uncle Jacob's half-witted schemes.

'That I would consider it and let him know. Which gives me another reason to revisit this house. But I will only come when you are here.' He took the ring box from his pocket, removed the ring and placed it on my finger. I took both Leo's hands in mine.

'Leyb,' I said.

He glanced along the route Matilda had taken towards the scullery. He leaned forward and brushed my lips with a feather-like touch of his own. 'Behold, thou art fair, my love; behold, thou art fair; thou hast doves' eyes.'

That must be from the scriptures, too. I would find it in Pearl's Bible, even if it meant reading it from cover to cover. Perhaps there was a name that meant dove. What might its gematria be?

Twenty-two Letters

The following morning, Aunt Emily, Uncle Jacob, and May were visiting a friend of Uncle Jacob's to offer condolences in respect of a family bereavement. I sat in my room, gazing out of the window at the rooftops with their chimneys belching smoke. My intention had been to draw together proposals for Leo's and my research. We had so little time to submit a new one and my mind was empty. In his telegram, Leo had said, *It might be possible to decompose arbitrary signals into combinations of simple harmonic waves.* He had found a promising book in the British Library, but we had not managed to examine it. 'This is the sound. The song,' Pearl had said.

I tried to remember what had been in Leo's notes that had led to his developing an equation involving Hebrew letters, but it was as though someone had reached inside my brain and plucked out the thoughts. Could there be repeating series of numbers in sound waves? Could there be merit in researching the phenomenon of the patterns I had observed in the fog? Could our research concern the mathematics of sound? Leo and I had planned to return to Oxford together on Monday, on the nine-fifteen train. Two more days, in the company of my family, to be endured. Only two more days to plan our research.

Sound and mathematics. Leo had said everything

seems connected, as though nature plays its own music with numbers instead of notes. I took up a pen and paper, the page as white as a newly dead body. Before I could write, the thought had vanished, like a bubble bursting.

Perhaps reading something different would provide a distraction. I reached into my bag and took out Pearl's Bible. Using the concordance in the back, I found the sentence Leo had quoted to me as he left. It was from the Song of Songs. The verse following it was: 'Behold, thou art fair, my beloved, yea, pleasant: also our bed is green.' I imagined it referred to lying on grass, but in November it would be too damp. Perhaps Leo and I should buy a green bed coverlet, for when we were married.

I turned again to the page Pearl had marked with a red ribbon. The red heifer had to be slaughtered, burnt, and the ashes used in water for purification. I turned to the next page. Anyone touching a dead body was unclean, whatever that meant, but could be cleansed using the ash water. I must ask Leo if that was still done.

Pearl had said the Bible's language flowed and had rhythm and that was so, but for all that, what I read was a translation. Was it really the same text, or could the translators not avoid putting their own meaning to it? Might it have a different tone in Hebrew? Perhaps the very sound of the words had a resonance, apart from their meaning? And there was gematria, of course. 'Find the gematria,' Pearl had said. I would learn Hebrew, despite my lack of aptitude in languages. I had struggled with French when I was in school, and in the end the teacher allowed me to sit at the back of the class with *The Uses and Triumphs of Mathematics*.

There was a knock at the front door. I left my room and

peered over the banister as the maid let Leo into the hall. He smiled up at me, holding two books and a newspaper. I ran downstairs and, taking his hand, led him into the parlour. I shut the door. Leo put the books and paper on a table and we held each other close.

When we moved apart, Leo picked up the books. 'These are for you. First, this one.' He passed me *The Talmud*.

'Thank you,' I said. 'Talmud? Ah, yes, that law book with text in the middle of the page, and commentaries around the edges.' I opened it. 'I am pleased that this book is in English, although I know nothing of jurisprudence. I thought there were many volumes to it?'

'Yes—this is an overview. There have been a number of eminent female Talmudic scholars. And here is *Introduction to Biblical Hebrew*.'

I smiled. 'I'd thought about this very subject.' We sat on one of the sofas and I looked inside the Hebrew book. It began with instruction in the letters. There were twenty-two consonants, many of which seemed to be identical to each other. I peered at the page, and noticed differences between them. Some had different versions if they came at the end of a word. The vowels were various dots and lines above and below the consonants.

'It seems to have a very complex writing system.' It was written from right to left. I traced the first of a line of letters with my fingertip. 'Is the language itself as difficult?'

'Compared with French, for example, yes. But you will not be speaking it, only reciting prayers and reading from the Bible. With a mind such as yours, I am certain you will become its mistress in no time.' Was reciting prayers to a deity in which you did not believe any worse than reciting poetry?

'Will you read some, please, so that I can hear the sound?'

Leo took the book from me. It fell open at a page marked *The Irregular Verbs*. My heart sank. He read, pointing to the words as he went. 'Oh dear—it means "As for man, his days are as grass; as a flower of the field, so he flourisheth".' He looked into the distance, brow furrowed.

I touched his hand. 'What's the matter? Is the memory of our horror looming over you?'

He put his arm around my shoulder and pulled me close. 'No more than usual. No—despite all that has happened, I have just realised that I am happier now than I have ever been in my life.' We kissed again.

We stopped and I drew breath. 'I too am happy, Leo, but for one thing—our research proposal. I cannot concentrate on mathematics. My mind returns over and again to the terror we endured.'

'My mind feels as though it has become derailed too,' he said. 'There is no escaping the memories. Everywhere I look... see here.' He took the newspaper from his pocket, *The Illustrated London News*, and opened it towards the back. He put it on the table and pointed to an article towards the bottom of the page, no more than a few inches high, headed 'Charnel House found in Central London.' The article began, *Horrors heaped on horrors is a phrase which inadequately describes the revelations in connection with the findings at a warehouse in Tanyard Lane.* It continued, describing the shocking appearance of *people's former loved ones, numbering over one hundred, whose peace had been disturbed.* Leo and I received a scant, nameless mention *discovered by two passers-by*. The bodies had been removed to a nearby mortuary, but their identification had not been possible.

'My poor Pearl,' I said. 'There is nothing of her left to identify. Only her last words, which I don't understand.'

'I have found it all overwhelming, but it's worse for you, of course.' Leo took my hand. 'We must not let this horror distract us from our purpose. We must not let it beat us.' He closed the *News*.

'But how? I wish it were as easy as turning a page. Time, they say, is a good healer, but even if it were true, we have none. It is less than a month until we have to submit our revised proposal to Professor Milton. If we do not, our research appointments will be terminated.'

He sat upright. 'We find the thoughts invading our minds, do we not? Whether we wish it or not? I have a suggestion that you may find unwelcome and even consider insane. May I?'

'I can't imagine what that might be, but remember Mother may come downstairs at any minute, and I have enough troubles without unseemly propositions.'

He frowned. 'You need not worry about that. I think we must revisit the scene of the horror. To prove to ourselves that all is well now. To move onwards.'

I looked away. 'Oh, Leo, I do not think I can do it.' My chest felt tight, and I could not catch my breath.

'We not only can, but must. The bodies are no longer there—they rest in peace, now. And the newspaper made no mention of the fog. That too must have cleared from the cellar, so we will need no protection to our breathing if we go by day. We will prove to ourselves that there is nothing remaining, and I am sure that will enable us to dismiss the thoughts. Then we will also find peace. At least consider it, please. We must be brave.'

I looked away and took as deep a breath as I could. 'I am uncertain as to whether I have any courage left. And why should it work?'

Leo took my hands in his. 'The thought of it is worse than the actuality. We will see there's nothing to fear. Will you trust me? I won't let any harm come to you. I will protect you.'

All the months, all the years I had spent, battling the likes of Milton, and his sex, who were convinced women were ruled by their emotions, were not trained to think intellectually or oriented to do so properly. Certain that the female brain could not manage anything more complex than counting on their fingers. Was my life as a mathematician to be snuffed out, because of the actions of other men and their treatment of the dead?

I held my forehead in my hands. 'I feel in so much turmoil I fear I will explode. I feel so debilitated that I am unable to confront my family's prejudice—as you may have noticed. I do know I cannot continue like this. Very well. I will try anything.' I rose. 'Let's go now.'

'Here I see the valiant woman who argued with Milton and who, with her head held high, told him to make up his mind.'

'That woman feels depleted of all moral fibre. But perhaps if I feign fearlessness hard enough, it will become true.'

'You don't need to be fearless. To be brave is to act, despite one's fear. Can a person be said to be brave, without fear?'

'I don't know, and I'm afraid I cannot turn my mind to

its consideration. Another time, perhaps. Let's finish this.'

I put on my coat and we stepped into the street. The pavement seemed to shift under my feet as though I stood on the deck of a ship. I took Leo's arm and tried to concentrate on breathing.

'You're shivering,' he said. 'Do you wish to return to the house for a warmer coat?'

'No, this one will suffice.' I felt sweat run down my back.

We stepped down from the omnibus and walked until we reached the end of Tanyard Lane. My chest felt tight, and I thought I would choke.

Leo took my hand. 'Take courage. This will only take a few minutes. Then, we will be able to think of research ideas on the omnibus back to your house, rather than staring from the windows.' He led me down the deserted alleyway at a brisk pace.

The outer door of the cellar had been nailed with strips of wood in an X shape. Leo pulled at one. It came away from the doorframe. He removed the other.

'Shoddy workmanship,' he said, 'But they have done us a good turn.'

'Some poor carpenter must have fixed them badly, in his haste to get away. I can't blame him.'

Leo pulled the door open, and we entered. With each downward step we took towards the inner door, a raw, tangibly malevolent force tightened its grip.

We reached the bottom of the stairs. Leo reached out a hand towards the door.

I pulled his arm back. 'No—I must do it.' I dragged the door open. This time, no foul odours rushed out. Standing on the threshold, we peered inside.

The bodies were gone. The machine nowhere to be seen. But, condensing from the air itself, the fog billowed, curling out of the cellar and around our feet, as though it knew we were there.

Three Hundred and Forty-one

We stopped dead. The hairs on my arms and the back of my neck stood up and goosebumps rose all over my body. An ancient, primal, and malicious force engulfed me. I held my breath and staggered backwards.

Leo threw an arm round my shoulders. 'Stand fast and true.' Did he also feel the concentrated hatred directed towards us? Together we stumbled into the cellar, onto a floor still covered with slimy residue. The air seemed to vibrate, as though a train with an infinite number of carriages passed beneath. The fog appeared in the air as though from an invisible source, billowing like the sea, wave after yellow wave rolling towards us, winding around our ankles.

'Very well,' Leo said. 'We have seen that the bodies are gone. We need do no more. Let us leave, before the fog rises above our heads. The walls and door should contain it. It must have seeped in at nightfall but could not retreat at daybreak.' He grasped my hand. 'Come.' He turned towards the door, pulling me after him.

I dropped his hand and stood still. 'I am as agitated as I was before we came—surely you are, too?'

He nodded. 'As yet, I feel no emotional release—but perhaps we should not expect it to be instantaneous.'

I was consumed by the sense that my enemy was here,

and to leave would be to recoil from it, to allow it to win. 'Look,' I said, 'not only is the fog contained here, but it seems to be created here, from the very atmosphere of this benighted place.'

Leo looked around. 'I do not see how that can be.'

The fog rolled across the floor and soaked into the walls. It poured out again from the centre of the ceiling, snaking to the top of the mould-covered walls, sliding down to the floor, rising to the level of my knees. I swiped at it as though that might waft it away.

'It's as though the fog is alive. As though it is aware of us, watching us, following us. As though it means us harm. Do you remember what Pearl said? "many bodies, such impurity"?'

He took my hand. 'I remember.'

I looked away from him. 'All those people, all of us who lost their loved ones, twice. Once to death, and then to these vile men. We have nothing and nowhere to mourn. Our poor dear ones' bodies taken, treated without respect, and now disposed of.'

And leaving me to dream again and again of Pearl, of gematria, the number three hundred and forty-one recurring time and again. Tears filled my eyes.

Leo passed me a crumpled handkerchief. 'I will not say that I know how you must feel. How could I? But I do know how I should feel if it happened to someone precious to me.'

I blew my nose and offered him the handkerchief back. He indicated that I should keep it.

'Pearl also said, "it is no delusion". What is? Do you think she meant that the impurity had power of its own?' I paused and took a deep breath. 'I never thought I would say this about May, but maybe she was right. Maybe ritual impurity does create some intangible force.'

Leo placed his hands on my shoulders and turned me to face him. 'I am very sorry for your distress, but what you have just said merely illustrates the effects of grief on the balance of the mind.'

I shrugged his hands away. 'Are you saying that I am deranged?' I snapped. I continued before he could reply. 'You will be telling me next that you didn't hear Pearl's body... Pearl speak. How do you explain that?'

Leo looked into my eyes. 'I cannot, other than as some form of shared delusion. Perhaps because of the toxic effects of the fog.'

I clenched both hands into fists. 'So, now we are *both* mad? I tell you, I think the residual impurity is causing the fog. It originates here. In this cellar. It spreads through the earth. Remember when you started the machine up? It made Pearl speak. It gave the fog renewed energy. It must somehow have made the impurity worse. Neither the bodies nor the machine are here now, but the impurity must remain. It is magnifying itself.'

Leo stroked my cheek. 'My poor, dear love. Let us apply Occam's razor. I will see whether the fog is entering through a gap in the wall, that I might be able to block. I see something in that corner.' He tramped to the farthest end of the cellar. The fog changed direction, and seemed to follow him.

I stayed in my place and looked around. As I stared at the wall closest to me, a stain emerged onto its surface. It had not been there when we entered. The scarlet colour of the stain contrasted with the grey green of the mould surrounding it. It was shaped like a cow. A scarlet cow. I moved closer. Smaller figures manifested underneath the cow shape. Not shapes, letters. Could they be… Hebrew?

'Leo!' As I called at the top of my voice, the fog thinned and Chladni patterns formed in it, as it had done when Pearl sang. As it had done the night we were lost in it. I stopped to draw breath. The patterns vanished and the fog thickened. 'Come here at once!' I called. Now a different thin pattern formed in the fog. I fell silent. The fog grew dense.

Leo plodded back to me, as though weighed down by the fog. 'There is no point of entry. All I found were folding tables leaning against a wall, that those swine had not yet used.'

I grasped his arm. 'Did you notice those Chladni patterns in the fog when I called you?'

He coughed and shook his head.

'Watch.' I called his name again. A pattern of four circles, like glaring eyes.

'An interesting phenomenon. Turning to practical matters, I could find no point of entry for the fog.'

'That doesn't surprise me. It's creating itself inside this place, penetrating the walls and then condensing out again. But look at this wall—here's a pattern that emerged from nowhere, like a photograph being developed. It's shaped like a cow. A red cow. And I think the letters underneath it may be Hebrew.'

Leo approached the pattern 'There is a trick of the mind, that recognises shapes where there are none. That part might be one of a cow's horns.' He reached out a fingertip but snatched it back. 'I see nothing else.'

'No letters? What do you see there—only a smear of scarlet?'

He moved closer once more. 'I see nothing whatsoever.'

'But you must see it! If only I could read the letters. Wait.' I pulled a piece of paper and a pencil from my bag and copied what only I could see. The fog slid up the wall, covering the pattern.

'There!' I pushed the paper under his nose. 'What's this?'

Leo looked at it and smiled. 'Amazing. One glance at a Hebrew primer and you wrote two words.'

My throat tightened. 'I *didn't*. I copied it from the wall. I saw it. I'm not lying to you. Now—what does it say?'

As fog wound its way around my ribcage, he took the paper from me and read. 'It says—*poro odumo*. Red cow.' He folded the note and put it in his pocket. The fog recoiled for a second, then moved towards us once more.

'Or maybe *red heifer*?' I said. 'To remove ritual impurity?'

Leo nodded. 'Yes, but to remove it from people and vessels. What use is that to us?'

I threw my hands into the air. 'But do you not see? Now we must determine if it will work for buildings. Pearl said, "only the song of the red heifer can conquer it". I think that the answer lies in sound. You saw the effect of my calling you. The fog thinned. The sound of my voice must have lessened the impurity.'

Leo smiled. 'You told me that all your life people have told you that the meaning of your name is "fair speech". How right they were.'

My throat tightened as I resisted an urge to stamp. 'That has nothing to do with it. Look.' I yelled his name again. The fog formed into patterns. I shouted *red heifer* in

English, then in Hebrew. More patterns. 'Now you try.'

'I am sorry,' Leo said. 'I sought only to lighten the mood.'

'Well, you didn't. Please don't speak nonsense.'

Leo's mouth set into a line. 'I should not be the only one here if I did. Are you now suggesting that we could shout the impurity away?'

I decided to ignore the insult. 'No, but sound seems to diminish it. If only I could work out a means to use it. Please, call out.'

'Hello!' Leo called, but it had no effect.

'Try again, calling your own name,' I said. 'Perhaps it is an effect of words themselves.' Still no effect. 'Your voice is too deep. Pearl said "only the song of the red heifer can conquer it. Could there be a song? Do you know any Hebrew prayers or songs about cows?'

He shook his head. 'Enough of this. I fear your imagination is getting the better of you.'

This time I did stamp. 'Mr Roentgen discovered X rays—such as were used to take a picture of my broken tooth. Did his imagination get the better of him? And Mr Becquerel found that some substances can emit a force. Did his imagination get the better of him?' My voice grew louder. 'The Curies called that force radioactivity. Were their imaginations getting the better of them?'

Leo raised a hand, his mouth set in a line. 'Please do not shout at me. I dislike it, and it lends no additional—if you will excuse me—*force* to your arguments.'

'I apologise. But perhaps ritual impurity is some sort of radiation that reacts with the air to cause the fog.'

'But why would that not happen in any place where there were many bodies, such as in a mortuary?' Leo said.

'I think that because there, bodies await eventual burial, at which peace would be bestowed on them. There must be similar words to grant such repose, in all ideologies. I do not believe in God's peace, but I do believe in letting the dead rest. But here, they have been stolen from their graves, the peace disturbed.'

'Yes, but why should this have such a catastrophic effect?'

'Perhaps alone it would not, but in addition, the body snatchers deployed their contraption in an attempt at communication, at enslaving the life force somehow. You saw the effect it had on the fog, and on Pearl. The machine must have reversed the effects of a blessing for peace given at the funerals and allowed impurity in to fill the void.' I stopped and drew breath, with a wheeze.

'We should leave now,' Leo said. 'The fog is affecting you.'

I put my hands on my hips. 'I am going nowhere. Allow me to finish. The snatchers stole bodies repeatedly. Over a hundred times, that's how many the newspaper said were removed. More, if we include the dead snatchers themselves.'

Leo raised his eyebrows. 'Let us imagine for a moment that you are right. What do you suggest we do?'

I took his hands between mine. 'We must purify this place. The red heifer plays an essential part—if I only knew what that is.'

'According to Leviticus, it had to be slaughtered, burnt and used to create purifying water,' Leo said. 'And the text goes on to say that if a person is not cleansed on the third and seventh days, then they would be permanently unclean. This is what would have happened to the snatchers.'

'And so they were. Not only were the bodies impure, but impurity also spread from the snatchers, who magnified it with their machine, until the entire cellar was contaminated to the extent that the impurity creates itself. We may have added to that when you started it up.'

Leo frowned. 'I doubt the few seconds it ran for would have made any practical difference.'

'I'm not blaming you. It enabled Pearl to speak to us. Now, we need a way not only to stop the impurity growing but also to remove it.'

Leo shrugged. 'There's more detail in the Talmud concerning ritual impurity, but it has nothing to do with sound.'

'Perhaps creating the cleansing water is only one way to achieve it. Could it be that a note of the frequency that Pearl sang would eradicate the impurity? Can you remember the note?'

'It was F natural. But, a musical note as sung or played on an instrument is a mixture of the fundamental tone and harmonics, they're multiples of the fundamental tone. Which would be the one that worked, among all that were sung? Perhaps you and I should sing together—we could begin with a perfect fifth.'

I moved closer to him and linked my elbow through his. 'I would love to sing with you, at any time but now. I feel sure that what is needed here is a single, fundamental tone. It is somewhere in the note that Pearl sang. Where's your frequency mechanistic generator? The one you demonstrated at the musical evening?' I gasped. 'Oh— don't tell me that you have taken it back to Oxford.'

'No. It is not that easily portable. It is still in my room

in Aunt Matilda's house.' He bent to kiss me.

I jumped back. 'Later. You must bring the generator here. I will go to my uncle's house and make us masks—when we return, the fog will be above the level of my head and perhaps even yours. I have an idea for a mask that it will not be able to penetrate.'

'Really,' Leo said, 'this appears to be a great deal of labour with no likely outcome. I remain unconvinced.'

I squeezed my eyes shut and turned my head. 'Then you leave me no choice but to act alone. I will go to Aunt Matilda's house—I am sure she will allow me to take the tone generator. I trust you will not stand in the way of that.' I turned and trudged away, through the waist-high fog, towards the door.

'Wait,' Leo called after me. 'I did not say I would not take part.'

I ran back to him and threw my arms around his neck.

He wriggled free. 'Later, you said. The fog is rising—let us continue this discussion outside.'

We stepped through the door and back up the stairs to the street. He drew some money from his pocket. 'Take a cab to your uncle's house, and back.'

I stood on tiptoe and kissed him quickly on the cheek. 'Thank you. We must come back immediately. I feel there is no time to waste.'

Leo sighed. 'Very well, despite the fact that the fog will probably reach above my head by the time we do. I do not think that what you suggest will make any difference, but I stand by you.'

I kissed him again. He did not object.

'Ritual can be a powerful thing,' he said. 'Perhaps carrying out this one will have the desired psychological effect that will enable you to come to terms with what we have seen.'

'I will prove you wrong. I must.'

'That remains to be seen—but it may help me, too. It will take time, as we must run through the entire range of tones the generator can produce, one by one, until, as you think, we find the one which removes impurity and thereby the fog.'

I shook my head. 'No. I have an idea where to begin. What is the gematria of *red heifer*? That is the note that we must generate. That is the song. That is the sound of gematria.'

Leo pulled the note with the letters I had copied from his pocket. He ran his finger along the letters, muttering numbers. He looked up.

'The gematria is three hundred and forty-one.'

Count to One Hundred

I returned to the house, to make protective masks for myself and Leo. People already resorted to wrapping scarves around their faced but once removed, the scarf was fog-stained yellow inside and out. Better defence was essential.

I opened the front door wide enough to peep into the hall. From the absence of boots, coats and umbrellas, I deduced Uncle Jacob, Aunt Emily, and May were still away from the house. I required a sheet and Betty the maid's cleaning paste. I must be speedy, and silent.

I crept into the scullery. If Cook or Betty were there, or worse still Nurse Wilkins, I would have to tell them I had come to get a drink of water, or some similar tale, and wait until they had gone. This would delay everything. Leo would be waiting for me and the weather might have worsened. In my mind's eye he stood at the top of the cellar steps, rainwater dripping from his hat and, worse, falling onto the tone generator. I must make the masks soon. If our work was not completed before nightfall, the fog would surely be too strong, and it would have seeped out of the cellar and up through the ground. I looked at my wristlet watch. We had some three hours at our disposal. Would that be enough time?

The scullery was empty of people. The jar where Betty

kept the paste stood half full, next to the range. I snatched it, and a knife lying next to the sink, and inched back out to the hall and upstairs. I reached out to open the linen cupboard.

'Euphemia, is that you?' Mother called from her bedroom. I held the jar and the knife behind my back and peered around her door.

She lay on her bed. 'Where have you been? You were not at luncheon.'

Lying to her did not come easily. I paused, hoping it was not for too long. The words tumbled out. 'Leo and I... went to a café... for tea and cakes.' Perhaps her tiredness would enable this to slip past her, undetected. If not, she would deploy her Holmesian questioning and soon have the truth from me. And if Leo did not believe me, how could she?

She raised her eyebrows. 'For lunch? I hope you will live better than that, once you're married.'

'Certainly!' I said, with a forced laugh. 'Leo is an excellent cook. Actually, I've just returned for a book I promised to lend him. I'm invited to Mrs Lazarus's house for afternoon tea.'

'I hope that will be enjoyable.' Mother yawned. 'You will have had a surfeit of tea today. Now, if you'll excuse me, I wish to sleep until Nurse comes in to clear my chest. Postural drainage and percussion, she calls it. So helpful, but so strenuous. Please shut the door behind you.' She closed her eyes.

I left her and entered my bedroom where I placed the jar and the knife on the floor and slunk down the landing to the linen cupboard. Its door squeaked open. I found an old single sheet that had been put sides-to-middle. Less likely to be missed, and at least I would not be ruining one of the better ones. On the middle shelf were pillowcases, and on the lowest, summer curtains and greyed old lace ones.

Footsteps on the stairs. Nurse Wilkins. I shut the cupboard and dashed back into my room with the sheet. I paused, holding my breath. Mother's bedroom door opened and shut. I waited until I heard Mother coughing, ripped a strip about a foot long from the top of the sheet, which I spread across the floor. I knelt and, using the knife, smeared Betty's paste across a six-inch area of the sheet and folded it over. I picked it up and held it over my nose and mouth. I could not breathe.

I sat back on my heels. What was it about the paste that made the fog stains disappear? There must be more to it than any abrasive property since scrubbing did not appear to be part of the cleaning process. Could I make the paste thinner? With water? Must I return to the scullery? I picked up the jug from my washstand—there were a few inches of that morning's supply left. This, I poured little by little into the jar, stirring as I went, until I had produced a liquid thin enough to soak into another strip of sheet.

I removed the strip and folded it into a pad. I held it to my face. I managed to inhale and exhale through it, but it had to be held with one hand. I must find a way of securing it. I laid it on the floor, opened the door a few inches and looked onto the landing. Nurse must still be with Mother. Back to the linen cupboard. I took out one of the lace curtains and rushed back to my room.

A strip of lace curtain wrapped around the soaked pad, tied round the back of the head, left both hands free.

Would the voice be audible through it? There was no way to test it. I made a second lace-wrapped pad for Leo.

As I looked around for something, preferably waterproof, in which to carry the pads, the front door slammed, footsteps pounded up the stairs and May burst into my room without knocking.

'Oh, hullo Euphemia! You're back,' she said.

'So it seems.' I tried to stand between her and the mess on the floor.

She pushed past me. 'What's that you've been doing with all those bits of material and lace?' She held a finger to my lips. 'No—don't tell me—you've been trying to make a wedding dress and a veil. Couldn't you find better material?'

I brushed her hand aside. 'You guess correctly, but I was merely practising.'

May giggled. 'Well, this is the first time you've expressed any interest in needlecraft. I must say, Leo is having a good influence. But what's that smeared all over your face? It's on the linoleum too. And my hand.' She pulled a tiny lace handkerchief from her cuff and wiped her finger.

I lowered my voice. 'Well, it's a secret, so don't tell anyone. You won't, will you?'

She shook her head, pushed the handkerchief back inside her sleeve, and drew closer. 'I like secrets. Just you and I will know.'

'Well.' I looked right and left. 'Good, there's nobody around to hear. I'm making a new cleansing poultice for the face. I don't want anyone to know about it till I see if it works.' I tied one of the pads across my face. 'Do you see? Can you hear me properly?'

'Oh yes! Do you know, you could pull the veil up over your eyes, if you wanted to soothe them too. I see you've made one for me!' She reached down towards the second mask.

I clutched her arm. 'Don't take it yet. I must see how it works overnight. You wouldn't want to use it if it irritated the skin. What would you do then, with your face covered in blemishes?'

She threw up her hands. 'I'd die, that's what I'd do. Anyway, the secret of your experiment is safe with me. Do let me know what happens. Such poultices can work very well.'

'It not only can, but must,' I said.

She left the room and I heard her go downstairs.

I tore off another piece of sheet, laid it in the bottom of my Gladstone bag, placing the masks on top. I pushed the remains of the sheet and the curtain, along with the jar, into the bottom of my wardrobe, picked up the bag and tiptoed downstairs. Any moment now, Aunt Emily would burst out of the parlour demanding to know about the mess I had made turning my bedroom into a laboratory.

I snatched my coat and ran outside, not wishing to delay leaving the house even by the few seconds donning it would take. I rushed down the street in search of a cab. One stopped outside the end house, and I waved, dashing towards it. The driver waited, and I clambered inside, flopped into the seat, and drew breath.

We clattered past people going about their business, as though it were any ordinary Saturday afternoon. Carts and carriages passed us. A woman trudged along carrying a wicker basket brimming with vegetables. A young man strolled arm in arm with an elderly woman. People entered and left shops. All oblivious of the task facing me and Leo. Supposing I pushed my head outside and shouted that we were to eliminate the fog? What would be the result? A one-way ticket to Colney Hatch?

I stood at the entrance to Tanyard Lane. Leo was nowhere to be seen. I moved down the alley, but he was not there either. What should I do? I stood by the steps leading to the cellar door. We had agreed to come back at once. Surely, given the time it had taken for me to create the face pads, he should have been here first.

I returned to the top of the alley, where it met the street and looked around. People made their way along the pavement, but Leo was not among them. I looked at my watch and paced. I would not check the time again till I reached the next turning.

Had only five minutes passed? If I counted to a hundred, I would allow myself to look at the time again. Ten, twenty… it must have stopped. I shook it, held it to my ear: still ticking. Carriages rattled past. If I saw three black horses, then Leo would come. One… two… a woman, head covered by a shawl, stopped, and asked whether I was lost. I told her I was in no need of help and set off down the alley once more. What could have detained Leo? He had said he was unconvinced, but that he would take part. Had he reconsidered? Should I find my way to his house? But supposing I passed him on his way here, and did not even know?

I stood at the top of the steps. If there were an even number of them, Leo would come. I shook my head. How could one have any effect on the other? I must stop this superstitious nonsense. How many steps were there?

As I looked down, a regular clattering, such as might be made by wheels banging across cobblestones, came from behind me. Any moment a shout would come, accusing me of trespassing. I tried to think of an excuse for why I should be there. None came.

Heart pounding, I turned. It was Leo, pushing a small wheelbarrow containing a bulky object covered by a sack.

I dashed to meet him. 'Where have you been? I thought you had changed your mind.'

Leo stopped pushing the barrow and fanned himself with his hat. 'I do apologise, but I had extreme difficulty finding a cab driver who would agree to transport my machine as well as me.'

I peered under the sack. The machine's glass bell-like sound enhancement devices appeared intact, and he had remembered the dry cell. 'You tested this, I trust?'

'Not to have done so would have been most unscientific. Fortunately, Aunt Matilda was away from the house so I received no complaints about the noise, as she would have called it. And the gardener will not need the barrow today.'

'Move up,' I said, grasping one of the handles of the barrow. Together we pushed it to the end of the alley.

'Now I must carry it down the steps.'

'No, *we* must. I will brook no suggestion that as a woman, I am not fit for the work.'

'Very well, but please be careful. I would not want you to damage your back.'

'I won't. Now let's get on.' I grasped one edge of the base of the machine, Leo took the other and we lifted it off the barrow. We inched our way sideways down the steps. At the bottom we paused.

'It's even heavier than it looks. Let's put it down for a moment. I think we ought to retrieve the barrow before someone makes off with it. It'll help once we're inside. I'll let you do that.'

Leo ran up the steps two at a time and returned, wheeling the barrow down with a series of thuds. We placed the machine on it.

'I have made us masks, to protect us from the fog.' I pulled them out of my bag and gave one to Leo.

'What a curious object,' he said, touching the pad with a fingertip. 'What is this liquid it's soaked in?'

'Something our maid uses to remove stains left by soot and fog. I don't have time to talk about the detail. You will have to trust me.'

Leo held the pad over his nose and mouth. 'Like so?' Muffled, but audible.

'You must secure it by the pieces of lace curtain. Allow me.'

He turned around. I reached up and tied his mask on. 'Not too tight? It must not slip.'

'No, this is acceptable. Now I will tie yours.' He did so. 'Imagine—this might be looked upon as some outlandish betrothal process. We have tied each other's masks, therefore our souls are as one.'

'If only converting to Judaism were that simple.'

He frowned, above his mask. 'Do you regret your decision?'

'Of course not! Now, we must waste no more time. Let us enter. I hope the fog does not reach our eyes, but if it should do so, pulling the lace up may offer protection.'

Leo opened the door and we pushed the barrow into the cellar.

Three Stars

The air inside the cellar vibrated. The fog, which had been at the level of my waist when we left, now reached to my shoulders. It was as though I was caged in yellow fog. Wisps reached up and touched my mask. It did not penetrate it, but I recoiled.

Fog submerged the barrow and tone generator. How could we operate the machine? Even if we were to kneel on the floor, we would not be able to see.

'We must set up one of the tables the snatchers left and lift the machine onto it,' Leo said. He moved across the cellar, through the fog.

If I did not stay close enough to touch him, to feel something real, to feel love, the concentrated hatred pulsing from fog might swallow me. I hurried after. 'Let me help carry it,' I babbled. I gripped one end of the table, thick with fog-grime. 'Where should we put it?

'In the middle of the space. The sound will be transmitted in all directions.' His shaking hands belied his calm voice.

He grasped the opposite edge of the table and we hauled it to the centre, wading through the fog as though it were a filthy sea, and managed to stand the table upright. Any delay would make our work more difficult, if not impossible.

Trembling, I reached down through the fog to the barrow and grasped one side of the tone generator. Leo found the other side and we lifted it onto the table. I removed the sack.

The upright glass cylinder at the centre of the generator was filled with clear liquid. A copper cable as thick as my thumb ran from the top to a smaller box where the glass bell-shaped devices, which transmitted the sound, were mounted. Leo turned one of them to the ceiling, and the other to the floor.

He bent to retrieve the dry cell that provided the power, connecting it to two smaller cables coming from the generator and pressing a button. The glass bells glowed, and a tone rang from them.

'Middle C,' Leo said. '261.626 Cycles per second.'

'If it isn't three hundred and forty-one, I do not care,' I said. 'Please. We must be quick.'

He slid a lever at the side and the note rose in pitch, in the manner of someone playing a sliding whistle.

'This is 341 Cycles per second.'

The fog rippled but did not disperse. No patterns formed.

'Interesting,' Leo said. 'The note with this frequency is higher than E but lower than F. There is no note in between the two, at least not on a keyboard instrument. But this is such a note.'

I took him by the shoulders. 'This is no time for a lecture. It must work—there is nothing else. Can you make it louder?' My heart pounded.

Leo slid a lever on the side of the generator to its halfway point. The volume of the tone climbed. The ripples in the fog turned into waves, the peaks higher than before, the troughs lower.

'Take courage.' I heard Pearl's voice, in my memory. The fog was no less present, but my heart slowed.

'Louder!' I shouted, above the sound.

'I can only do this until the dry cell runs out of power, but…' Leo pushed the lever to the maximum point. The liquid in the cylinder bubbled and turned straw yellow.

The shuddering in the air grew, and the fog vibrated. On top of it a throb, like the pulse of a giant heart, set off a trembling through my body. My hands shook in step with the vibration.

The fog waves pulsed into jagged shapes in time with the throb. A flash of bright yellow light filled the cellar, lasting only one second. 'Don't switch the machine off!' I said, clinging to Leo's arm.

'I haven't,' he said. 'Look around.'

The fog had disappeared, leaving not a wisp.

Leo switched off the machine and disconnected the cell. We slid our masks down below our chins.

'The vibration the machine produced must have been the same as the fog's natural resonant frequency,' Leo said. 'Strong enough to abolish the impurity, break up the fog and disperse it.'

'No more need be done,' I said, taking his hand.

'Yes, our work is complete. You and I have done a wondrous thing.' He said, hopping from one leg to the other.

'Dance with me!' I shouted through my laughter, throwing my arms round his neck. I pulled him towards me, and we kissed. Eventually we broke apart, drawing in great gasps of air. I rested my head on his shoulder, eyes closed.

With a gasp, Leo recoiled, pointing behind me. I spun around. The fog was rising once more, not as tendrils but as a solid yellow curtain.

My mouth dried and my throat closed, as I tried to scream. I forced out words. 'We have failed.'

With shaking hands, we replaced our masks. The fog inched towards us. We might be able to run from the cellar before it reached us, but it would never stop its inexorable progress. It would penetrate the walls and floor, spreading, always spreading. Now in London, but soon through the entire land. Now by night, but soon by day also, poisoning everything in its path. And nothing could stop its progress.

'Pheemie, I am sorry,' Leo said. 'Truly so. We tried our best. But I do not think that it is a lasting solution. Not without a permanent supply of power to the machine so that it can run constantly.'

'All my ideas, all those dreams of numbers—it was merely a delusion,' I sobbed, tears running inside my mask. 'Pearl speaking—all of it—I must have been deranged to have imagined such a thing.'

He put an arm round my shoulders. 'It was all real and true. But it was not enough.'

I wiped my eyes on the netting of my mask, pulled away from him and turned to the generator, sliding levers, and turning knobs on the machine, as though that might make it spring into life.

'Leave it,' Leo said. 'You will break it. Although, I do not suppose that would matter.'

'There must be something else we can do.'

The fog rose in a dense, yellow layer, now reaching our knees. 'There is.' Leo clutched my arm. 'Run!'

I pulled away. 'No. We must try again.' I grasped the cell and reconnected it. I switched the generator on. The same tone came from the glass bells.

'More power!' I shouted. I turned every dial to maximum, slid every lever as far as it would go. I turned the glass bells so that they faced the fog. Beyond the note produced, a loud hum began, setting off throbs through the floor. The liquid in the cylinder in the machine turned dark brown. The solid wall of fog writhed and convulsed. The humming grew ever louder. Light blazed from the glass bells, brighter than the midday sun at the height of summer. I screwed up my eyes and pulled my mask up to cover them, as though that might help against a brightness that passed through closed eyelids. The vibration of the hum shook me to my bones. The air itself pulsated.

'Stand back!' Leo shouted.

I opened my eyes and jumped, as the glass cylinder and the two bell-shaped glass devices shattered, showering the liquid contents of the cylinder and broken glass over where we had just been standing. The light vanished. The fog was no more. Neither was the tone generator.

I blinked at non-existent spots as, in silence, we lifted the remains of the frequency mechanistic generator onto the barrow. The thick cable, which had connected the glass bells to the cylinder, had burnt through. We pushed the barrow outside into the early evening air and carried it up the steps, with its contents. We paused at the top. I glanced back at the cellar. No fog emerged.

'Leo, *now* is the time for dancing.'

'And for music!' He broke into singing, 'No more fog, no more impurity' to the tune of some operatic aria. Not

Wagner, I trusted.

'The Soldiers' Chorus, from Faust.' He stopped and drew breath.

I looked down at the barrow and its mangled contents. 'I'm so sorry, Leo. Your wonderful machine.'

'When I made it as an entertainment, a toy, I could not have imagined it would have such a destiny. But—perhaps we have abolished the impurity and its symbol, the fog.'

I took his grimy hand. 'Can the machine be repaired? If anyone could do so, it would be you.'

He shook his head. 'I doubt it. I might be able to construct another one if required, which I hope it will not be.'

'The proof of this will become clear once it grows completely dark,' I said. 'If the fog does not come, then we have won. I imagine the sun has set already so we won't have long to wait.'

Leo took the handles of the barrow and we walked until we found a small open space where we sat on a bench.

'In the Jewish tradition day begins at sundown, not midnight,' he said. 'According to the Talmud, three medium-sized stars together in the sky signify nightfall.'

'Which stars? I am not sure I would recognise them. Perhaps to be certain, we need to wait for night.' I pulled my coat tighter.

Leo put his arm around my shoulder. 'We need not. It's any three stars, or even planets, it does not matter which. It's just a way of measuring darkness.' He looked at his pocket watch. 'It is ten minutes past four. The sun must surely have set. We should not have too long to wait.' He wiped his fingers on his soiled mask and pushed that into his jacket pocket. 'I must remember not to mistake this for my handkerchief.'

I smeared some of the liquid from my mask onto the back of my hand, stained yellow from the last rally of the fog, and scraped at it with a fingernail. This left a track of clear skin. I rubbed at it with the mask. The liquid from the mask wiped away, taking the stains with it. I replaced it in my bag.

I rested my head on his shoulder and we sat in silence.

A star appeared in the sky, low and bright.

Leo pointed at it. 'That's Venus. How appropriate for us, the goddess of love.'

I nudged him. 'You and your nonsense. That star always appears first.'

'Not always. And, it is a planet, but that doesn't matter. We only need see two more.'

The moon rose, less than half full but not yet a crescent. 'Two!'

'The moon doesn't count.'

'But it's a kind of planet. Doesn't it count if it's less than full?'

'Not even when it's gibbous. Do you know, the word gibbous was first used in the 14th century and comes from the Latin word *gibbosus*, which means humpbacked.'

'Only you would think of that, at such a time. And I am so lucky that you're mine.'

A yellow star appeared overhead, followed by another glowing red. I looked around us, searching for the familiar yellow wisps emerging from the ground. None came. 'Leo, I hope I don't speak prematurely, but there is no fog.'

'It is almost unbelievable. After so long, coming night after night. Now, nothing.'

'And you and I have done this, together. Whatever the future should bring, it will always be ours.'

He took me in his arms, and we kissed. We separated and he took my hand. 'We must write about the mathematics of this for our research proposal. We must also include a diagram of a mask plus the details of their construction, and their efficacy.'

'Yes. We will not seek fame, but our work should not be lost. Supposing it should be needed again?' I looked around again, as though expecting the fog to loom behind me.

'Let's hope it will never be needed.' Leo stood and pulled me to my feet. 'It is time to go. First, I need to find another cabman who will be prepared to transport the barrow.'

I brushed the back of my skirt. 'I will come with you. Then you can escort me home. But only if you come inside the house and give your regards to whoever is there.' This man, his unique fusing of mathematics and music, is mine. Every inch of him. Would it be unseemly to declare so out loud to whoever I found? Would I care if it were?

'As though I would expect you to travel alone,' said Leo. 'It will give us a few moments longer together. Visit me tomorrow and we will draft our research proposal. Then we will return to Oxford the day after and submit it to Milton.'

We left the park and headed for the main road. A cab rattled towards us. Leo flagged it down and the driver not only agreed to take the barrow but climbed down from his high seat to help fit it inside. Leo gave him my address. 'Right you are, sir. Fog's late!' the driver said.

'Indeed!' Leo said, smiling at me. I grinned in return

and held his arm.

'It is as though some higher power smiled upon us,' Leo said.

I didn't believe that, and surely, he would not expect me to. Was I to pretend I did? I made no reply. We stepped in, sat, and the cab moved away.

I grasped Leo's hand. 'We did it. We truly did.'

'Together. It is our child. Our first.' His face reddened. 'Pardon me—I've spoken out of turn.'

I patted his hand. 'You have not. But I rather think that's a discussion for another time.'

'Yes—next comes your conversion.'

I did not wish to think about that, nor what I must do to achieve it, but rather I wanted to turn over in my mind the work we had already done that day. I did not reply, and leaned well back in my seat, capable of little else than yawning.

'We must arrange to meet the rabbi, sooner rather than later,' Leo said. 'I imagine Aunt Matilda knows people who can help with that.'

'Let's consider our research proposal first.'

We sat in silence. The realisation washed over me that nothing would be the same for me again.

Two More Days

By the time the clock on the church across the square chimed seven, I conceded I would be unable to sleep. I sat up in bed, yawning, eyes gritty, as the maid clattered in to fill my washstand jug with hot water.

I had heard each hour chime, and each hour I had arisen from my bed to look through the window, in the general direction of where I thought Leo's house might be, to determine whether the fog had returned. The view across the sky had remained clear all night. Had Leo also spent a similarly sleepless time?

Shivering and alone, I climbed out of bed onto the former living room rug, relegated to my bedroom. I washed, dressed and stepped onto the landing as Nurse Wilkins came up the stairs with a cup of tea for Mother.

'I will take that in.' I took the cup.

'Very well,' she said, as though reluctantly granting me permission. 'I shall return in half an hour to administer Mrs Thorniwork's medicines.'

Mother's eyes were closed. I placed the cup on her bedside table and crept towards the door. She called good morning. I turned. 'I'm sorry I woke you up.'

'You did not—I was merely resting my eyes. Now, I would like to sit up.' I moved towards her bed. 'No, let me do it. I really believe I could hoist myself up without aid.'

She achieved it and lay back on her pillow. 'I fell asleep without nurse's sleeping draught, for once. I feel as though I have slept for a week.' She coughed.

'Allow me to pass you your cup, at least.'

'Thank you.' She took a sip. 'If it does not rain, I believe I might ask Nurse to take me to the gardens, for a change of scenery.'

'I will do it.'

'But have you no plans for today?'

'Well, yes, Leo and I are to rewrite our research proposals, then resubmit them when we return to Oxford. But I can take you when I am back from his house.'

'Then, it will be dark. Another time.'

'May I sit with you until Nurse ejects me?'

Mother raised her eyebrows. 'Of course, but why this sudden interest in me?'

I sat, twiddling my fingers. 'I feel a need for company and you're my mother. Is that not reason enough?'

We sat in silence. I picked up a book lying on Mother's bedside cabinet. It seemed to be a play, called *Tosca—an opera in three acts*. 'It says "Enter Angelotti in prison garb, harassed, dishevelled, panic-stricken, well-nigh breathless with fear and hurry",' I said. 'Do not let Nurse see this. She might consider it too exciting for you.'

'You are interested in Puccini? This is an unexpected turn of events.'

'I don't really know his work, but Leo once sang something about my hand being cold.'

'Ah yes.' Mother sang a few notes of the same song but was overcome by wheezing.

I leaned her forward and patted her back. 'Oh dear— Nurse will hear. I don't want her twisting her face up, giving me one of her looks. Not that you can really tell.'

'Do not be unkind, Euphemia. She takes good care of me.'

'And so she should, for the money Uncle Jacob pays her. Which reminds me—what of his investments?'

'I believe he is considering withdrawing his funds from the scheme in which they're currently invested.'

'Our funds, you mean.'

'Very well, our funds. He takes the view that the financial future lies in medicines.'

'Yes—he tried to persuade Leo to invest in some purported treatment for consumption.'

Mother took my hand. 'Leopold again.'

'Yes—I don't care what we say about him, as long as we talk about him.'

'My dear girl. I remember that sentiment. But,' Mother turned towards me and, took my other hand and kissed them both, 'Are you certain that you are doing what is right for you?'

I pulled my hands back. 'Of course, I am certain.' Wasn't I? 'Why do you ask?'

'You are to be a proselyte. How can you, as an atheist, make yourself believe? Have you had some divine flash of inspiration?'

I waved my hand. 'Is that what concerns you? Then it needn't, I wouldn't have to believe in Judaism, it's only that I need to know more about it. What's behind it, intellectually. Scientifically.'

'Are you sure that is correct? I have heard that Judaism does not actively seek proselytes, but surely you have to believe in God, at the very least.'

'I believe that it will be like reading theology at

university. One would not have to believe in the religions one studied.'

'I hope you are right. I do not think you would be able to live a life of pretence and lies.'

Nurse knocked at the door and entered, carrying a tray bearing different sized brown glass bottles. I went downstairs to find something to eat and decided to boil an egg. I tried to remember as best I could what Leo showed me, and discovered Betty's cleaning paste was most efficacious at removing stains left by a pan that has boiled dry, and an exploding egg. I seized my coat and left for Leo's house, before complaints about the smell of burning began.

I arrived at Matilda's house at about nine o'clock. Leo answered the door, suppressing a yawn. 'I do apologise, but I did not sleep well. I kept a watch for the fog.'

'I too, albeit unintentionally, but there was none.'

As soon as I stepped inside, he pulled me into his arms, and we kissed. He smelled of soap. We separated and, grasping my hand, he pulled me along the hall towards the dining room.

'Quickly! My aunt has gone out.' He opened the door and ushered me inside. 'In here, before she comes back.'

I raised my eyebrows. 'I thought that she might be out, but I am here to work.'

His face reddened. 'So am I. It isn't that we can't work when she is here, but I want us to get as much done as possible before she returns. She is bound to find an infinite number of reasons to come in and disturb us. I think she fears we might behave in an unseemly manner.'

I sat at the table in the centre of the room. 'Really?

Would she feel the same if I were of your faith?' My voice grew louder. 'Perhaps she feels you would use me for some sort of practice, before you reject me for a genuine Jewish woman.'

Leo took a step back. 'That is an outrageous slur. I should have thought better of you. I meant no insult. It's just her old-fashioned etiquette, and faith has nothing to do with it. She would behave the same if any bachelor and spinster were alone together—within a certain age range, of which I am unclear.'

I stood and kissed him. 'I am so sorry. But this is all so new to me. Let us begin work. We need to complete the proposal today if we are to return to Oxford tomorrow.'

I sat again, and Leo joined me. 'Now,' I said. 'We need to include material on the Fourier Transform. What was it that Euler said? We should use that as a starting point.'

'*Would Aunt Matilda feel the same if you were of my faith*, you asked,' Leo said. 'It's *our* faith, now.'

'I don't think that's what Euler said. Now let's not get distracted.' We set to work.

The doorbell rang. Leo rose. 'I must attend to it. The maid is visiting her sick mother, again.'

He returned. 'The postman, with a package for my aunt.'

He sat again, and we tried to remember what we had been writing. We had covered another page with notes, when there was a knock at the front door.

I rose. 'Let me go,' I said.

'Oh no, I couldn't. You are a guest. Also, you're not the lady of the house.'

I put my hands on my hips. 'Once I am the lady of our house, we will have a servant whose sole role is to answer the door and do anything that arises from that.'

Leo smiled, and left the room again.

He returned and, sighing, took his seat. 'The fish man.' He picked up the paper we had been writing on.

I pointed to a paragraph he had scribbled. 'I think we have already said that earlier, and more eloquently, as well.'

Leo set his mouth into a line, seized his pen, and scratched out the paragraph.

'Be careful,' I said, 'you've made a hole in the paper...' My words died away under the force of Leo's frown.

He read through the paper, muttering as he went. After some time, he paused. 'I think we have a type of skeleton. Now to put flesh on it.'

We examined the bones that were the outline paper.

'This will make good reading,' Leo said, raking his fingers through his hair so it resembled a curly halo. 'Now, I consider that it would be arresting to the reader if we were to start by comparing the Fourier Transform with eating a cake and thereby being able to determine its recipe—'

The front door opened, closed, and Matilda called Leo's name from the hall. He said a word I had not heard anyone of his station say before and hurled his pen down on the table, splashing ink over its top.

'I beg your pardon?' Matilda put her head round the door and blinked at me. 'Oh, Euphemia. I didn't realise that you were here.'

It would not only be stating the obvious, but probably considered impolite to reply that yes, I was, so I wished her good morning.

'We have a lot of work to complete, Aunt, before we

return to Oxford tomorrow morning,' Leo said, dabbing at the ink with his handkerchief.

Matilda frowned. 'Must you return tomorrow? I have just visited Rabbi Kenig. He is holding one of his evening discussions for those wishing to convert, the day after tomorrow. I told him that you would both be pleased to attend.'

My throat tightened. 'But we cannot go to Oxford and then return here, there would not be time,' I said. 'If the Rabbi holds such meetings regularly, perhaps we could join the next one.'

Matilda drew herself up to her full height, somewhere near my shoulder. 'Oh, I don't think Leopold would want to do *that*, dear,' she said. 'It would be most impolite to decline the invitation. What sort of impression would it give?'

'Really, Aunt,' Leo said, through gritted teeth, 'you might have consulted us before accepting on our behalf. But still, we have enough time before the submission date for our paper that delaying our return will not cause problems.'

My mouth felt dry. 'I think we also have time for a cup of tea.'

'Oh, how unfortunate,' Matilda said. 'The maid is not here.'

'Very well,' I said. 'I shall make it myself.' I rose and headed for the kitchen.

Leo followed me inside and shut the door. 'I need to show you where the tea and the rest of the components are.'

I clenched my fists and leaned my forehead against the wall. 'I cannot believe you agreed to delay our return. And without discussing it with me.'

He put his hand on my shoulder. 'We do not want to get a reputation of being... ah... difficult. It might make the conversion process harder.'

I shook off his hand. 'Why should it?' I snapped.

'Do turn around,' Leo said. 'I would rather talk to your face than the back of your head.'

I complied.

'I am not saying it would, but I just do not know. I am sure, though, that we cannot afford to make things any harder than they might already be.'

'What do you mean? Do you doubt my ability? I am as capable of rigorous study as any would-be proselyte.'

'More so. However, there must be more to it than that.'

'Well, we will find out in two days, won't we? Thanks to you.' I turned from him and opened cupboard after cupboard, until I found three cups. 'Find a tray, will you? And where's the kettle?'

'I'll boil the water, provided you won't think I doubt your ability.'

I took his hand. 'I'm sorry, Leo. I do love you; you know that. It's just I don't want to lose momentum in our work. I want us to submit the proposal as soon as we can. I am impatient to see Prof Milton's reaction.'

'I also want to submit, but this delay could be a blessing in disguise. It will provide another night to see whether the fog returns.'

I sighed, but I could see the sense in what he said. 'Very well. But we must return to Oxford on the morning after we have visited the rabbi.'

After tea was made and drunk, we plunged further, without interruption, into the mathematical aspects of sound and music until drowsiness overtook us at around four. We agreed to stop, and that I would return the following morning to polish the section on the masks and the paste, which would put the finishing touches to our proposal.

When I awoke the next day, the air was clear. I left the house and walked to catch the omnibus to Leo's house, deciding to take a route through the park. Mist accumulated on the grass, but it was only a normal London November morning vapour and by the time I reached the exit, the sun had risen enough to chase it away.

Seventy Volumes

A maid showed us into Rabbi Kenig's drawing room, where we were to wait for the rabbi to join us. The room had a polished wooden floor, and a roaring fire overheated the place. Charcoal drawings of desert scenes and ancient buildings, plus a portrait of Her Majesty, hung on the walls. A bookcase covered the wall facing the door. A grand piano stood in one corner. Would we be required to sing?

Various ill-matched dark wooden chairs were set out in a small horse-shoe shape, some with books resting on the seats A woman about my age sat in one, next to a man who sat drumming his fingers on the arms of his chair.

'Good evening. We are Euphemia Thorniwork, and Leopold Lazarus,' Leo said. 'How do you do?'

'Very well, thank you,' the woman replied. 'I'm Edith Blanchflower. I'm converting. This is my fiancé, Reginald Offendort. You must be new.'

'Yes,' I said. 'I don't know what to expect—does Reginald always have to attend?'

'For the first few months, yes,' she said.

I looked at Leo and raised my eyebrows.

He touched my hand. 'I will go anywhere if it is with you.'

I felt my face grow warm and turned away to examine

the books on the shelves. It would be too much to hope that they included a mathematical text that I could discuss with the rabbi, but perhaps he liked Conan Doyle, as Mother did, and we could converse about that. As far as I could tell from their spines, all the books appeared to be Hebrew.

'Is this some sort of encyclopaedia?' I whispered to Leo, pointing at two shelves packed with identical-looking black leather-bound tomes.

'They're the Babylonian Talmud,' he said. 'This edition evidently comprises seventy volumes.'

'I feel extremely ignorant.'

'You are not, don't worry.' Leo lowered his voice. 'And I'll wager you know more about ritual impurity than Rabbi Kenig does.'

I clutched his hand. 'We will not have to talk about that, surely.'

Before Leo could reply, the door opened. I jumped back from the bookcase as though caught in some illicit act. Rabbi Kenig entered. He was aged around fifty, with dark hair and long sideboards, but was otherwise clean shaven. He wore a black skull cap. Leo rummaged in his pocket, pulling out handkerchief after handkerchief like a stage magician, until to my surprise he found a skullcap of his own, made of creased dark blue velvet, which he placed on the back of his own head.

The Rabbi took his place on a low chair, covered in tapestry, set at the head of the others. 'Mr Lazarus I already know. And this must be Miss Thorniwork,' he said. We nodded. 'Sit down, please.'

Leo and I picked up the books on our seats and did as requested. I opened the book that had been on my chair:

The Authorised Daily Prayer Book of the United Hebrew Congregations of the British Empire. It had Hebrew text on each right-hand page, with what I supposed must be an English translation on the left. It opened at the opposite end from an English one.

Kenig cleared his throat. 'Welcome, proselytes and companions. "Proselyte" comes from the Greek translation of the Hebrew word "ger" which itself means "one who has arrived." Miss Thorniwork, this *siddur* is for you. I assume Mr Lazarus already has his own.'

What was he going to give me? 'Thank you,' I said, looking at Leo.

'It's that.' He leaned across and touched the book I was holding.

'This is our daily and Sabbath prayer book, Miss Thorniwork,' Kenig said. 'We call it the *siddur*, which has the same root as the Hebrew word for order. Here is a list of other suggested reading material.' He handed me a piece of paper. I slipped it and the book into my bag.

'Now, let us begin,' he said. 'Mr Offendort and Miss Blanchflower, I am aware that you have already heard this, but revision is never a bad thing. I should like the four of you to travel together along the road, so to speak.'

Reginald smirked and Edith simpered.

Kenig continued. 'The word "Israel," referring to the Jewish people, means someone who wrestles with God. Judaism is not a religion whose members go door-to-door seeking converts, or who stop people in public places seeking to impress on them the need to become Jewish. It is, in contrast, a religion that is glad to provide instruction about itself to all who seek knowledge. It means learning about Jewish culture, religion, and history. All of these and more are the strands of Jewish existence. Learning is central to Jewish life.'

I relaxed as much as my chair would allow. Seeking knowledge—that was as I had expected. Mother need not worry.

Kenig raised a cautionary finger. 'But conversion entails a commitment to a fully observant and practising Jewish way of life. Changing one's faith, in particular when it involves taking on the stringent standards of Jewish observance, is a huge undertaking. It should not be pursued because of some idealised notion of what it means to be a Jew or as a gesture of personal sacrifice for the sake of love.'

I was doing it for the sake of love, but it would be no sacrifice. I nodded.

'There should be no ulterior motive other than the genuine desire to join the Jewish people and its destiny. Do you know, a man once asked about conversion, because he thought becoming Jewish would give him better connections in the banking business? The Jewish people welcomes sincere converts. But—'

Unable to retrain myself any longer, I cleared my throat. 'Rabbi Kenig?' Leo glared at me.

Kenig frowned. 'Yes, Miss Thorniwork?'

'I apologise for the interruption,' I said, 'but how long does conversion usually take?'

'A minimum of two years of study and living a Jewish life is generally recommended, though individual circumstances may vary,' Kenig said.

The discussion, more like a lecture or tutorial since Kenig did most of the talking, turned to an outline of the requirements of the Sabbath. In addition to studying from books, it would be important to experience Sabbath meals with observant families and to watch how food was prepared.

'Can I join in your Sabbath meal, in your house?' I whispered in Leo's ear.

'I do not think ours is—'

Kenig hushed Leo and put his finger across his lips. If I must attend the house of strangers, Leo must come with me.

While all this was sinking in, Kenig told us to familiarise ourselves with the Jewish calendar, about which festivals and fasts fell when. The months were lunar, with leap months added to keep within the solar year. There was a nineteen-year cycle for that, plus a seven-year cycle to determine the Sabbatical years during which all land in Palestine must remain unworked, plus a fifty-year cycle to determine the Jubilees. There was also a twenty-eight-year cycle involving some other aspect, I forgot which. I smiled to myself and considered how I might combine all these cycles into a single equation.

After about an hour's further discussion, Kenig stood. 'Before we finish, I would like to discuss a text with Mr Offendort and Mr Lazarus.' He took Leo and Reginald into the parlour, leaving me alone with Edith. I leafed through the daily prayer book and found the marriage service. It appeared that the bride did not have a speaking part and that the groom had to break a glass at the end. Would Leo have to throw his into a fireplace, as though he were a Russian?

'I wonder if we can expect tea?' Edith said. 'Kenig gave us a reasonable cup last time. I expect he forgot about it today, absorbed as he was in study. On the other hand, I have heard that a rabbi is meant to try to dissuade a convert, so who knows?'

Perhaps that was why he had emphasised the amount of study required. If so, that held no fear for me. 'I suppose it would depend on what sort of tea it was,' I said. 'Some blends might dissuade you if you had to drink them,' I said, remembering the lapsang tea at Madam Galdora's, with all the nonsense that had happened with the tealeaves.

'True,' Edith said. 'I'm glad you're here, it'll be good to have a bit of company. Would-be converts don't come along very often, not that I'm surprised.'

'You said you started your conversion in September,' I said. 'Have you attended many of these meetings?'

'Yes, I've endured about six of these.' She got up and sat next to me in the chair Leo had vacated.

'What do you mean, endured?' I said. 'Do you find it difficult to grasp the subject matter? To discard the faith in which you were raised?'

She waved a hand. 'What, that wishy-washy Anglicanism? I never gave it much thought and I never went to church. And as for this, I'm not particularly involved, especially with all this God stuff. Religion really isn't a thing I can be doing with. I've been blessed with a good memory, that's all. It'll get me through the final meeting with the Rabbinic Court.'

'But how are you making yourself believe in Judaism? Or is it just happening by itself?'

She raised her eyebrows. 'My dear Euphemia, you don't think I believe it, do you? I'm doing this for Reggie. His family aren't very observant. He's no more religious than I am, except for wanting his children to be Jewish, "not

294

wanting to break 4000 years' worth of tradition", you know.'

'Leopold also wants Jewish children.'

'That seems to be the last thing they cling to. Even if they don't know much about the religious stuff, they do know that,' she said with a nod. 'The first time we came here, Reggie was terrified that Rabbi K would ask *him* questions. I'll keep whatever requirements he wants us to, at home. Some of the festivals are rather nice, but the services are so long.'

'How long is long?' I tried to remember the last time I had been in a church but could not.

'Well, on the Sabbath—that's Saturday—the service goes on for about four hours, only the women tend to drift in part way through. But on the Day of Atonement—I started in September, just before it—we were in the synagogue all day. Of course, some people—the ones who are born to it, only attend on that day. Once a year!'

'Once a year should be manageable.'

She shook her head. 'Oh no, *we* have to outdo them, at least while we're converting. You'll have to attend regular services every week, on Saturday mornings at least.'

I looked at my watch. Surely Kenig had finished whatever he was doing with the men?

'I will get the first train from Oxford.' I hoped there would be one suitably early on a Saturday.

She gasped. 'You can't do that! Didn't you hear what Kenig said? On the Sabbath you're not allowed to do any kind of work, which for some reason includes travelling by any artificial means. You will have to walk.'

I would have to find a synagogue in Oxford. 'But you'll be in charge of your children's Jewish education,' I said.

'How will that be for you if you don't believe it?'

She shrugged. 'Who does? Just recite the words.'

I cast my eyes down, 'I'm not sure I can do that,' I quavered.

She raised her eyebrows. 'You love Leopold, don't you?' I nodded. 'Well then, of course you can.'

Not only can, but must, as Leo so often said.

Kenig, Leo, and Reginald returned, and the meeting ended. They were to be held every two weeks. Leo and I walked to the omnibus stop. Leo told me that Kenig had engaged him and Reginald in a detailed study of a text about marriage.

'I thought the meeting went well,' Leo said.

'Yes.'

'Kenig is an erudite man. And the other couple are not uncongenial. I trust you found something to talk to Miss Blanchflower about.'

'Yes.'

'She might keep a companionable eye on you. That would not be unhelpful.'

'No.'

Leo stopped and took my hand. 'Pheemie, is something the matter?'

I looked down at my feet and kicked at a pebble. 'No... just a slight headache. Also, I'm preoccupied with how Prof Milton will react to our proposal.'

'We will discover that very soon. He will be impressed, I am certain. Do you have doubts?' Leo said.

I gasped. 'Doubts?'

'Yes—that Milton will be impressed by the proposal.'

'Oh no—the mathematics and the uniqueness of it will amaze him.'

We waited, shivering. Our breath was visible in the night air, and no fog competed with it. Leo waved his arm. 'Look! You can see all around us. Soot covered buildings, filthy streets, everything. And people trudging along as though being able to see their way was a commonplace matter.'

'Yes.'

'Oh dear, more monosyllables. Your poor head. I hope we do not have to wait long for the omnibus.'

'Leo,' I said, 'Are there synagogues in Oxford?'

'I don't know—I've never noticed any. I always come back to London to Kenig's, for the few services I attend.'

'But if there aren't any in Oxford, what am I going to do? Edith Blanchflower said I would have to attend every Saturday and that I had to walk there. I don't want the whole process to fail before I've started.' How might I feel if it did?

Leo put his arm round my shoulder and hugged me. 'Don't worry. There must be a community there, or nearby. Perhaps they meet in each other's houses.'

The omnibus pulled up and we climbed inside. I sat in the only empty seat, between the window and an old man muttering to himself. Leo stood in the aisle, clutching onto a rail as the omnibus rattled over the cobbles.

We stopped, and the man next to me rose. Leo waved a woman, staggering along the aisle towards us, into the seat. She turned to the window, leaned across me, and waved to someone on the pavement. 'Not that long ago I wouldn't have been able to see our Elsie,' she said to me, her breath scented with methylated spirit.

'Or breathe,' I said, wafting my hand in front of my face.

The woman closed her eyes and seemed to fall at once into an open-mouthed sleep, lolling against me so that her head lay against my shoulder. I nudged her and she spluttered, opened her eyes, moved away about an inch, and fell back into her stupor. I recoiled from her and turned my head to gaze through the window, which afforded me a clear view of the buildings we passed. No fog. Leo and I had achieved this. It was our doing. If I were to tell anyone this, who would believe me? The mathematics must convince Milton. It must.

The omnibus slowed again, and the woman awoke with a methylated snort. She rose and swayed to the door.

Leo dropped into her place. 'How unsavoury. But never mind, we must love our neighbours. Did you know that's from Leviticus? Jesus took the idea from there.'

'Good for him,' I said. 'I hope he referenced it.' I closed my eyes. The omnibus proceeded along the road to Uncle Jacob's house. Tomorrow Leo and I would return to Oxford. But where was I headed? Would I arrive?

Thirty-nine Types of Work

Leo and I sat next to each other in an empty carriage, aboard the eight o'clock train to Oxford. Our proposal lay safely in my travelling bag, held flat inside the pages of a large copy of *The Book of Jewish Beliefs*. We would hand it to Professor Milton as soon as we arrived at Huxley.

'I hope Milton is there,' I said. 'He does not always attend his office on Saturdays—I am not certain my nerves will be able to withstand two days' additional delay. After we have handed in the proposal, we must discuss the detail of our research, on the assumption that he will support it.'

Leo laid his document case on the seat next to his. 'He can do no other! It confirms the ability of equations written on pieces of paper to know nature.'

I took a notebook and pencil from my bag and scribbled an outline for the work. Writing—that was something Jewish people were not supposed to do on a Saturday, on the Sabbath. So was riding in trains, as I had already discovered. Yet, only a few weeks ago Leo and I had travelled together from Oxford on a Friday evening, when the Sabbath began. He gazed through the window, where the sun was rising over the crowded buildings near the tracks.

'I've been looking at the *Jewish Belief* book,' I said. 'It tells me that there are thirty-nine types of work you can't do, including planting, threshing and winnowing. I've never seen you threshing or winnowing, but I'll wager you and Aunt Matilda don't keep all the requirements of the Jewish religion.'

'Well, no, we don't,' Leo said. 'Not all of them. For example,' he took his jacket lapel between finger and thumb, 'It is possible that this garment is made of a combination of wool and linen, in which case I should not wear it because such a mixture of fabrics is forbidden.'

'When—not on the Sabbath? Is that too considered to be work?'

'It applies all the time, but I do not know why. You might look it up.'

I took the *Book of Jewish Beliefs* from my bag, our proposal still inside, and turned to the back, but there was no index. I would have to plough through the lot (although ploughing was also a forbidden activity) before I found it, and there was so much else to be learned before the matter of tailoring. 'I am not surprised that conversion takes as long as it does. And all of this will be demanded of me. That is unfair. I will be more observant than you.'

Leo leaned back in his seat. 'Your point is well made. Religion, after all, is all about belief. One could ask why a person who believes in the Jewish religion isn't considered Jewish—even without the conversion?'

'I don't speak of belief, but rather of performing all the rituals. Why are those born to the faith who don't believe and don't keep any of the practices still considered Jews?'

Leo took my hand. 'What you need to understand is that Judaism is not only a religion. We are a people who have a shared history, who are bound together. Other religions are usually only concerned with belief and practice, whereas Jewishness does not go away due to lack of those. Converting is like being adopted into a family.'

'You haven't answered my question,' I began. The door to the corridor opened and a man entered the carriage and picked up a copy of the *Westminster Gazette* lying on the seat in the corner. He sat opposite us and opened the newspaper.

I slid the book, with our proposal still inside, back into my bag, nudged Leo with my elbow and nodded towards the front page of the paper. On the left, near to the corner, was a small heading: 'Extreme weather conditions found responsible for nightly London fog, now dissipated.'

'Stuff and nonsense.' Leo said.

'I beg your pardon?' the man lowered the paper.

'I apologise for disturbing you,' Leo said. 'I disagreed with the statement in that article. The one about the London fog.'

The man looked at the page. 'Weather!' he snorted. 'It has been a normal autumn and winter. And this has never happened before.'

'I quite agree,' I said. 'It is most unscientific.'

'It is certainly wrong,' the man said. He leaned towards us, looked to his right and left, and spoke in an undertone. 'I know what caused it.' I held my breath. Not the Jews, not that again. How did one get inured to discrimination? Could one? 'The fog was sent by God. To punish those who ply their trade,' he paused and leaned even further over, '*by night!*'

'Such as night soil collectors?' I said.

The man's face reddened. 'No, that is *not* what I meant. It is not a fit subject to discuss further, in the presence of a lady.'

He fell silent and returned to the newspaper. I glanced at the back of it, filled as it was with advertisements for patent medicines, support devices and invalid furniture. Leo shook his head and peered out of the window again. After some ten minutes, the train pulled into Didcot station. Our fellow passenger rose, pulled a pamphlet from his pocket, and handed it to Leo. 'You will find all you need to know within.' He raised his hat to me and left the carriage.

Through the window I saw him hurrying along the platform. Didcot—our journey was almost complete. My heart gave a jump. 'What did he give you?'

'I don't know. You read it if you like, I have no wish to do so. The man is a fool.'

'Why? Because his explanation of the fog is faith-based? How does that differ from what you, I mean we, are meant to believe?'

'Because *we* have demonstrated what caused the fog, and what abolishes it,' Leo said. 'Do you think the man would change his opinion if we told him? I doubt it.'

'No—how can you instil belief in a person, where there is none? Where there can be no proof, but faith alone?'

'But our abolition of the fog can be explained by mathematics and science. Unlike whatever this says.' Leo handed the booklet to me, frowning. It was *The Bible—our Guide to Money Problems*. I did not open it.

'Don't look so downcast,' I said, taking advantage of our now-empty carriage to kiss his cheek. 'I'm nervous too. Let's think about how we might develop our Fourier work.'

Leo leaned his head back again and closed his eyes. I

returned to my note-making. I scrawled an equation, but it looked incorrect.

'Leo,' I said. He did not reply. I shook his arm and repeated his name.

He sat up with a start and a splutter. 'I am sorry—I was considering Riemann integrals.'

'You were asleep. I've got a question, if you don't mind.'

He yawned. 'Of course I don't. Does it concern integrals?'

'Probably not. At a Jewish wedding, why does the groom have to break a glass?'

'I'd have preferred a question about Riemann, because I don't know the answer to this one. I think it's either to show that joy must always be tempered, or to scare away demons.'

I slipped an arm around his neck. 'When we are married, our joy will be magnified. And as for demons, I'll be leaving my family. Except for Mother—'

Leo kissed me, in a way that he had not before. It was unexpectedly exciting. I arched my back so that I pressed against him.

The carriage door opened, someone let out a gasp, and slammed it shut again. Leo pulled away from me. 'I am sorry. But my emotions are running high today. I find it impossible to read.'

I straightened my hat. 'I cannot set my mind to anything.' I pulled the Jewish book out of my bag. It fell open where our research proposal lay, at the page of blessings to recite before and after eating different sorts of food. More for me to remember.

Leo peered at the book. 'I wonder if there's a blessing to say after seeing fog?'

'There's bound to be.' I sighed. Was there one for kissing? Would you have to say it beforehand, thereby removing spontaneity? I would learn it.

Leo took a copy of the daily prayer book from his briefcase.

'Do you always carry that with you?'

'No, but now that you're converting, I thought I should be on hand to help you.' He leafed through the pages and muttered, 'on witnessing lightnings... on seeing falling stars... lofty mountains... great deserts... there are a great deal of blessings that apply to natural phenomena, but I am afraid fog is not among them.'

More for me to learn. The train slowed as we approached Oxford.

Leo turned over another page. 'Here is "On seeing a sage distinguished for his knowledge of the Law". That'd be Jewish law, of course. And here's "On seeing wise men distinguished for other than Sacred Knowledge".'

'No need to recite that when we see Milton. Do you think that abolishing the fog using gematria counts as sacred knowledge?'

'That will be a matter for the rabbinic authorities,' Leo said, 'because once our research is published it will be reported in the newspapers and they, like everyone, will know about it.'

'If Milton accepts it.'

'I am certain he will. Do you not also believe it?'

The train stopped. The end of the journey.

'I am no longer certain what I believe,' I said.

Pairs of Words

It was still morning when we arrived in Professor Milton's office, which was unoccupied, but with a coat and hat hanging on a stand in the corner. I removed the research proposal from its pages inside the book and placed it in the centre of the desk.

'Is there a blessing for success?' I asked.

'I don't know, but if there ever was a time for prayer, this is it.' He looked at me, eyebrows raised. Was I supposed to recite one?

'I've never prayed in my life, and now is not the time to set my mind to it. I will say that I hope the Professor has not departed, leaving his coat and hat in this office.'

We walked outside and sat on a bench in the quadrangle, facing the lawn in the centre. The chill air set my eyes watering and nose running. I looked at the doors on the other side of the lawn, willing Milton to come out. Leo drummed his fingertips against the armrest. The Wagstaffe clock across Broad Street struck the quarter past the hour.

Leo passed me a handkerchief, crushed into a ball. 'For goodness' sake, use this. You have been sniffing since we sat down.'

'I'm sorry—I didn't realise.' I teased a clean corner of fabric from the ball shape. It bore Leo's initials, LRL. I dabbed an unembroidered part against my nose and handed it back to Leo, but he told me to keep it, so I stuffed it into my bag. 'What's your middle name?' I asked. 'I have none.'

'It's Richard. Which apparently means "strong in rule".'

'Not a Biblical name?'

He shook his head.

'Although, it wouldn't matter if it were, after all my Uncle Jacob isn't Jewish, and…'

Movement in a doorway opposite caught my eye, I stopped babbling and stood for a better view. Two students whom I did not know walked out, chatting as though it were an ordinary Saturday. Which it was, for them. I walked to the edge of the lawn, plucked a few blades of grass, and let them fall. I paced.

'Do sit down,' Leo said. 'Try to calm yourself.'

I sat. Leo took a book from his pocket and read from the beginning. He turned a page and I tried to look across to see if it was a mathematical textbook. I hoped it was not another religious book—my brain felt like a pan of water on a hotplate, and to try to add a single additional piece of nonsense would make it boil over.

'What are you reading? Is it enjoyable?'

'It's *Daniel Deronda*—Aunt Matilda lent it to me. I cannot set my mind to mathematics today. It concerns, among other things, a Jewish gentleman and the possibility of a Jewish homeland. I can't say whether it's entertaining, since you have only permitted me to read one page.'

'I am sure I am very sorry. I won't say another word.'

Along the path behind us, footsteps crunched on

gravel. I turned my head towards the sound. It was Parbold, who strolled round to the front of our bench and wished us a good morning. Leo returned the greeting.

'Have you seen Professor Milton this morning?' I said. 'Is he in college?'

'Yes, I passed him in the corridor about an hour ago. He was going into his office.'

I jumped to my feet. 'Did you see him come out again?'

'No, but I wouldn't have. I went to my room. Why are you so concerned about his whereabouts?'

'That is none of your business,' I said, my hands shaking.

Leo placed his hand on my arm. 'Sit down. Let's be civil.' He looked up at Parbold. 'We have just submitted our revised proposal.'

Parbold smiled and nodded. 'Hence the nerves and the ill-temper. He has accepted mine, of course. I am just on my way to the library to delve further into the theory behind it. He accepted Spaulding's too, and Standish's.'

'I am delighted for them,' I said through gritted teeth.

'Oh, come-come,' Parbold said. He moved towards the bench. I put my bag on the space next to me. 'There is no reason why he should not accept yours, this time.'

'Other than the fact that he thinks very little of women and Jews.' I said.

'I am certain that your work will be good enough to overcome all of that.'

Why should Parbold have any comprehension of it? He ambled away around the green.

Leo resumed his percussion, humming under his breath, but loud enough for me to recognise the 'Radetzky March'.

I sighed. 'Must you do that?'

Leo stood. 'This is helping neither of us. As far as we can tell, Milton is here. Let us go and take tea.'

'In your room?' We might find a refuge in the clink of ill-matched cups and the smell of paraffin from the stove.

'I have no milk,' Leo said. 'But in any case, let us put distance between ourselves and this place and visit *our* tearoom—the one in Turl Street.'

'That is a good suggestion—worry has parched my mouth. Do you agree to our going to see Milton as soon as we return? Just to be certain he's received the proposal?'

'Yes,' Leo said. 'Of course, after he has, we will have to wait for his decision. But at least we'll know we have cleared the first obstacle.'

We headed for the doorway leading onto the Broad. As we were stepping through, someone behind us in the quadrangle shouted 'Wait!' and we stopped and turned. It was Baravelli—Milton had no objection to foreign students—crimson faced, thudding towards us along the path. He stopped and leaned forward, hands on his knees, gasping for breath.

'I am pleased that I found you. Professor Milton has commanded me to send you to him at once.'

Leo took my hand, and we ran.

I knocked on Milton's office door.

'Come!'

We stepped inside. He looked up from the desk, which was scattered with the pages of our proposal.

'I think you would do well to sit down,' he said, pointing to the wooden chairs facing the desk.

I could do little else, as my legs had turned to water.

'I have delayed my weekend departure especially to be

able to speak to you,' Milton said, stone-faced.

Leo and I smiled at each other.

Milton continued. 'I believe that congratulations are in order.'

I gasped and clasped my hands. 'You have accepted our proposal, already!'

'I referred to your engagement,' Milton said. 'It is fortunate for you that Huxley College is not among those institutions that require married women to leave their posts.'

I shuddered. This had not occurred to me. What would I have done if that had been a stipulation?

Leo thanked him.

'Shall you marry soon, Lazarus?' Milton asked, as though I were not part of the arrangement.

'No,' I said, 'ours must be a long engagement. I am receiving instruction in the Jewish faith.'

'Really?' Milton leaned forward across the desk. 'I had thought you a confirmed atheist.'

'I am,' I said.

'Well, your new studies, if I can call them that, must explain the pure tommyrot in this fever-minded research proposal of yours and Lazarus's. I had thought them a sign of lunacy. Ritual impurity causing fog? Foggy thinking, more like. You can do better. I would rather walk down the Broad on my hands than put my name to this.'

'We did not ask you to do either,' Leo said.

'Do you accept the proposal?' I asked. Perhaps Milton was poking fun at us, having his little joke about Jews, before saying yes.

'I do not,' Milton said.

I gasped and turned my face towards Leo. He stared

and covered his mouth with the palm of his hand.

I stood and walked to the door. 'Then clearly, my time at Huxley is at an end.' I looked towards Leo, still seated.

'Now, now, Miss Thorniwork, I did not say that,' Milton said. 'Please be seated.'

I returned to my chair.

Milton leaned back in his. 'Without wishing to damn you with faint praise, I consider the two of you to be among the brightest of this current group of researchers, despite your racial and biological disadvantages. Because of this I shall give you a third and final chance to submit a proposal. "What I tell you three times is true," as Mr Carroll informs us in "The Hunting of the Snark".'

I stood. 'I don't see the relevance of that. What we described in our previous two submissions *was* true.'

'Miss Thorniwork. Please.' Milton gestured towards the chair. 'Build on your Fourier concept. That is truly interesting.'

I put my hand on Leo's. That had been his idea.

'Also,' Milton said, 'Omit any references to respirators in your proposal, ingenious though the properties of the alleged fog repellent were.' He took a diary from his desk and thumbed through the pages. 'Let us discuss it no further. Return in two weeks with a proposal that I shall feel able to support. That will be the seventeenth of December. A week before the festive season, although that may not matter in your case. Lazarus—or perhaps I should ask you, Miss Thorniwork—when is the Jews' Christmas?'

I sat opposite Leo at the table in his room, my shoulders hunched, heedless of the tea cooling beside me. 'We were so sure. What will we do now?'

'We still have two weeks to come up with something,' Leo said. 'There is the Fourier Transform, of which Milton seemed to approve. Or, what about the prime number idea we were considering, before...' His voice grew faint.

I put my hand on his. 'Before we eliminated the fog. This will always be our great achievement. Even if nobody will ever believe us.'

'We know it is true.' Leo pulled some books from the shelf.

'Leo, I must breathe fresh air. Let's go and sit outside again.'

Leo brought the books, and we sat on the same bench in the quadrangle as we had earlier. He opened one. 'Now, we must start again. We can draw strength from resting this afternoon, but shall we meet at nine tomorrow morning in the library? We have no time to lose. I am sure Rabbi Kenig will understand if you do not devote yourself to Jewish studies for two weeks.'

I put my hand on the page he was examining. 'Leo. I cannot do this.'

He took my hand and kissed it. 'Nonsense, Pheemie. It's just another Milton rebuff. We can do it, and we will.'

I pulled my hand away. 'It's not that. It's the conversion. I cannot believe in God, and without that, although I can learn to keep and perform all the requirements to the last detail, it will be no more than play-acting. It would be deceitful.'

'Are these your true feelings, and not just the effects of our disappointment?'

'Yes. I have suspected it for a while. I cannot pretend to

be what I am not—it would drain the life from me. And from you, too. When you proposed marriage to me, did you assume that I would convert?'

He did not reply but sat with pinched lips.

'Would you have asked me to marry you, if you had not made that assumption?'

'I'd have loved you, as I still do. But no.'

I removed the engagement ring, took his hand, and placed the ring in his palm.

'Then, I release you from the contract of engagement that is between us.'

Leo's hand closed around the ring. He stood. 'This grieves me, but I can see no alternative. Goodbye, Euphemia.' I watched as he walked away from me, out of my life.

Could we still work together? For the love of mathematics? I doubted it. Could I bear to no longer be able to touch him, but instead to endure his ever-chilling behaviour? How could I bear it when he courted another?

I remained on the bench. Students passed me, shivering, but I did not notice the cold. I picked at a loose thread in my skirt. It ran down, leaving a hole. What did I care? I turned my face from what little sunlight persisted.

Parbold wandered towards me. 'Hello, Euphemia. Still here?' he said, in a jaunty tone. 'Where's Lazarus?'

I could not answer, but began to cry. It was an ugly affair, my heaving great inward breaths, while Parbold stood by awkwardly, saying 'there there', 'now now,' and other pairs of consolatory words. I must have looked a fright, but what did it matter? Eventually, my sobs slowed. My nose streamed and Parbold offered me his

312

handkerchief. I waved it away and rummaged in my bag for one of my own, but the one I found was Leo's. Leopold's. I cried until no more breath was left in me.

Into the Twentieth Century

A week later I saw a notice on the common-room wall. It was Leopold's, inviting applications for a research partner 'required owing to unforeseen circumstances'. Poor Leopold, he must have been so sure of me. As I had been of him. Should I remove the notice? If he could not be mine, then he could be nobody's. I let it remain, chiding myself for such thoughts. I did not wish to make it difficult for him to work, nor did I wish him ill. Plus, there were no other female mathematicians in Huxley (or anywhere else, as far as I knew), Jewish or otherwise. But, eventually, he was bound to be introduced to a woman more suitable than I. Julia, or someone like her, was probably already on her way to see Matilda.

I spent the next two weeks trying to find a new topic for research I could carry out alone. The time passed as a grey haze, filling my mind with cotton wool. Parbold invited me to work with him, but I declined, having interest neither in him nor his subject.

Three days before Christmas, Professor Milton summoned me to his office.

'Miss Thorniwork,' he said. 'Lazarus—'

A lump grew in my throat. My eyes filled with tears.

He tutted and raised his eyebrows. 'Here, take this.' He passed me a handkerchief. Was that to be my lot in life, a collector of men's linen? I had not had the heart to discard Leopold's, which I had laundered and hidden in the bottom drawer of a chest I seldom needed to open, at Uncle Jacob's house. I doubted the opportunity to return the handkerchief would arise.

'I have been considering a number of possibilities for solo research,' I said. I did not add that I had rejected each one.

Milton continued. 'I have accepted Lazarus's solo proposal on Diophantine sets over polynomial rings.' I was pleased for Leopold, with a pang of sadness—I would have liked to research that subject. He must have been unable to find a partner. 'But I feel *you* research more methodically when working with another. I want you to join a new student, Ernest Mummery, whose proposal I have already accepted. Raise him to your level. I am sure that in return he will keep you from any flights of fancy.' He picked up his pen, looked down and started writing.

I cleared my throat. 'What is the research topic?'

He looked up. 'I shan't tell you. You must find Mummery, and he will reveal the subject to you. Let it be a surprise. He is probably in the library.' He waved his pen at me. 'I understand that you refused to work with Parbold. You *shall* work with Mummery, or I will have no choice but to review your position.'

I returned to London for Christmas.

'I wasn't sure whether you'd be celebrating,' May said on Christmas morning, as the family and I sat beside the tree, decorated with ornaments she had made by hand. 'When I bought my presents, you were still, er.' Her face reddened. 'But I got you this, anyway.' I opened the small package she handed me. Handkerchiefs, embroidered with the letter E. 'I wasn't sure what last initial to choose,' May began. Aunt Emily gave her a nudge and a sharp look.

The exchange of gifts continued. Mother rose from her chair on the other side of the room, walked across unaided and sat in a chair next to mine. She took my hand and spoke in an undertone. 'I doubt you are in a celebratory mood. But this agony will abate, with time. I promise you.' She kissed my cheek. I hoped she was right.

By March, I no longer awoke in tears as the awareness of what had happened came beating down on me. My pain at losing Leopold had faded to a dull ache that would flare up from time to time into a stab that left me weakened and breathless. I returned from Oxford to the family home on the twentieth of the month, the day before my birthday. I could not bear the thought of waking in my lonely room at Huxley, and I wanted to be with Mother.

She had been growing stronger day by day since the fog had gone. Since we had abolished it. She had purchased tickets to see the opera *Tosca*. It appeared to end in a woman jumping from a window, and I declined the offer to attend with her, leaving Aunt Emily to try to make sense of it.

Early in the morning on my birthday, Mother and I took a stroll along the street arm in arm. She no longer needed my support, but I needed hers. Other former invalids appeared from their houses, blinking at the early spring sunshine, like shoots emerging from the ground.

We sat on a bench in the park. I picked up a newspaper someone had left there and opened it at a page of advertisements for patent medicines and household cleaning preparations. My eye was caught by a drawing of a smiling housemaid holding up a rag. 'No more elbow grease for me! I use Miracle Miltonite!' the caption read. 'Based on hypo. It removes soot and other stains with a mere flick of a cloth.'

So, there had been a part of our proposal Milton felt he could put his name to, although at two shillings a tub, how well would he fare? At least our paste, or rather Betty's, had seen the light of day. I must tell Leopold, he would… but that would not be possible.

Mother looked at the newspaper. 'We are lucky that Uncle Jacob cannot see this. He might choose to invest in the product instead of that tuberculosis jollop he is currently engaged with, and I think our money deserves a rest from being moved hither and yon.'

Uncle Jacob had withdrawn our money from the Shares in Prosperity scheme he had had such faith in, making neither profit nor loss. Mother, with newly returned astuteness, had insisted that, rather than his paying me an allowance from the whole as he had been, he must set a sum aside for me, separate from the rest of the money. She had called it 'protecting your money, and your future, with a circular fence.'

When we arrived home again, a letter had arrived for me. Of course, it must be from Leopold. The whole thing had been a terrible mistake, a bad dream. My illusion was shattered when I realised it was not his handwriting on the envelope. I opened it to find a greeting card, showing a dachshund standing on its back legs, a red ribbon tied around its neck, holding a walking stick in one paw and a basket of flowers in its mouth, with 'Birthday Greetings' written above. It was from Parbold, who had managed to obtain our address. Or, perhaps I had given it to him—the few conversations I had had with him faded from my memory as soon as his mouth closed. I cast it aside.

I could not face returning to Oxford. Mathematics held no joy for me now. I lay on my bed wishing my life could return to how it was before Leopold, in the nineteenth century. Now it was the twentieth, which was supposed to be a time for new attitudes and thinking, but I saw no miraculous changes to the world. I would never have imagined I'd look back fondly on those times, where the only problem was that of trying to please Milton. At least he seemed content with the progress Mummery and I made, as we waded through the treacle of an unexciting but worthy project.

May entered my room and handed me a package. 'Many happy returns!'

'Thank you.' I turned my head away and closed my eyes.

'Go on, open it. I made it specially for you and I've just finished it.'

I obliged. It was a handkerchief, 'To my dear cousin,' embroidered on one corner. I would soon have enough of the things to tie together and perform conjuring tricks.

I stood and embraced her. 'You are so thoughtful,' I said. I supposed that she meant well, and I resolved to try to think more kindly of her.

We sat on my bed.

'Try to cheer up,' May said. 'Tell me about that young man you're working with now. Perhaps he can mend your broken heart. Is he very handsome, perhaps with sparkling eyes and curly dark hair?' Both of which Leopold had possessed.

'He has light brown hair, as straight as a yardstick. I have not noticed his eyes, but in any case, I shall never marry, now.'

She took my hand. 'But you have loved, and now that you know how to do it, you will be able to do so again. You'll change your mind when you meet the right person.'

'You told me that before, and I did meet him,' I said, looking away. 'Now all I feel is an aching hollowness. If that is love, I do not wish for it again.'

May stood. 'Leopold wasn't right enough. Father will find someone for you who isn't losing his hair. Now, I'm going downstairs. Don't come into the kitchen until I tell you to.' She left the room.

I sat at the window, scribbling notes. I paused and looked outside. *Don't think of Leopold. Yes, do, because you can't help it.* He was there in my head, the way he spoke and dressed, the way he cooked, that smile. It filled my mind. 'Leopold,' I said, just for the sake of hearing the name.

I looked back at the pile of books on the table. On the top was Durège's *Elements of the Theory of Functions of a Complex Variable with Especial Reference to the Methods of Riemann*, which Leopold and I had argued about at our first meeting. I put down my pen and walked downstairs.

I stepped into the kitchen. The smell of burnt cake stopped me in my tracks. 'Oh dear,' May said, standing by the table. 'I'd hoped you wouldn't come in till I'd finished. I wanted it to be a surprise.'

'What, you wanted to choke me?'

'No, silly,' she said, pointing at the table. 'That.'

'That' was a cake, covered in runny white icing, which

had flowed over the blue-patterned china plate on which it stood, onto the table. A red smear, which might have been writing in some arcane language, had spread itself across the middle.

'It was meant to say Happy Birthday.' May pouted. 'Look, this is a pretty decoration.' She stuck a gold bird into one of the smudges. It fell over and sank into the icing.

I sat at the table and patted her arm. 'Thank you. It was a truly kind thought. I am sure it will be very tasty.'

'Let's have tea,' she said. She filled the kettle and placed it onto the range. 'That hotplate doesn't feel very warm.' She opened the door at the front. 'Oh—the fire's going out. I must've put too much coal on. Never mind— I'll fix that.'

She picked up a can of paraffin that stood next to the range.

'No, May!' I shouted, but it was too late. A whoosh of flame shot outwards. She jumped back and slammed the door.

The smell of cake and paraffin caught the back of my throat. In a moment, I was back in Leo's room at Huxley College. He had just cut the cake he'd made. He had used a wooden ruler in place of a knife. I saw him filling the primus stove with paraffin and lighting it. I hadn't believed anything worse than financial problems could trouble me, then.

'Have you gone deaf?' May said. 'I asked you, are my eyebrows burnt?'

'Leo,' I said.

'Oh, he's gone. You released him—now forget him. I told you, Father will find someone for you. Someone who can afford a bigger diamond.'

I stood and bolted through the kitchen door and up the stairs to my room. I rooted through the bottom drawer, pulled out Leo's handkerchief and stuffed it into my pocket, leaving the drawer open. I clattered back downstairs.

'Goodbye, May!' I called from the hall.

'Where are you going?'

'Oxford!' I shouted, as I grabbed my hat and coat from the stand in the hall. 'I am a woman of the twentieth century.'

'But you haven't touched your cake!'

As I entered the Huxley quadrangle late in the afternoon, Spaulding approached.

'Where is Leopold?' I asked him.

'What do *you* want with him?' Spaulding said.

'That is none of your business. Please answer my question.'

He shrugged. 'He is lecturing, in the main theatre.'

I hurried to the theatre and slipped in at the back. Leo stood at the front, facing the board, deriving a complex set of equations. The students scribbled in their notebooks.

Leo put his chalk down and looked at the students in the front row. 'Now, let us make haste. I must catch the five ten train to London. I can take, perhaps, one question.'

I stood and raised my hand. 'I have one.'

He looked up and raised his eyebrows. 'Ah, Pheemie. Many happy returns of the day.'

I gave a silly little wave, feeling my face redden.

He smiled. 'You have saved me a train journey. Now, what is your question?'